RISINGSON

John Alexander Crawford

I dedicate this book to D, C and I as a heartfelt appreciation of their unconditional love and unrelenting support.

RISINGSON - TABLE OF CONTENTS

PROLOGUE

PROLOGUE

Even though it was only half past four, it was already completely dark. It was also blustery and cold, with the constant threat of rain. While the inclement weather may have been a deterrent for some, it was of no concern to Lauren Smith.

Lauren had rushed home after an early finish at work in order to get ready, she was hugely excited as she sat in front of the mirror fixing her long strawberry blonde hair. Due to ongoing financial constraints, Lauren had a limited wardrobe and was once again utilising her best threads from previous milestone events, such as her cousin's wedding and her grandparents' ruby wedding anniversary.

The conditions outside were irrelevant to Lauren. This would be apparent to anyone taking the merest interest, with her outfit being more suited to a balmy summer evening, her white stilettos and matching handbag usually worn in warmer weather. She was pleased with her hair and makeup and was getting a lift to the pub from her friend's dad, so the lack of more appropriate winter clothing was not important to her tonight.

The venue of choice, The Railway Tavern, was nothing to write home about. Advertised as a hotel, it consisted of a modest number of perennially vacant rooms upstairs, with a small bar below at street level. In the pub, there was a pretty average selection of beers and spirits behind an L shaped wood-panelled bar, with a smattering of tables and chairs strewn around the medium-sized room. Between Dunfermline, the much larger town to the east, and the adjoined villages of Oakley and Comrie, there were plenty of other pubs to pick from, but Lauren Smith had picked this very spot for her first night out since turning eighteen.

In fairness, it wasn't all Lauren's idea. This was where her friends from work came most Friday nights, with tonight being a rare not-to-be-missed occasion. It was the pub's annual Halloween party, although that wasn't immediately obvious as very few patrons had bothered to wear anything remotely resembling a costume. This was possibly because it was the Friday *after* Halloween or people just couldn't be bothered with the extra effort required. For all the event lacked traditional fancy-dress wearers, it was not short on patrons in normal clothing, with the bar area significantly busier and much noisier than usual.

After initial trepidation about coming to this event, Lauren was glad she had ventured out. The evening had been a resounding success with Lauren even trying her hand at some karaoke, which was well outside her typical comfort zone. Her confidence in participating, first as part of a group of her friends and then as a solo performer, grew as the night went on and was fuelled by a not insignificant number of vodka and cokes.

The evening had flown by, and Lauren didn't want to leave, even when her friends were themselves heading home. As the bar emptied out, drunken strangers became fast friends, as those who had opted to stay moved seats to form new groups. As closing time approached, there were only a handful of revellers left. Maybe it was the alcohol talking, but Lauren felt entirely at home in this place tonight. She wasn't typically an outgoing sort, usually choosing quiet nights at home with her mum and dad instead.

Lauren was very close to her parents. Even more so after the difficult times they'd experienced in the last few years. Until recently, her dad had been a long-term absentee from work, due to the miners' strike, her mum having to pick up work here and there as a cleaner when she could. Even Lauren herself changing her career plans, dropping out of Lauder Technical College to become a trainee hair stylist to help contribute some money to the household. As it turned out, in Lauren's case, this had been a very good move. She had found her home at the hair salon and really enjoyed what she did. She'd made good friends and genuinely looked forward to work each day.

Her night out had been great fun, and Lauren felt a genuine warmth from the regulars she'd befriended tonight. The bar staff had now joined the table she was at and there was talk of a 'lock in' so they could keep drinking after the pub had officially closed. Lauren had had her fill, however, deciding she couldn't manage another drink, saying her goodbyes while loudly promising to return next Friday night.

As she walked from the warmth of the bar into the cold and wet night, the full effects of the alcohol she'd consumed hit home. Unsteady on her feet, Lauren knew she needed to get some food in her, but nothing would be open at this late hour, so getting home and making some toast was her only option.

It was less than a mile to her house and, typically, Lauren would walk, but the combination of the abysmal weather and how she felt, she decided to use the telephone box outside to call her dad for a lift. Her dad would be none too pleased, but she knew he would do it. As she steadied herself to run the very short distance from the front steps of the pub to the phone box, two white car headlights turned on, highlighting a thousand rain drops in thin lines between the vehicle and where she stood. With the bright light causing her to partially shut her eyes, Lauren couldn't see who it was, but, in anticipation of a very welcome lift, she walked over to investigate.

Chapter One
December 14th 1985

The evening was cool and crisp. Ideal conditions for walking the dog as well as for some clear thinking, and that's exactly what the troubled mind of Sergeant William Hamill needed. In a police officer's career, it is said there's always one case that haunts them, and he was the living, breathing proof of this very fact. Usually, however, it's an unsolved case that niggles away at them long after they've retired. but Hamill was many years away from hanging up his boots, and this case was only a mere six weeks old.

As he crossed the street, Hamill looked back at his cosy-looking house. He could see his wife Janet waving from the upstairs window, her silhouette visible thanks to their bedroom ceiling light beaming behind her, so he gave her a quick wave back in acknowledgement. As he turned towards the woods just along the road from him, another dog walker, Tom Slater, passed by, heading in the opposite direction, nodding and saying "Evening, Bill" but Bill was already deep in thought and could only muster the merest of acknowledgments in return.

Upon reaching the end of the row of terraced houses, he turned left onto the adjacent grass field, his huge frame momentarily caught in the glow of the streetlight as he passed underneath it. Hamill lumbered over the grass banking towards the treeline, reaching into his coat pocket for his metal torch. It wasn't exactly hard to find as it was a foot long and weighed a tonne, which he very much liked. It was highly unlikely, but if he did come across any trouble on his walk then the torch would be a handy weapon. He swapped the orangey glow of the streetlights for the darkness of the woods, his substantial shadow following him in a second later. Hamill flicked on the torch to light his way.

The sergeant was dressed for the season. A flat cap resting on top of his thick salt and pepper hair and his heavy winter jacket protecting him from both the cold night air and the numerous thin tree branches that were now protruding into his path. As he walked through the woods, there were no thoughts of Christmas. Lauren Smith was all he could think about. The young woman had been missing for over a month and there hadn't been much evidence for Hamill and his colleagues to go on. It was as if she had vanished into thin air. The village police branch had interviewed all the patrons of The Railway Tavern, the pub she was last seen in, but nothing of note was uncovered. This included Lauren's colleagues from the hair salon, who were in tears as they detailed having convinced her to go out in the first place. They also interviewed the pub's owner, Samson 'Clint' Westwood, who wasn't there that night, the bar manager, the other staff, as well as any suppliers to the business. Nothing. Despite the relatively short distance from the pub to her parents' house, she never came home.

Sergeant Hamill left the well-trodden pathway through the woods, breathing in as he squeezed through a gap in the fence onto the railway tracks. Turning his torch off again, as there was now enough natural light for him to see his way. He preferred to walk on the tracks, even though there was an alternative route, a tree-lined dirt path which ran adjacent to the railway line. Going that way at night, even on a clear night like tonight, would require using his torch the entire way until he reached the other side of Pitgarvie Primary school, where the streetlights would be shining again. He liked that the moon and stars were lighting his path on the railway tracks tonight.

Things were extremely quiet and still. There would be no trains until morning, when the colliery was open again and the long caravan of wagons would meander their way from the pit to the depot. Tonight, instead of coal trucks, there was only the light of the moon illuminating the tracks, creating two silvery parallel lines ahead of him as he walked. Aside from the occasional rustle of leaves from the trees which ran along either side of the railway line, the only sounds were the footsteps of the sergeant and Millie the dog, as they both alternated from walking on the wooden railway sleepers to trudging on the gravel in between. Hamill and Millie liked their evening walks, although he occasionally begrudged walking her when the weather was less accommodating. Millie wasn't even his dog, she was Sam's, his son. A birthday gift from his wife and him, around five years ago now.

He pondered the case as they continued to walk. What had happened to Lauren? Had she been picked up as soon as she left the pub, or had she been intercepted as she walked closer to her home? It's possible she left the village of her own accord but there was no evidence to support this theory, and, during subsequent police interviews, her family were adamant she wouldn't just up and leave. Plus, that begs the question, where on earth would she have gone? Her entire world was Oakley and the people who lived there. Understandably, with the passage of time, everyone now assumed foul play.

Scotland had seen a spate of child abductions over the last few years, but Lauren was eighteen and much older than the victims in those cases. Sergeant Hamill and his team had almost certainly ruled out any connection for that reason. The police had stood shoulder to shoulder with the community for weeks to trawl the vast amount of farmland and woodland areas which surround the village and not one footprint, or piece of clothing, or discarded item from her person was found. In fact, there had been so little evidence, the local station had resorted to canvassing every house in the village, which had turned up nothing of note and had only seemed to unnecessarily agitate a number of the local population. Their interviews of the pub staff and customers had been thorough but had been unproductive. Aside from the bar manager, Steven Morrison, nicknamed Bairn, as he had been completely bald since his teens and looked like a grown-up baby, nobody had any criminal history. The fact that he had spent some time in prison for a series of minor offences was neither here nor there as all staff and a number of customers had remained in the bar for hours after Lauren's disappearance. They were all each other's alibi, and the police had no reason to suspect any of them were lying.

Even the owner of the pub, Samson Westwood, who had the sort of reputation that the owner of a large number of pubs and clubs in the area would be expected to have, also had an alibi and was miles away at one of his other businesses. Murky reputation or not he had no apparent connection to Lauren or her disappearance.

Hamill had left no stone unturned, following up every lead, the issue was there just weren't very many. Against his better judgement, he even visited old Mrs Young last week who had a 'theory' about her next-door neighbour. But they searched his house, shed and garden, and found absolutely nothing. Nothing at all. In Hamill's opinion, it seemed far more likely that she didn't like him because his dogs barked too much.

The landscape ahead of him was changing now. Sgt Hamill was leaving the single-track section of the railway, heading towards a significantly broader area with multiple sidings to one side of the main track, where there were a large number of coal wagons sitting. Even though Hamill walked this way most nights, the sheer size of the metal wagons always astounded him when up close. The lumbering mechanical beasts were quiet now, but they'd be on the move again first thing in the morning, drenching the surrounding environment in creaking, groaning and clanging as they headed toward the colliery to be filled. He wondered how much longer they would be here given the pit was scheduled for closure in the next twelve months. This would lead to more uncertainty and unhappiness for the village populous, but he couldn't go down that road as he had other, more immediate, worries on his mind.

As the landscape ahead changed so did the night sky above. Hamill stopped for a second to appreciate the beauty of the, now, unobscured stars, and also to wait on Millie to empty her bladder. It was chilly enough that their breath was briefly visible before dispersing into the cold night air. He could smell the coal burning in fireplaces across the village, although he had to imagine the thin plumes of smoke emitting from chimneys as all the houses were currently hidden from view. His distraction from the case didn't last long.

What troubled Hamill the most is why her, why here? Nothing like this ever happens in Oakley. It was a small village in a quiet part of West Fife with under two thousand inhabitants who all knew each other, went to school, work and church together. The village was small and typically uneventful. It had three pubs, a couple of cafes, a handful of shops, including the hairdresser where Lauren worked, a couple of car repair workshops and that was about it. It was a village with an industrial heart, but it was also very rural, surrounded by farms and forest. In his eighteen years in the job, he'd dealt with speeding tickets, car accidents, minor thefts and animal disappearances, the standard fare for a village of this type, but never anything like this.

Sergeant Hamill went through the village population in his head, just as he had done many times before when canvassing the residents, asking himself who, locally, could do anything like this. The answer was still nobody. People were generally happy here and it was the antithesis of the stereotypical view of miserable miners and their downtrodden families. While the village had grown rapidly to satisfy the demands of local collieries, the houses were well built and people had pride in their village, took care of their gardens and, on the whole, looked out for one another. He knew them all to some degree and he just couldn't pick one who was capable of this.

Just like anywhere with a population of a reasonable size, there will always be oddballs, strange characters and quirky individuals who might be regarded as a little offbeat, but nobody comes even comes close to being a likely suspect for an abduction, or worse. Did that mean it could be an outsider? Almost certainly so. But Lauren was a homebody who worked in the village, and socialised in the village, so there was no tangible, obvious connections to the surrounding area which amounted to anything which merited further investigation.

The only conclusion he could come to; it was a random act and that she was in the wrong place at the wrong time. Most probably right outside the pub as an opportunistic motorist passed by on the main road and took advantage of her when she was slightly worse for wear, after possibly one or two drinks too many. It annoyed him this was the best he could do but a theory was all he and the rest of the local police could muster, and for now they would have to settle for that.

His nightly constitutional was nearing the halfway point as he approached the end of the rows of coal wagons, with the moonlit roof of the sawmill peeking out from behind them. Again, with the assistance of his torch, the sawmill would be where he would cut through to Station Road and walk up the hill back to Hill View and his home.

Hamill allowed himself to think about other things for a moment. He thought of Christmas and spending some quality time with Janet and Sam. He briefly thought of the gifts he had bought and stashed in the attic, the meal they would eat in front of a roaring coal fire and, hopefully, a few quiet days off. He also thought about Lauren's family and how bleak Christmas will be for them without their beloved daughter.

As they continued on towards the sawmill, Millie gradually started tugging on her leash, building to a strong pull and causing Sergeant Hamill to lurch forward somewhat. Millie was a Border Collie and strong for her size. She increased her speed and was now pulling him rapidly towards the last coal truck in the row, Sergeant Hamill reluctantly following as an unwilling jogger, Millie's sudden change of pace having taken him by surprise. "Millie!' he shouted. but she had a scent and was locked on, and continued to pull him along faster than he would like. Luckily, she stopped as suddenly as she started, homing in on something on the ground. Sergeant Hamill again pulled out his torch from his coat pocket, shining the light onto the gravel beside the track as Millie started to tuck in. "What the hell?" he softly muttered in muted bewilderment as he observed a small pile of wet dog food on top of a railway sleeper. In all his years walking this route, and all the odd things he had seen, this was a new one on him. Before he could pull Millie away, the food was entirely gone - wolfed down in record time. Millie was an eat first, ask questions later, kind of dog and Sergeant Hamill hoped that the food was at least fresh, which would make this incident no less bizarre if it was.

Before the sergeant could ponder the curiousness of the dog food being where it was, the silence was shattered by an ear-splitting metallic screech. As he swung around to see what was happening, he quickly realised that it was too late to move, or even cry out, as the metal door of the nearest coal wagon swung open from above and was falling at pace directly towards him. Sergeant Hamill's legs buckling beneath him as he prepared for the inevitable. The downward motion of the door creating an outward blast of cold air and ending with a loud but dull thud. Then everything was still. The only sound now was Millie's leash scraping along the gravel between the tracks as she disappeared into the darkness.

Chapter Two
In Memoriam

Oakley Church wasn't particularly welcoming. Its grey sandstone exterior was complemented nicely today by a foreboding grey sky and, of course, a grey austere interior. It was probably not unlike the majority of Scottish protestant churches, and, on this particular Friday, it was the busiest it had been for many a year. It was standing room only, but it somehow felt soulless and empty.

It wasn't just the church which had a dark cloud over it. The whole village seemed to have been in a state of eternal gloom, which began when Lauren's disappearance came to light, followed not long after by the premature death of Sergeant Hamill, both events dovetailing nicely with the depressingly futile battle to keep the local colliery open.

Sergeant Bill Hamill was part of the fabric of the local community, and it just seemed so very wrong that he was gone. The church had been well used during the last few months, having been the focal point for Lauren's vigil and now, just a few months later, playing host to a memorial service for a much-admired man taken before his time.

Bill Hamill's passing had left a void in many peoples' lives, but it left a gaping chasm in his family's. Their whole world revolved around him, they did everything around his schedule, appreciated his important role in the community, with the respect that people had for him transferring to the family as a result. But now everyone looked at them with nothing but sadness and pity.

The funeral had been a small, family affair immediately after Christmas at Dunfermline Crematorium but there had been some local pressure on the Hamill family to have a larger memorial service once the fatal accident inquiry had reported, and once things had settled down for them. Today was that day.

Bill Hamill's death had been widely reported in the media, as well as in follow up coverage as the resultant inquiry was taking place. Given the accident took place on National Coal Board land, their lawyers were claiming it was trespassing, but the fact that Sergeant Hamill was the principal police officer investigating Lauren Smith's disappearance, coupled with the fact there is no signage warning potential trespassers to 'keep out', the inquiry ruled that his family should receive additional compensation for his death. Of course, the family hadn't seen a penny yet and had no word on when they would. Even with his dad's police pension and his death benefits, things were tight for Sam and his mum, but today was not the day to think about this.

Despite three months having passed since the accident, the Hamills were still feeling very raw. When Sam first heard the news about his dad, he had suppressed his feelings. A feat he managed to maintain for about ten days, but when Christmas arrived, Sam couldn't hold in his emotions anymore, finding the numerous family get-togethers over the holiday period too much, and he just broke down. It's likely there was an element of catharsis about finally releasing all the built-up grief. This was repeated on his sixteenth birthday, a month ago. His large family getting together on these occasions did nothing more than underscore the fact his dad wasn't with them anymore. And here they were again, all together one more time. He sorely missed his dad, but Sam hoped they could at least get some closure on things and move on with their lives after this.

Sam looked down at his shoes. There was no chance he would see his face in them. They were unpolished and dull, which would not have impressed his father at all, who always had gleaming shoes and boots, for work and for any formal family event. Otherwise, Sam was looking extremely sharp. His grandparents had bought him a suit, shirt and tie for his dad's funeral, and he was wearing this ensemble again today. His hair was also combed, and he even used a decent portion of his giant tub of styling gel to keep it in place. His unpolished school shoes aside, he felt he was looking good.

Conscious of the large gathering of people behind him, Sam didn't want to shift in his seat too much, but he was really uncomfortable. 'I suppose they don't believe in cushions at this fucking church' he thought to himself as he adjusted his position for the umpteenth time. Even worse than the hard wooden pews, was listening the

Minister droning on about his dad, especially since it was obvious, he was using time worn cliches the whole time and clearly didn't know his dad well at all.

Sam shouldn't complain, his family weren't exactly prolific church goers. His dad's religion was pretty much his job. His mum was the only one of them who went remotely regularly but in recent years her attendance had waned, and her husband's untimely death will not have done much to restore her faith.

Sam eyed his surroundings. This building did not seem an adequate place to celebrate his dad or indeed his larger-than-life personality. With its grey walls, stone floor and bare, wooden pews, the atmosphere created was dour instead of the preferred upbeat commemoration. Unfortunately, the church was the industry standard around these parts, and so was the service.

Sam leaned slightly forward, looking along the row to his grandparents, both sets, his aunts and uncles and his friends, who were sitting, heads bowed at the very far end of the pew across the aisle. His pals looking understandably sombre in their school uniforms, and not remotely well groomed which raised a wry smile from him. Nothing new there, he supposed. He took a fleeting glance behind him and caught a glimpse of a few well-known faces to him; old Mrs Young, Mr Thompson his old primary school headteacher, the Browns from next door. Pretty much everyone he could think of was there, even Lauren's parents.

Sam then caught the eye of Margaret Stafford for a brief second, who was with her parents, instantly remembering the embarrassing incident that took place on the bus in the immediate aftermath of Lauren's disappearance. Sam and the boys, like everyone else, assumed Lauren had just gotten drunk and had simply gone home with someone she'd met. As time went on, that theory waned and the terrible reality of her disappearance became more apparent. However, in the first day or so most people naively suspected there was nothing sinister to it. He and his friends were all sitting in their usual seats at the back of the lower deck of the bus and they were joking about Lauren's 'abduction', mainly because that's not what they thought had really happened. There is a girl at school who has extremely hairy neck and forearms, Mary Scott, who they, not very originally, nicknamed Hairy Mary. They were kidding around, speculating what would happen if she had been the one abducted with Sam impersonating her dad as if he was on the news, at one point mockingly shaking his fist in the air in faux anger, shouting at the abductor "If you touch as much as one hair on her... back" to much amusement from his cronies. Nobody else in the immediate vicinity found this funny at all, however, and as he caught Margaret's gaze, she looked at him like Medusa looked at her next victim. Sam felt instant shame and had thought of this incident often over the subsequent months, particularly as Lauren's disappearance turned into an actual abduction investigation. Even though he liked her a lot, Sam had done a sterling job avoiding Margaret until now, but upon seeing her, the shame and regret returned with a vengeance, and he felt himself turning red.

Moving on, he continued his quick scan of the guests, spotting his dad's colleagues from the police station. Usually so full of fun and quick with humourous anecdotes, they now sat stony-faced and silent. His thoughts again turned to Lauren, as he had spent many of his weekends since his dad's death putting up lost dog posters around the village for Millie and saw the large number of posters on lampposts and in shop windows appealing for information on her disappearance. He almost felt guilty putting up his posters next to hers, but he loved Millie and desperately wanted her back. He was respectful to Lauren's posters, ensuring he didn't overlap on hers, instead ensuring his posters only went over the top of those highlighting other things, such as upcoming jumble sales and missing cats.

The Minister reached the end of his lengthy address, finally wrapping up proceedings. Then it was time for Sam and his family to make the necessary but horrendous walk down the middle of the aisle back to the church doors, nodding in appreciation to the same people they had already seen, would see again outside, and probably see once more at his house afterwards. Even though Sam was the saddest he'd ever been in his sixteen years on earth, his emotions were all on the inside. He felt that he had to put on some sort of pretence to convey the appropriate amount of outward emotion to everyone who was looking at him, wiping away a few imaginary tears as he walked.

Outside on the church steps, a good number of locals came up to pay their respects in person, which pleased Sam as that meant they likely would not be coming back to the house. Bert the Bookie was first, then Davie, the Secretary of the Miners' Welfare, who, of course, had to get in a dig about Sam's family not holding the wake there, followed by Vince the chip shop owner with his wife and daughter, and a horde of others. Just as they were about to head back to theirs, Lauren's parents walked over. They looked totally drained but wanted to say thanks for everything Sergeant Hamill had done in the search for their daughter and give Sam and his mum their best. Lauren's mum gave them both a tight hug before departing.

After the rest of the attendees dispersed and the Minister had wished them well, the Hamills felt like they could now head home and await whoever was going there. Sam's Uncle Tam, his dad's brother, was across the road simultaneously waving and pointing up the hill from the church, indicating where on the street they needed to go for their lift. After the short drive, they arrived outside their house and couldn't see anywhere remotely close to park as everyone who was coming was already there. Sam sank down in his seat. He was hoping for a handful of people and to get this final part over and done with, but it looked like another decent shift from him would be required.

The house was completely mobbed. It was a small, terraced house, like every other in the street, and holding a medium-sized event was always going to be challenging. Oakley was typically a very safe place, and the guests had probably just checked if the door was locked, which it wasn't, and wandered in. It was mostly family and close friends, in any case, who knew their way around. There was the usual spread for this type of event; little sandwiches, sausage rolls and mini pies, along with a tea urn – borrowed from the police station - and the booze table, for those who fancied a tipple. Lager cans were outside stacked up against the coal bunker, which would keep them suitably cold.

All of Sam's relatives were there. All of them. He was met with a human wall of hugs, pecks on the cheek, handshakes and hair ruffles. His aunts and uncles complimenting him on his handsome looks and getting sentimental about his dad, and the fact that Sam had his eyes. He wasn't tall or heavily built like his father, rather he was relatively short and slender by comparison, but their pale blue eyes were identical – a fact that Sam had been reminded of frequently throughout his sixteen years. It seemed like a herculean task, but once he felt like he had spent an appropriate amount of time with everyone, he moved on to the next gathering, through in the kitchen.

As he entered the room, his dad's colleagues –
Constables Bob Seton, Andrew Redpath and Davey
Sneddon - from the cop shop were holding court, telling
funny stories about his dad, which was actually very nice
and helped lift the mood. Some of the stories he'd heard
before and some were new. The one about a local man
who carried a single patio paver from a building site in
Porterfield every night until he created his own patio at
home was his favourite. Apparently, his dad was so
impressed with the effort he just let the guy off.
Naturally, after some time, the subject turned to Lauren
Smith.

Everyone agreed that they were completely baffled by
the case, as Seton, who was the elder statesman at the
station, moving his thinning grey hair off his forehead
and clearing his throat, as if he was about to say
something important. Not far from retirement, he had
been a police constable all his long career and was quite
happy with that. "They're sending an Inspector out from
Dunfermline." Everyone looked up, surprised by this
news, especially the fact it was coming from him. Seton
was now struggling to conceal his delight after clearly
being the only one of the group with the gen. "How do
you know this?" asked Sneddon. Seton responded that
the inspector had paid the station a visit earlier today
when he was on duty and explained that there was now
also a missing girl from Dunfermline and that they are
setting up a task force to see if the cases were connected.
"Another one?" said Redpath. "Yep, afraid so. A

sixteen-year-old from Abbeyview." Redpath followed up with "what do they have so far?" Perhaps realising that he really didn't have any other details, Seton cleared his throat again saying, "we're all to get fully briefed in due course." Everyone, including Sam, who'd been listening intently, nodded in sombre agreement.

It was getting late and the number of revellers at the house had dwindled dramatically. There were only a few members of his family left in the other room, plus Constable Redpath and Sam's pals still in the most fashionable part of the house. None of the boys were looking their best now, having been downing cans for a good few hours. The combination of a full day of school, the memorial service immediately after, and a night of drinking beer, the lads were now looking extremely dishevelled. Shirts were untucked, ties were off, shoelaces untied and their hair – Gub aside, whose head was always shaved 'down to the wood' – was looking greasy and unkempt. This messy and unattractive lot might not look the best, but they were everything to Sam, although, obviously, he could never tell them that. After his dad's accident, he relied on them so much, but he didn't know if they realised how important they've been to him. Here they sat openly drinking cans of beer in front of the local police, but it didn't seem to be a cause for concern to the constables, or indeed the boys.

They were a tight-knit group and pretty much did everything as one unit. Sam's closest pal was Tommo, Mark Thomson, and they'd been friends since nursery

24

school. Even when they were separated by going to different primary schools, they still played together after school, went to the local scout troop for a few years, and played in the same football team. They were tight. The other two, Hugh Watson (Shug) and Robert Gibson (Gub) lived very close to Tommo. Shug a bit further up Wardlaw Way and Gub in the adjacent, and rather unoriginally named, Wardlaw Crescent. Sam's mum and dad had always approved of his friends. Maybe it's because they didn't get into too much mischief, Sam was especially careful on account of who his dad was, or maybe his parents knew they were all from good families.

Just when Sam thought he should go through to the sitting room and check in on his mum and remaining family members, the conversation turned to his beloved Dunfermline Athletic. The Pars were having their best season in many a year and, if they could keep it up, they could be looking at promotion to the First Division for the first time in years. Sam was an avid fan. He and his pals would get the bus to town to see them play - well, not Tommo so much, who was a Celtic fan but would go with the rest of them occasionally. Sam hadn't been for a while, though, for obvious reasons, but he would tune in via the radio whenever he could and would park himself in front of the tv on a Saturday at 4.45pm for the scores coming through.

"Johnny Watson's going to fire us to promotion!" shouted Shug, drunkenly, as everyone else turned to look at him.

Just when Sam was going to slate him for being wasted, Gub joined in "Don't forget my favourite player, Shaggy Jenkins!" as he lived up to his nickname by stuffing three sausage rolls in his massive mouth at once.

A half-hearted, and exceedingly off tune, version of Walking Down the Halbeath Road then started but ended as soon as it began. The alcohol was definitely taking its toll on the lads. Sam was glad he hadn't had as much to drink as the others. It had been a very long day. The good news was the latter part of the day had actually flown by; the bad news was that it was now 10.30pm and he really needed the remaining guests to go home.

Even though it was a Friday night, Sam had a game plan for Saturday morning. He had been scouring the village and the surrounding areas for signs of Millie for the last few months. Sam reckoned she had been spooked by his dad's accident and had run off. It was the only explanation as there was no sign of her near the scene at the time, or any time since. The village is surrounded by either farmland or forest on all sides and Sam's plan was to cover every piece of ground until Millie is found, although he was running out of places to check.

With the agenda for tomorrow fresh in his head, he set about trying to cajole the last of the stragglers out the door. He had managed pretty well to ease people out of the house without seeming rude, but Tommo and Shug were the last two and, having not seen their friend much lately outside of school, they wanted to stay. "Aw, c'mon man, it's Friday night" said Tommo while highlighting his high level of inebriation by overuse of elaborate and increasingly meaningless hand gestures.

"I have an early start tomorrow, sorry" replied Sam.

"To do what?" Shug chimed in.

Realising that looking for his dog again sounded a bit weak, Sam felt it better to lie. "I have to help my mum."

That nugget of misinformation was the party killer he required, and the lads, along with Redpath, who had been in the other room, immediately left, not wanting to interfere with Sam's family time. As they were walking down the front steps Tommo turned back "What about Sunday?" In an effort to usher the two of them off, Sam said yes.

Chapter Three
The Black Hole

Sam's most prized possession burst into life. The radio on his Pioneer stereo system had been set to power on at 6.45am, the cowbell and bass from the Pet Shop Boys' West End Girls filling every corner of his room. Always a gamble to set the radio to turn on but he was very pleased with the song, as it could have easily been a song he didn't like or, even worse, the DJ talking or the news. The only downside was that he didn't have the stereo turned up as loud as he'd have liked, given the early hour.

Even though Sam was feeling the effects of the late night before, he thought to himself 'what a pleasant way to wake up', as he lay in bed trying to let his eyes adjust to the darkness. It was certainly much better than the piercing electronic chirps of an alarm clock.

Additionally, he vowed to himself to buy the 12" of that record next time he went into town. Sam had bought the stereo two years ago by saving money from his old paper round, and it was, by some margin, the best money he'd ever spent. It has a turntable, double cassette decks, the radio and a graphic equaliser, which, after some initial experimentation, now has all the sliders all the way to the top. It's definitely state-of-the-art but the best thing about it is it's very loud, with 100-watt speakers.

After lying in bed for the duration of the song he had to force himself to make a move. It was cold in his bedroom and still pitch-black outside, but he dragged himself out from under the warmth of his covers. He needed to get going. Despite probably having already woken his mum with the music, Sam quietly got ready, putting on a long-sleeved t-shirt, jeans and old trainers and turned his bedroom door handle as slowly as he could, as if that would be somehow quieter. Because he didn't know if his mum was up yet, he decided he would grab breakfast from the paper shop instead of at his house. He sneaked into the bathroom, urinating as quietly as he could, then washing his hands and quickly splashing some water on his face. He crept downstairs and eased out the front door, which was directly across from the foot of the staircase, while simultaneously putting on his parka. It was a fairly chilly morning, showcased by his breath steaming up the glass on the outside of the front door as he was pulling it shut.

He walked along the garden path, quietly manoeuvring the front gate back into the latch as he left and taking a mental note of the surprising number of cars from last night's revelry that were still parked outside. His dad's was always there, it hadn't moved since his death. Sam was still too young for his licence and his mum didn't have one, so there it sat. His mum wanted to keep it until Sam passed his test, but Sam wasn't sure if he wanted it. Sam couldn't wait to get his wheels, but a cream-coloured Morris Ital wasn't what he had in mind. Sam did, however, covertly sneak out to turn the engine over every few weeks, just to make sure it was still running.

In total, there were another seven or eight cars parked in front of his house and across the road. Sam hoped the owners would just pick them about without feeling the need to check in on him or his mum.

It was about a five-minute walk to the shop and Sam encountered precisely zero people on his short trek. Presumably because it was still dark, and sensible people wanted to wait until daylight before they ventured out. Aside from Mr Das, there was nobody in the shop either. This was ideal as Sam was on a mission and didn't wish to be waylaid by idle chit chat.

Mr Das made the best morning rolls. Sam ordered a bacon and egg roll with brown sauce and left Mr Das to prepare while he gathered other provisions from the shop. Two bottles of Red Diamond Cola from the chill cabinet, one for now, one for later, a banana and, his favourite chocolate bar, a Texan. Not exactly the breakfast of champions and not too healthy either. Sam, though, was in good physical health, lean and muscular from his footballing activities plus he covered a lot of ground on foot since he wasn't driving yet. While his dad had been both tall and broad, Sam was built like his mum and was, at 5ft 8, a good few inches shy of his dad's height. That could change with a late teenage growth spurt, but Sam was fine with his current physique.

Unperturbed by the lack of nutrition in his food purchase, Sam slapped his money down on the counter with Mr Das, in return, presenting him with his hot bacon and egg roll inside a brown paper bag and the rest of the items in a plastic carrier bag as he set off down Station Road towards the sawmill. Sam could have gone the scenic route along the railway line, but he didn't like going that way since his dad's accident.

The sun was starting to come up and the village was beginning to stir into life, with a few cars now on the main roads. As he walked, he peered over the trimmed hedges into people's gardens on his route. With the dawn sun rising in the sky, everything was briefly bathed in a sort of half-light, like looking at everything through lace curtains. It was nice to be walking in the fresh air munching on his warm roll and, for the first time in a long while, he could actually feel a little heat from the sun on his face as it rose higher in the sky. In a flash, the roll was gone and Sam washed it down with a freezing cold bottle of cola, which was eye-wateringly fizzy, letting out a loud roar of satisfaction when he was done to an audience of no one.

Now that Sam had digested his early morning fuel, it was time that his walk had an accompanying soundtrack. He fumbled in his jacket pocket for his second most prized possession, his Aiwa portable cassette player. A Christmas gift from his mum and dad, which was even more coveted as his dad wasn't around to see him open it. Sam had wanted a Sony Walkman, but his minor disappointment didn't last long when he turned it on and could hear the impressive sound quality. He had also been lucky enough to receive a good number of new cassette tapes for it – a coordinated effort by his mum and dad to rope other family members into the main gift theme.

He put his headphones on and pressed play on the cassette player. The album of choice for this mission was Kraftwerk's The Man Machine. the electronic bleeps of The Robots filling his ears as he walked down the steep hill to the bottom end of the village, depositing the empty bottle and the now crumpled up paper bag in a bus stop rubbish bin as he passed by.

It had been almost three months since Millie disappeared and, if Sam was being realistic, she was probably gone for good, especially if she had slipped her collar and her ID tags had come off with it. If that was the case, he was just hopeful that she had found another family and was being well cared for. However, he did not want to give up looking and refused to stop until he had some sort of closure on the matter, one way or another. Hence the trip into the woods today. Despite school and his various part-time jobs, and being mostly limited to weekends, Sam had scoured pretty much all of the village and most of the surrounding area since Millie disappeared but today was the first chance he'd had to venture out to this particular part of the forest.

He took the shortcut through the sawmill with the unmistakeable smell of recently cut wood filling his nostrils. The mill was closed today but he could easily imagine the high-pitched screaming of the numerous saws, which would be running all day during the week.

After leaving the sawmill, Sam wandered onto Coal Board land, crossing numerous sidings and then walking over to where the old Dunfermline – Alloa line intersects with the colliery branch junction. While the colliery line was still in use. there were no trains on a Saturday, and there were rarely trains on the passenger line as regular service had been discontinued a long time ago. Despite the lack of trains, Sam was careful to walk to the side of the tracks so there would be no unwelcome surprises while he was wearing his headphones.

Sam's plan was to search the large forest on the far away side of the main line so he shouldn't need to be by the tracks for long in any case. As Sam wandered along, all he could see before him was what looked like never-ending railway tracks sandwiched between thick forests. From where he was, the forest looked like it would go on forever, like an excerpt from a film shot in the seemingly endless tree-lined rail system of the American northwest, but in a mile or so the trees before him would be replaced by farmland.

The area Sam was walking to was only a couple of miles away from his house, but it felt like another world. Since eating his breakfast, he had walked for around half an hour, and he was already on track six, the final track, on his Kraftwerk tape. No matter though, he was about to enter the woods and thought it better to put the cassette player away in his plastic carrier bag while he searched in any case. If he was being entirely honest with himself, the woods looked dark and creepy, and he didn't want to explore them while having any of his senses impaired.

Sam climbed the steep slope to the edge of the woods, stopping for a second as if he needed to convince himself to continue walking forward. As he entered the forest, his world immediately switched from light to dark. Once his eyes adjusted to his new surroundings, he started shouting, interspersed with whistling, for Millie and listening for any sort of response. The woods were incredibly dense, and trees were all Sam could see now in every direction.

After the initial climb up the steep bank to enter, the ground was much closer to level here. And, as Sam continued moving forward, he arrived at a sinister looking pond which was surrounded with brick at the water's edge and, almost all of the way around, a barbed wire fence. The water looked black and, coupled with the rather extreme security measures, the pond looked very foreboding.

As he took in the surroundings, Sam was suddenly very aware that there were no sounds in this part of the forest. It was eerily quiet. No birds singing, no insects flying around, everything was very still. Even the water was motionless, it was like staring into a black hole. As he looked up, the tree limbs looked like black bones against the light blue sky behind. Sam wasn't particularly superstitious but there was something which seemed otherworldly about this place. He could sense it, and he assumed all other living things could sense it too.

This wasn't the first time he had been here. Sam and his pals used to come up to this part of the forest regularly to build camps and play 'japs and commandos' when they were younger. Unlike other streams and ponds around the area, there was no desire for hijinks anywhere near the dark water, and certainly nobody ever thought about venturing into it. Throwing a large stone or stick into the murky liquid was as much as anyone over did, almost as if they didn't want to disturb whatever dark spirits were under the surface.

Sam wasn't sure if it had a proper name, but they all just called it the black hole. Neither Sam or his friends seemed entirely sure what this pond is or was. It certainly wasn't natural and had been created for some other purpose, and was now left as a creepy reminder of its prior function, whatever that was. It wasn't big, maybe fifteen to twenty feet across, but what it lacked in distance across it appeared to make up for in depth. Aided by the shade of the trees, the water looked so dark that it could almost be oil in there. Could it be an old air vent for one of the local mines or maybe even a drainage channel? He would try and remember to ask his grandad, who would likely know.

There were numerous urban legends relating to various landmarks around the village and this one had more than its fair share. Sam and his friends had been told numerous stories about events which had supposedly happened there. There were claims that it was haunted, as well as being the scene for a multitude of mysterious accidents. It was said farmers used to dump their dead cattle in it, it was also said that a dog was lured into it, running in at high speed, pulling its unfortunate owner in behind it. According to that particular legend, neither the man nor the dog were ever seen again. The only tale Sam and his friends were inclined to believe is that a boy was swimming in it and got tangled in grassy vegetation under the water and drowned. It was for this reason alone that they never ever went in and no doubt why it had, at some point in the past, had an impenetrable ring of barbed wire installed around it. It seemed as though the passage of time had meant that the section which was farthest from where he entered the forest was now in disrepair leaving that side somewhat accessible, not that anyone in their right mind would want to access it.

Sam didn't want to spend any more time in the area around the black hole, so he continued walking through the woods, continuing his calls for Millie as he went. There was now another pretty substantial incline to contend with as the forest rose up away from where the pond was. He hadn't really thought about it before, but the forest was not terribly deep in this area and Sam could now see a band of light, where the trees ended, up ahead of him.

Sam eventually exited the darkness, discovering a field on the other side he was fairly sure he hadn't seen before. When they were younger, the boys all assumed that there was nothing else but forest covering a significant area of ground, but they were clearly not very well informed.

Sam was trying get his bearings, as he had not walked in a straight line through the woods, but he assumed that this was a dormant farmer's field near to the Pitgarvie Estate. It certainly didn't look like anything useful had been planted here for some time and the field was overgrown with what appeared to be long grass. In contrast to the black hole area, there were birds and insects in abundance in the field. He could not only see them, but the most noticeable difference was the noise, with a cacophony of chirping and buzzing filling his ears.

Sam wanted to get a better idea of where he was, so he walked through the tall grass hoping to get to higher ground, where he could possibly see something that could help him identify his location. As he reached the highest point near the middle of the field, he noticed that there was an old cottage in the distance further along the treeline to his left. From his vantage point, it looked abandoned, so he changed direction to further investigate, continuing to shout for Millie as he walked.

As he got closer to the cottage, he could now see that the exterior was surrounded with what appeared to be old appliances, left outside to rust, accompanied by numerous black rubbish bags and various other pieces of detritus scattered around. Sam thought he knew every inch of Oakley and the surrounding countryside, but he hadn't ever heard anything about this cottage, and he was compelled to check it out.

Sam's eyes were fixed on the strange building ahead of him, and he was maybe about fifty yards away when he felt a tickle on his wrist. As he looked down, he saw a small tick crawling on the back of his hand. With his other hand he picked it off and, while it was crawling on his index finger, he used his thumbnail to push down into its back, in an attempt to kill it, and then flicked it away. No sooner had he gotten rid of it then another tickle, this time on the other hand. Was it the same tick? No, because much to his horror, as he looked down, he saw dozens of minuscule black dots crawling all over his trainers and on his jeans. He let out a loud shriek.

Sam must have accidentally wandered through a tick nest, as they were all over him. He took off his parka and swung it around in the air, in an attempt to rid himself of the tiny eight-legged life ruiners. He dumped his jacket on the ground and furiously started swiping his legs with his hands but there were too many. He had to think quickly, he needed to rinse them off before any latched onto his skin, then there's no getting them off without tweezers and, even then, they could give him one of the many diseases they carried.

Sam picked up his jacket and his plastic bag and ran back the way he had come, swiping and slapping his skin and ruffling his hair as went. He felt a tick on his neck, stopping briefly to pick it off, and then started running again. He knew that if they latched onto him water would no longer be any use, so he had to act fast. Sam needed to get to the burn on the other side of the railway line. There was an area within the Comrie Burn called the Dookin Dam, which was deep enough for him to jump in and rinse the ticks off.

Sam was running at full pelt, almost out of control, down the hill back towards the railway line when he had to stop again to get another tick off his face. He was starting to panic now and sensed he was still a good five plus minutes away from the burn. He was closing in on the black hole and, in his desperation, made a snap decision to jump in where the barbed-wire fence had fallen down. He would be in and out pretty fast, Sam thought. He threw his jacket on the ground again and plopped the plastic bag down next to it. He took his shoes, socks, t-shirt and jeans off and flapped them around in an attempt to rid them of the crawling beasties. Sam didn't have time to check closely as he could feel another tick on the side of his neck.

He took a deep breath and jumped in, fully submerging himself for a few seconds. The water was bone--chillingly cold and, when he resurfaced, he let out an expletive-filled scream which echoed around the woods. Had there been any birds resting up on the tree branches they would definitely have flown off en masse as a result.

Sam attempted to combine treading water with brushing off his arms and legs with his hands, but it resulted in mostly just flailing around. He was trying not to think about all of the terrible things that had supposedly happened in that pond and then, just as he was getting ready to swim to the edge and climb back out, he felt it. His heart sank and sheer panic consumed him. Around his foot and ankle Sam could feel the strands of something organic brushing across his skin, tickling him and beginning to wrap around his lower leg. If he got tangled up just like the urban legend described, nobody would hear his distant screams, and he would surely drown. He was not going to go out that way and virtually launched himself out of the water like a leaping salmon to escape.

Sam checked himself for ticks, looking very closely at his soaking underwear, they seemed tick free. However, he decided to dispense with them as the thought of putting his jeans on over wet underpants would not be too pleasant. Instead, he squeezed as much water from them as he could and, after removing his portable cassette player, and the rest of his leftover provisions, placed the underpants in the carrier bag. Sam carefully depositing his tape player and snacks in the deep pockets of his parka, then checking his t-shirt and jeans for the pesky parasites once again. He flapped them around once more for good measure, but he couldn't see anything. Sam also double-checked his jacket and shoes and as far as he could tell, no ticks. He would get also get a bath when he got home to ensure complete success.

A sudden realisation fell over him that he was completely naked in the middle of the woods. While it was highly unlikely anybody else would be stupid enough to be in this sinister setting with him, he decided he'd better expedite getting dressed and get out of there, just in case. He had no difficulty pulling his t-shirt on but that couldn't be said for his jeans. Pulling them over his wet legs was a challenge but he managed, now motivated by mild panic, as he half jumped and hopped in order to pull the thick denim up his thighs. Once they were on everything else was a breeze. Sam quickly brushed off the debris on the soles of his feet, putting his socks and shoes on, which he, of course, like everything else, checked first. He felt ever so slightly more composed now but was ready to get out of there.

As he walked away, Sam scarcely looked back at the pond, beyond checking he had all his possessions with him. From the shade inside the woods, he could see the end of the dense grouping of trees ahead. As he walked briskly down the hill away from the black hole, it got gradually brighter, and he continued to check his person for any creepy crawlies, but he couldn't see any. Before long, he was back out in full daylight, taking a right turn back towards the railway junction, and constantly examining his person for ticks as he went. One thing that entered his head is that he would have to break his own rule about avoiding the railway siding as he didn't want anyone to see him looking like a drowned rat on the main street. If anyone was walking along the railway line, Sam would have looked quite the sight trudging back along the tracks looking like a drowned rat with his soaking wet underwear swinging beside him in a plastic bag, never mind in the centre of the village where the streets would be busy with people running errands.

As he left the main line and cut back towards the colliery line, Sam could see the sawmill where he had entered the railway property and, more ominously, just beyond that, the siding where his dad died. He had been determined to avoid this section of the railway, but it was now unavoidable.

Sam was walking about as far away from the sombre site as he could get, but, as he neared the line of stationary coal trucks, he couldn't help glancing across the tracks to where the tragedy unfolded, ultimately stopping to look over at the place where his dad took his last breath. There was no obvious sign that anything had ever happened there at all. Maybe that was a good thing, he thought.

Sam always worked hard to keep happy memories of his dad in his head, but, at this moment, it was impossible. Sam also thought about how much he missed him. His dad was a fairly quiet man and was always working, but he was a big presence, even when he wasn't around. One thing his dad would often say was that he was looking forward to taking him for a pint, when Sam was legally able. Sam thought about this frequently. Especially now that it's not going to happen.

It had become a sore point for Sam that he wasn't closer with his dad and could never be now. He wistfully wondered if meeting for an occasional pint would be the thing that brought them closer together. His dad didn't watch football, so that was never something they shared.

Maybe this was how it was for everyone who's lost a loved one? Sam realised he was descending down a bit of a rabbit hole with this train of thought and his attention shifted to Millie. This was her last known location as well.

His trip to the woods had provided neither sight nor sound of her and he was running out of local places to check. In fact, many of them he'd already checked multiple times. He continued along the railway towards home feeling pretty downbeat and, while checking his clothes for tiny arachnids again, thinking of how desperately he needed a piping hot bath.

He walked into the woods near his house and up the grass banking back to his street. He observed that a few people had come to collect their cars while he was out, but a few were there still. As he walked in the door his mum shouted through from the kitchen. "Sam, you were up and about early?"
"I was, I'm going to get cleaned up and come and tell you about it." Sam replied.

Sam sprinted upstairs and ran the water long enough for the boiler to kick in, then slotting the rubber stopper snugly into the plughole. He wanted the water scaldingly hot, and the resultant steam was already filling the bathroom. Sam hung his parka on the back of the door and peeled off his sopping wet t-shirt and jeans, depositing them in the sink so as not to drip water on the bathroom floor. He pulled a bottle of Dettol out from the under-sink cabinet and poured a capful into the bathwater, giving it a slightly milky appearance and then, to be sure, another capful. Knowing his mum was safely ensconced downstairs, Sam sped naked through to his bedroom and put his stereo on, so he would be able to hear the radio through the wall, before running back through to turn the taps off. The bath was about halfway full now which was enough.

Before climbing into the bath, Sam removed his wet underwear from the plastic bag and dropped them on top of the other items in the sink. He gingerly stepped over the bath side and into the piping hot water. If he hadn't gotten all the ticks off before, this would surely do the trick.

It was almost too hot to get in the water, but he persevered, lowering himself in an inch at a time, and after a few minutes sunk down so he was fully submerged, washing his hair on his return above the surface and dipping under once more to rinse. As the bath water cooled, he considered topping it up, but he thought better of it and lifted himself out. One solitary tick was floating on top of the water as Sam pulled the plug out. He towelled himself dry and stood in front of his mum's full-length mirror to check himself one last time. He stood looking at his pale, naked frame, checking under his arms, twisting around to check his back and behind his knees. He moved in closer, checking his medium length brown hair and the scalp beneath, running his fingers through it just to be sure. Satisfied he was tick free he got dressed and went downstairs to speak to his mum, taking his dripping clothes with him to put in the washing machine. His mum knew him too well, as there was a steak bridie sitting under the grill. This was just the pickup he needed after his extreme outdoor experience.

As he sat eating his food, Sam told his mum the sorry tale of the ticks and his dip in the pond. Mrs Hamill moved on from her initial reaction of concern and scolding him for doing anything so stupid as jumping in that pond, to laughing out loud at what must have been quite the predicament. Eventually the subject changed to less exciting matters.
"Old Mrs Young is looking for someone to cut her grass, and I said you'd be ok to do it." Mrs Hamill said.
"Sure" Sam said while taking a bite of his bridie.
She continued "That's great, Sammy. Please remember to not mention anything about her cat. It's been missing for a long time; I think it probably got run over on the main road."
"Oh, I didn't know that" replied Sam in a surprised tone.
"You haven't seen the posters? They're all around the village." his mum said, as if to suggest her son was blind to have not seen any.
Sam then felt a major pang of guilt, having no doubt seen the posters without taking in any of the information on them. In fact, he probably inadvertently covered some of these up with his missing Millie posters.
"Ok, I will avoid any cat-related chat." Sam promised.

He decided the ill-fated trip to the woods was enough outdoor activity for the day and decided to retire to his room to make a new mix tape for his portable cassette player. This would be the soundtrack for his next adventure, and he planned to look out some classic synth selections for the tape, which included Ultravox, OMD, Visage and Depeche Mode.

Sam started leafing through his growing collection of vinyl, both 7" and 12", which were all propped up against either side of his stereo, which itself was on top of his chest of drawers. He took great pride in his records, his favourites safely housed in plastic protective sleeves.

After a few hours of making mix tapes, Sam heard his mum shouting upstairs, asking if he wanted to go with her to his gran and grandad's for dinner. He pondered for a few seconds and said yes.
"Get your skates on then as we're leaving now."
Sam shouted down that he was coming and proceeded to get his trainers on before they took the relatively short stroll down the concrete steps on the hill and across the playing field which led to the back of his grandparents' house.

Handily, Sam's grandad had installed a gate at the bottom of his long back garden, which saved them walking all the way around to the front of the row of terraced houses to enter the property. The downside of this innovation was they had to pass the large metal drum filled with liquid excrement which his grandad used on his vegetable garden. Sam always thought the drum was an odd thing to keep in your garden, but who was he to judge? His grandad's plants were the envy of the street and if he spent his time collecting cow and sheep dung on his morning walks then that was his business.

Both Sam and his mum held their breath for a few seconds as they passed the barrel and were rewarded for their efforts with an altogether better odour as they neared the back steps. The glorious smell of Sam's gran's homemade made steak pie, one of his favourites, filled the air. Sam always enjoyed his grandparents' company, but the meal would be the icing on the cake.

The steak pie was served with boiled potatoes, peas and gravy. Unlike his house, where they either ate at the small kitchen table or with the plates on their laps, his grandparents had a proper dining table, so the four of them could have a proper chat. It was nice to all sit together for a change. Sam and his grandad were now sitting, having organised everyone's drinks, while his mum and gran sorted the food out through in the kitchen. The TV was meant to be off, but the final scores were on the screen of his grandad's TV, which was 'CEEFAX enabled'. Dunfermline had a tough game at home against Queen's Park that they needed to win to keep up their promotion prospects. "Oh no!" they belted out in unison, Sam's grandad following up with "Absolutely rubbish!"

Knowing that they would immediately be asked to turn the TV off, Sam's grandad pre-empted this by rising from his chair and pushing the power button off.

"They got beat, then?" asked Sam's gran, as she carried two plates laden with steaming hot food through to the sitting room.

"No, drew nil, nil." Sam offered, clearly downbeat.

"Not a great result at all." Added Sam's grandad, shaking his head. "These are the games they've got to win."

Sam's mum and gran were not in the least bit interested so it was easy enough to move onto something else.

Sam immediately lifted the mood by telling everyone about his unexpected dip earlier in the day. His gran and grandad bellowed with laughter at the predicament Sam had found himself in. However, their faces changed when he neared the end of his story.

"You got tangled in some grass under the water? His gran asked in a concerned tone.

"Grass, reeds, something like that." answered Sam.

"And it was one of those air shafts?" inquired his grandad.

"I don't know what it's for, but it has bricks all around the outside and barbed wire around most of it." Was Sam's reply.

"That's what it sounds like. I've seen a few of them around. Said his grandad. "I've seen algae on top of the water but never grass growing from underneath that's definitely a first. I wouldn't advise any further swims in them though. They go down really deep and who knows what's in that water?" He continued.

Sam shrugged his shoulders "Definitely not planning on it."

Sam had enjoyed a really nice time with his mum and grandparents, and, after a good feed, Sam was ready for his bed, even though it wasn't particularly late. Sam and his mum took a pleasant nighttime walk back up the hill to their house.

"I know we were all laughing about it, but can you be extra careful when you're out wandering around the outskirts of the village. There are plenty of ways around here to get yourself in bother."

Sam nodded his agreement as they walked the last few yards home.

It was Sunday around 10.30am when Sam's friends
arrived at the door. Sam had completely forgotten that
he'd said he would go out with them today but, as he
was still in his t-shirt and pyjama bottoms, he invited
them into the living room while he bounded upstairs to
get changed. Before Mrs Hamill could finish taking the
boys' tea and biscuits order, Sam was back downstairs,
fully changed and the four pals were all walking out the
front door together.

Without anyone taking any decisions or making any
plans as to where they should go, they all turned, as if by
default, to walk towards the swing park. It was always
the natural choice when they had no prior agenda. As
they walked along Hill View, Gub asked Sam how he
was doing, which was the first time in three months any
of them had asked him that. The boys had been there for
Sam without really doing anything specific. Just general
help and always available with something funny or
entertaining to lift the mood.

Sam knew they all cared, but questions about feelings or
emotions were usually taboo in this group. "Fine…
fine." Sam said rather defensively. However, the three
amigos seemed entirely satisfied with Sam's answer and
were happy to move on. Sam adding "I'm starting to
think Millie isn't ever coming home. I'll try to keep
looking until the matter is closed, either way." Acting as
if the question was actually about the dog, as opposed to

50

his dad. Again, they all nodded empathetically. Sam then told them about the tick incident the day before, which had the gang chortling about it as they cut through the lockups on their way to the swing park.

All the hardware in the park was pretty much falling apart, due to a combination of mistreatment by the village's youths, the weather, and age. The benches were riddled with dry rot and the swings were either missing seats or had been deliberately tangled around the metal bar at the top of the structure which the swing chains hung from. There really was only one option left, so they all draped themselves over the little kids' roundabout while spinning around slowly and shooting the breeze.

As he slowly rotated around, Sam was getting a recurring view of the back of Mrs. Young's house at the bottom end of the park. Eyeballing her back garden, he could see her grass looked about three feet high. 'Well, *fucking great!*' he thought. 'His mum didn't tell him *that!*' When he tuned back in to what the rest were talking about, the conversation was about the best-looking teachers at school.
"Mrs Philips is lush" exclaimed Shug.
"Oh yeah, definitely" added Gub, clearly having given the matter some thought.
"My favourite is Miss Meldrum." Sam chimed in.
"Horrendous voice though" added Tommo, which killed the conversation somewhat.

Margaret Stafford and her pal entered the park from behind the lockups and walked across Sam's eyeline.

They caught each other's gaze briefly before looking away. This time Margaret gave Sam a wee smile, which was a welcome boost that 'hair gate' might possibly be in the rear-view mirror, before the girls continued on their way. A thought occurred to him. Girls didn't walk around the village by themselves anymore, always in twos or more since Lauren's disappearance. And with Lauren occupying some space in his head again, an unfamiliar voice broke his concentration.

"Hey, guys, a body's been found!"
Tommo stopped the roundabout from spinning by letting his foot drag along the ground as they all looked up.
"What?" inquired Shug
"A body's been found."
It took them a second to process what was going on but there standing in front of them was Chris McGregor.
"How do *you* know?" asked a sceptical Shug.
"I was down there by the level crossing and it's all police and ambulances down there. I heard one of the policemen say something about body recovery from the Comrie Burn."

Chris was a couple of years below them at school, but he was likeable and didn't have a reputation for exaggeration or duff info. They all looked at each other wide-eyed, knowing that the burn ran right past The Railway Tavern. None of the gang wanted to show enthusiasm or excitement, because it was obviously a sombre discovery, but this was really big news. Nothing like this had *ever* happened here. In unison, they all immediately jumped up and started jabbering at each other, talking in high-speed sentences, without making much sense.

This could put an end to the mystery that had haunted the village for five months, which is what became of Lauren Smith. It also presented so many questions… how had Lauren died? Was it an accident? Was it a deliberate act and, if so, who did it? The boys all knew that they had no option but to go to the scene and see what was going on.

Gub asked Chris, who was walking with them, "Who found the body?"
"Craig Nisbett and his wee sister, they were walking their dog along the railway line." Chris replied, clearly quite pleased with himself that he had the scoop.
Sam grimaced. His immediate thought was that neither of those kids would sleep tonight, or maybe for some time after. Not before too long, the group were leaving Forth Gardens and were at the steps at the top of the hill which led down to where the main road, the level crossing and the burn all intersected. The Railway Tavern was visible in the distance, directly behind the signal box. Fire engines, police cars and an ambulance were in attendance with their flashing lights illuminating the surrounding trees and nearby buildings in blue. Even in daylight the lights were quite dramatic. Once again, the typically quiet village of Oakley had its peace shattered by a major event.

They walked down the hill, closer to where the police cordon and all the emergency vehicles were parked.

They weren't the only ones who were being nosey, they could see other groups of people standing around waiting to hear any news. As they arrived at the scene, Sam could see Constables Redpath and Seton standing by their patrol car, talking. Also there, he surmised, was the new inspector who was mentioned after his dad's memorial service. Whoever it was, he was clearly in charge, doling out orders to the others.

The five boys positioned themselves as near to the cordon as possible, hoping to hear whatever news there was first-hand. As they waited for developments, they spent their time checking out which other nosey parkers were on the scene. Kirsten McCudden and her friend Suzanne Somerville were there, Mrs Watson and Mrs Bayne were gabbing away by the roadside, a bunch of little kids were riding in circles on their bikes, a few cars were parked at the side of the road gawking at what was unfolding, Mr and Mrs Gillespie were there with their dog and old Mr Slater and *his* dogs were there but he looked like he'd already had enough and was heading back up the road.

For the casual observer, another interesting sight could be seen. The rather flash motor of Clint Westwood himself was parked outside his pub. The cardinal red Rolls Royce Silver Shadow was often seen outside his various pubs and clubs around greater Dunfermline. An instant signal to anyone that he was loaded and wanted everyone to know it.

Westwood was an interesting character. With a name like Samson Westwood anyone would be forgiven for expecting to see a large, impressive looking athletic man with long flowing hair, but Westwood was a bald, overweight diminutive character in his late forties. The nickname 'Clint' was actually a joke to begin with, a play on his last name, and a tongue in cheek reference to the fact he was about as far removed from a leading man as you could get. Westwood didn't care about that, he liked it and made sure it stuck.

Sam let out a long, low whistle as he looked at Clint's car. "That thing is mint."
"I bet Clint is in there briefing Bairn about what to say to the cops." Shug said, with a wry smile on his face.
"Why do you say that?" a puzzled Sam asked.
"I'm half joking, half serious. One of the theories in the village is that Lauren did something to piss Clint off, so he got Bairn to remove her from the equation." Shug explained, while slowly running a finger across his throat.
"What? Get real." scoffed Sam. "Has anyone else heard this theory?"
Gub and Tommo nodded.
"Really? I know Bairn is supposed to be some hard case, but murder? How come the police didn't arrest him then?" Sam queried.
"We all heard he had an alibi, but he could have threatened folk to get them to say that." Tommo suggested, while shrugging his shoulders.
"Do you not think it seems like a really stupid place to leave her body if Bairn did it? The burn is directly

55

behind the pub he works in." Sam said, making a quite reasonable point which the others seemed to agree with.

While the foursome were having their spirited discussion, they didn't immediately notice another car arriving. It had driven all the way down to the level crossing, parking next to the emergency vehicles on the railway access road. All the various conversations suddenly stopped as the watching crowd realised it was Lauren's parents. They had obviously heard about the grim discovery and had come to be there when their daughter's body was recovered. The senior officer, who they assumed was the new inspector, swivelled around, his face turning ashen white.

As the friends looked on, it appeared as though he was rapidly giving orders to the constables with Redpath immediately intercepting the couple as they looked to walk down to the tracks from their vehicle. Mr and Mrs Smith looked understandably crestfallen as they walked towards where Redpath was standing, but rather than Constable Redpath ushering them down to the burn, they got back in their car drove away. How odd, Sam thought to himself.

Immediately after the Smiths' departure, the ambulance was driven from the access road onto the level crossing, the driver manoeuvring the vehicle and reversing up to where the road meets the tracks. The level crossing gates were then lowered so that cars could no longer pass. As the onlookers studied the scene, all eyes were trained on the area immediately behind the ambulance. None of them had any idea what was happening, but they had to assume it was something significant. Then, from behind the pub they could see a couple of medics emerge from the treeline and walk towards the ambulance. They were carrying a stretcher generating audible gasps from onlookers as it was carried into view.

The boys had positioned themselves at what they thought was a good vantage point, but they couldn't really see anything definitive. All they *could* see was what looked like a body covered with a blanket on the stretcher. And, just like that, the stretcher was loaded into the ambulance, which was driven away slowly with the lights flashing as the gates were lifted again. The mood had turned from excitement, not that anyone was outwardly showing any signs of that, to sadness.

As the numerous groups of onlookers started to disperse, Constable Redpath came over to Sam and his friends. It felt quite cool having a policeman leave the cordon to come over and talk directly to them, with the remaining gawkers now redirecting their collective gaze onto them.

"It's not her. It's an elderly male" Redpath said.
Their mouths collectively dropping open.
"Who?" asked Shug.
"We're not 100 percent sure, as we've had no missing person's report. but we think he was a regular from the pub and we're canvassing patrons now."
"What happened to him?" asked Sam.
"We aren't entirely sure, but it doesn't look like foul play. They're taking him for a post-mortem now, but we

think he might have drowned, possibly because he simply fell into the water while intoxicated. We were quite shocked when we heard about the discovery in the first place, as we'd searched the burn three times since Lauren disappeared."

"So, any more news about the missing Dunfermline girl? asked Tommo.

"Not a peep. Just like Lauren Smith, she just seemed to vanish into thin air." Said Redpath. "Anyway, better be getting back to help clear the scene."

This seemed like the obvious time for the boys to head off themselves. They walked Chris back up towards the swing park and let him head off - he couldn't wait to get home to tell his parents the news about the body. The rest of them sort of stood about for a bit and then decided to walk up to the main street.

The boys scuffed their way to the corner of Station Road, wandering down the street past the bookmakers and the police station next door to it. Both were usually shut on a Sunday, but they could see that the station lights were on, silhouettes moving around inside behind the smoked glass. They would undoubtedly be dealing with the dead body discovery which the boys had just seen unfold.

They crossed the street to the community centre and walked behind the main building to the grass fields to watch some of the youth football game being played between Oakley Under 15s and Steelend. Both Tommo and Sam had played for the Oakley youth team up until last year, when they were selected for Queen Anne's school team, and liked to keep tabs on how they were doing.

As they walked past the side of the building, the bulletin board gave them all an instant reminder of both Lauren's and Millie's disappearances given the sheer number of posters on it. The whole board was like a patchwork quilt of grief. Sam spotted one of Mrs Young's missing cat posters, which was one of quite a large number with the 'missing cat' message on it. His mum was right. Sam clearly hadn't been paying attention before but couldn't help but notice them now. Mrs Young's cat had been missing for almost nine months, many of the others seemed to have been for a while too. Sam wasn't too optimistic of any of their chances at making a return home at this point.

Sam clearly should have been paying more attention when the multitude of cat disappearances were the talk of the village, but he must have been focused elsewhere. Thinking back, he had overheard a few suggestions for the perpetrator in the missing cats mystery, possibly a fox or a Scottish Wildcat, some had even suggested a feral dog, which had some merit as there used to be a large one-eyed stray which roamed the village which required people out walking to take a large stick with them, although there had been no sightings of that particular creature for many years. Sam hadn't seen any of the proposed villains around the village so hadn't paid as much attention as he probably should have. He felt a bit guilty now, especially given how many reported disappearances there had actually been.

After watching the football for a short time, the boys all walked over to Vincenzo's, the chippy, for a bag of chips each. Vincenzo's was named after Vince himself and, according to local lore, had originally been called Torretti's but in a twist not unlike the infamous Dassler Brothers feud, Vince and his brother fell out in pretty major fashion, with the brother, Alfredo, moving away opening his own chip shop in High Valleyfield, unsurprisingly called Alfredo's. It was now lunchtime, and they were starving.

They peered in the window, which was completely fogged up with condensation, making it virtually impossible to see anything inside. There were a few clear strips where droplets of water had run down the window, allowing a narrow glimpse to see that Vince was working today and so was his daughter Angela, who was completely gorgeous and, therefore entirely out of their league. Undeterred, they tried to spruce themselves up before entering the shop. Sam ran his fingers through his medium length brown hair, trying to push it back from his forehead into some sort of style. Tommo and Shug both had long red hair, Tommo especially, which was also curly and there was nothing he could really do to improve it today, but he attempted to flatten it down, nonetheless. Gub's hair was shaved so short that it was almost a 'skinhead', so he pulled up his jeans and tucked in his shirt instead. This was all an exercise in futility as

Angela wouldn't be remotely interested in any case. Undeterred, they went in to buy their lunches.

The chip shop was fairly typical for an establishment of that type; a dual-purpose large glass display cabinet, which both showcased the fried wares and also kept the local yokels at a suitable distance from the staff. They all got chips, with standard issue salt and sauce, standing gawking while Angela wrapped up their orders. The general consensus was that they managed to conduct themselves in a positive fashion and made it back outside without embarrassment.

Once outside, the boys raced to unwrap their piping hot bags of chips as quickly as they could in order that they'd swiftly arrive at optimum eating temperature. As they were waiting, Mrs Young walked out of the corner shop next door with her tartan roller shopping bag. She said hello to them all and, seeing Sam, asked him if he was ok to cut her grass.
"It would be nice if you could cut it tomorrow, Sam." She suggested. "Ever since my grandson got his new job, he's always got something more important to do and it hasn't been cut since last August. It's so long, I'm embarrassed to go out the back!"
Sam needed the money and was also feeling bad for her because of her missing cat, so he nodded in agreement.
"What kind of mower do you have, Mrs Young? He asked.
"Oh, I couldn't tell you, son." She replied. "Just your typical lawnmower."
"Ok, I'll be over right after school tomorrow" he said.

And with that she raised her hand to give a wee wave, and she was on her way.

Their chips were now at a digestible temperature and the group started walking to the bottom end of the village, eating and chatting as they went. Sam was detailing his financial woes to his buddies. He had a couple of part-time jobs, he enjoyed cutting grass/weeding but that was mostly seasonal, and he was also a stock boy, restocking shelves at the Co-op a couple of nights a week. It used to be enough, but it wasn't any longer. His dad used to top up his wages with the odd fiver here and there and, obviously, that had been missing for a few months. The insurance money from his dad's accident still hadn't arrived and his mum had burned through most of the money that was in his parents' joint account while she looked for work.

The money from the grass cutting gig wasn't going to make much of a difference, but it all helped. Sam typically got a few quid for a spring clean, but he thought he could get at least £5 for this one, given the scale of the job. He didn't think there would be much chance, but Gub advised him to ask at the Co-op to see if he could get any extra shifts. They all agreed to keep an eye open for any jobs they thought would be useful for Sam, and, until then, he would continue to be highly frugal while looking for any little odd jobs here and there.

The next day, Sam didn't wait for his friends at the school gates like he usually did. He jumped straight on the first bus, as he'd promised Mrs Young that he'd cut her grass today and, in order to get it done before dark, he didn't have time to hang around. It was typically around half an hour by bus from Queen Anne High School in Dunfermline back to the village. and it would be getting dark around 6pm so he figured he'd have about two hours to get home and get over to her house to complete the job.

It was the younger crowd who travelled on this bus and Sam couldn't be bothered with any unnecessary chit chat, so he had already decided to be anti-social and listen to music for the journey's duration. He had come prepared and had a couple of tapes alongside his cassette player in his coat pocket. It was a choice between Sparkle in the Rain or New Gold Dream, both by Simple Minds. He plumped for Sparkle in the Rain.

From the second Sam first stepped foot onboard and flashed his bus pass, the sound of incessant chatter on the bus was already hurting his ears and he couldn't wait to get his headphones on. He climbed upstairs and sat at the very front, which he realised wasn't at all cool, but he liked having the big window to look out of. Headphones on, play button pressed, he was immediately lost in the crashing drums and dramatic piano of Up on the Catwalk.

The journey went quickly, thanks to the music and, apart from nearly jumping out of his skin when the bus clipped a large tree branch, thumping the front side of the bus right next to him, it was otherwise uneventful. He leapt off the bus at his usual stop, jogged the short distance home, dumped his bag and put some old clothes on, that were more suitable for his upcoming gardening duties. He grabbed an apple from the kitchen and walked down to Mrs Young's house via Forth Gardens then the swing park. He knew it would just be the back needing done as, just like his gran and granddad's house along the road from Mrs Young's, the much smaller front garden was paved.

Sam knocked at her front door, as he felt like he didn't know Mrs Young well enough to go around to the back door yet. She greeted him with a broad smile and walked him around the side of her house to her hut, which was positioned directly off of her back path, close to the house. Sam's eyes widened as the hut door swung open, it was full of very old gardening equipment. In front of him was an old push mower, which would be severely sub-optimal for this task. He turned slowly to look at her.

"Unfortunately, that won't work Mrs Young, your grass is far too long" Sam said through gritted teeth. "What about your next-door neighbour, would they let me borrow their mower?"

Mrs Young said "I wouldn't ask that old creep for anything. And I definitely would *not* want to know what he has hidden in his hut." Thinking quickly, he told her he could borrow his grandad's Flymo and immediately started heading along the road to his grandparents' house, which was only two or three minutes away.

Sam's Grandad was his mum's dad. He was a retired miner and was now a full-time gardener/man of leisure. William Wilson's time down the pit had taken its toll, and he had various health issues as a result of his job. He had only worked in two collieries; Solsgirth and Comrie, the latter of which was where he finished his career. He had been forced to stop working early through ill health and the only silver lining about that was he was already out before the miners' strike which tore the community apart only two years ago. There was a lot of conflict at that time, striking miners at odds with the police, as well as with the scabs who crossed the picket line. It was the first time Sam had felt widespread unease in the village. The only time until Lauren's disappearance.

Sam walked in the unlocked back door of his grandparents' house shouting "Hello, it's me."

"Come on through, son." His grandad shouted back from their sitting room.
Sam walked through to see his grandad sitting in his armchair. "I can't stay long, Grandad, I'm cutting old Mrs Young's grass this afternoon."
"It bloody well needs it! It's a joke, have you seen it?" asked his Grandad.

"Unfortunately. That's why I'm here as she only has a push mower" Sam replied, his eyes rolling skywards for effect.

Sam's grandad knew what was coming next and, after walking him back through to the kitchen, rummaged in a small drawer, throwing Sam the key for his hut as his grandson headed out the door towards it. "Thanks! Tell gran I'll see her when I bring it back" Sam shouted from the steps on his way out. His grandad's grass was looking pristine, like a bowling green, and the plants in the greenhouse, probably tomatoes, were looking supremely healthy. He reached the bottom of the garden, where the hut was situated, and unlocked the door to a veritable treasure trove of glistening gardening tools displayed before him. He grabbed the Flymo, locked the door and speed-walked back to the top of the garden, popping his grandad's key on the kitchen counter inside the back door. He had no time to waste.

Sam liked the Flymo. His mum and dad just had a normal electric mower, which was fine but the way the Flymo hovered above the grass was far superior, in Sam's view. Plus, it was the perfect mower for this job, he thought as he arrived back at Mrs Young's house. She opened her kitchen window as Sam passed her the extension cord, so it could be plugged in, and Sam could finally get started.

To begin with, Sam had to lift the mower in the air so he could gradually trim down the grass from the top down, before he could cut it in regular fashion. It was awkward as he had to keep the mower raised at knee level while avoiding severing the electrical cable, but he was making some headway. Her property, which was typical for the area, was comprised of a very short front garden on the street side and a very long and skinny back garden. The bottom end of the back garden buffering with the lower side of the swing park.

Sam had now managed to trim down, followed up with a proper mow, about four rows of grass. The new growth nearest to the soil was looking nice and healthy so it might end up looking alright, he thought. Sam carried on until he had about half of the lawn to go.

Cutting the grass was hard work, so Sam decided to take a short break. Sam asked Mrs Young, who was now watching him from the bench under her back window, for a glass of water before continuing. Sam was well over the halfway point now and it hadn't taken him as long as he'd thought, mainly due to the superior quality of the Flymo. As he lowered the mower down onto the grass at the bottom end, he noticed something poking out of the ground near the roots of the grass. He carefully mowed the tall stalks of grass down a bit further then abruptly stopped. It was an animal, and it was very dead.

It was only because of the ginger and white fur protruding from the soil that he could identify what it was; a cat. Based on his recent contemplation on the cat disappearances, Sam wondered if a wild animal had indeed killed it as it looked pretty mangled, the passage of time had not helped either with the poor creature looking pretty much like fur covered bones. He used the plastic edge of the mower cover to partially lift the carcass up from the soil. It was very easy to move as the soil was dry, the poor animal was smattered with dried blood, and it was hard to see which part of it was which. He took a deep breath and stepped away for a second, realising he would need to tell Mrs Young. He went to fetch her, knocking on her back door, as she was now back inside.

Sam steeled himself and took a deep breath. "I have some bad news, Mrs Young. I think I've found the remains of your cat at the bottom of the garden. Was your cat orange and white?"
"Ohh, nooo. My wee pal" she said her voice wavering as she spoke.
Sam didn't know what to say. "What was its name?" he asked her.
"Ginger Rogers, because of her colouring."
"A nice name" Sam said, somewhat insincerely. "You might not want to come over, as she's in a pretty bad way."
She really appreciated him saying this. "Thanks, son."
I'd like to remember her the way she was. Would you mind putting her remains in a box or a bag? This wasn't exactly part of the job description, but he knew it was the right thing to do.
"Do you have a shoebox or something similar? He asked. She went inside and gave him an old Clark's shoebox. After raking around in Mrs Young's shed for a

68

shovel, Sam prised the now dried up carcass of Ginger Rogers up from under the ground and into the box, a faded and tarnished pink collar and heart-shaped tag becoming visible as he did so. He was half looking and half looking away while performing this unsavoury task. It was in vain, however, as he had seen enough to have that image in his head for a good while. He placed the box down on the grass.

After completing this unenviable task, Sam double-checked with Mrs Young about the collar and tag, which she confirmed belonged to Ginger Rogers. He put his hand on her shoulder and gave his condolences again, although not really saying anything new, Mrs Young appeared to appreciate the sentiment. Not wanting to move on to the task in hand too quickly, he checked that she was ok, but he really needed to finish the mowing as daylight was running out, given the unexpected disruption.

After what he felt was an appropriate pause, Sam walked down to the bottom of the garden where the mower was sitting. He looked back at Mrs Young, who was back on her bench and still visibly upset, using a tissue to dab the tears from her eyes. He finished the last few rows of grass, which looked pretty good, considering it had been neglected for such a long time. The only section which didn't look great was the area where the cat's remains were. There was now a shallow hole there, and the area around it was more or less completely bare.

Sam walked back up to the back door, bringing the shoe box, the mower and the rest of tools up with him. He informed Mrs Young that he'd re-seed the bare patch sometime in the next couple of weeks, now that the frost was no longer likely. To show her gratitude, she gave him a twenty-pound note for his trouble, which made Sam double take for a second, as this was much more than he was expecting. She did have one last request, however. "Would you mind helping me give her a proper burial? Sam nodded a solemn agreement to this request, plus it was the most he'd ever been paid for anything, so he was happy to oblige.

She pointed him to an area with some plants near her shed and asked him to dig a hole right under a small tree to the side of her garden, which he did with the shovel he had borrowed earlier. As he placed the box in the hole she started to cry and repeatedly said "I'll miss you, I love you" to the deceased cat. Sam was almost in tears himself, not so much for the cat but for Mrs Young. It was a heart-wrenching scene. Before he re-filled the hole, Mrs Young threw a small fluffy mouse toy in on top of the box and then turned away. The whole episode had been too much for her and she went back inside.

Sam finished covering the box with dirt, then carrying a shovelful of excess soil down to the bottom of the garden to fill in the hole and even it out somewhat. When he finished, Sam knocked on Mrs Young's back door to say goodbye. She seemed a little better. She was sitting in her kitchen with a cup of tea and a biscuit and said thanks again for his efforts. It had been a long afternoon but as darkness started to fall, Sam headed back to his grandparents' house and, man, did he have a story to tell them.

After Monday's excitement with the dead cat discovery, the rest of the week had been extremely boring by comparison and, now that he had made it to Friday afternoon, Sam was ready for the weekend. The only interesting thing to happen between his couple of Co-op evening shifts and school, was Tommo had told Sam he had a job prospect for him. It was an evening job with a fruit machine company, and he would, to all intents and purposes, be simply accompanying someone while they drove around in a van emptying cash from the machines a few nights a week. It sounded ideal and, consequently, Sam now had an interview after school today in the Miners' Welfare with one of the bosses, who Tommo's mum knew. His boss at the Co-op had already told him that two nights a week was all they needed so he was hoping this new potential gig would work out and provide him with some much-needed extra cash.

On the bus journey home, Sam's crew were all trying to work out what plans they could organise for the weekend. Sam was focused on his job interview but hoped to be out with the boys afterwards, not that they had anything all that good planned. The best they could come up with was watching a video at Tommo's house with the traditional large selection of crisps and a few cans of juice. It would have to do.

The school bus pulled up outside the Co-op and the boys all jumped off. They said their goodbyes, Sam crossing the road, walking back the way the bus had come, towards the main road, past the bookies and cop shop with the others heading straight into Mr Das's to browse available videos. The Miners' Welfare Club was next on the left and he wandered in. Since his grandad was a retired miner, Sam had spent a considerable amount of time in this building throughout his life. The club did have some redeeming qualities, however. They had a monthly teenage disco that they all would regularly go to, they had 5p a game pool tables as well as darts, cards and dominoes, and hard and soft drinks, which were ridiculously cheap. In a village like Oakley, it was a great place to go if the weather wasn't good to while away a few hours, and many people often did.

As he walked along the path towards the front door of the club, Sam stopped for a second to gather himself. He looked at the non-descript building with its off-white roughcast exterior and took a deep breath. Why was he nervous? It was highly unlikely that this was to be a lifechanging moment. He exhaled slowly and walked in the front door.

As Sam entered through the main doorway, Steve Wilkins was waiting for him on the wooden bench inside the entranceway. He stood up and they shook hands. Steve stood out like a sore thumb with his long, thin face, pin striped suit and ultra shiny patent leather shoes. His hair was long and slicked back, not unlike Peter

Murphy's in the Maxell television advert. Steve seemed nice but had that sort of spivvy used car salesman demeanour, including stereotypical thin moustache. They walked through to a side room where he closed the door behind him, the two of them sitting down at an old card table.

"So, Sam, why do you want a career in puggie emptying?" Watkins said while placing his hands down on the green felt of the table. Sam certainly didn't want a *career* doing this and was struggling to think of an answer that didn't sound dismissive or rude when Steve burst out laughing. "Just winding you up, mate." Steve continued. "Karen Thomson already vouched for you, and I just wanted to meet you in person before offering you the job. There's not a lot to it. You accompany our driver, Derek, as he collects the cash, really as an extra pair of eyes. We have a new insurance requirement to fulfil, otherwise we'd still be just using one body to collect the cash. If you want the job, you're in." Sam wasn't daft, he knew he was the cheapest option. What the insurance company was recommending was protection, or muscle, for the driver and Sam knew he wouldn't be providing either of those. The company had a box to tick, and he was the low-cost solution.

Sam nodded. "What are the hours and the pay?"

"Friday 6-9 and Sunday 5-8." Replied Wilkins. "£10 a shift."

£20 a week wasn't bad at all, Sam thought, his Co-op pay was less for the same time commitment, although his weekends were going to take a pretty major hit, it would seem. Sam had heard that you should always sleep on a job offer but, on the spur of the moment, he said yes. The money was too good to turn down.

"Welcome aboard and you start tonight." Steve added.

"Tonight? Oh, I assumed it would maybe be next week." replied Sam.

"Afraid so, we have a requirement to do this right away for our insurers and we should have done this a few weeks ago." Sam reluctantly agreed. "You'll get your pay on Sundays; I'll make sure Derek brings it. Will I tell him to pick you up here or somewhere else?"

"Yes, here sounds fine to me," said Sam. And that was that. He had planned on doing an hour looking for Millie tonight, but he'd have to go tomorrow now.

Sam said goodbye to Steve and sped home via the lane beside Mrs Young's house, briefly admiring her neatly cut back grass as he galloped past. In a matter of minutes, he was home, bursting in the front door and giving his mum a fright. He explained to her as he was grabbing a sandwich that he'd landed this new job, and that it started tonight.

"Good for you, Sam! I'll make one for you, if you want to go and get changed?" she offered.

75

"Great, thanks mum," he said. Sam hadn't thought to ask if there was a dress code but couldn't imagine why there would be, as he laid out his newest jeans, hooded top and his best trainers – Adidas ZX450s, which he always wore when trying to make a good impression. He turned on his stereo and thought about putting on the radio for a second but then decided on the 12" of Blue Monday to get him in the mood for his new gig. The thumping base was pretty much shaking the walls as he brushed his teeth and gave himself a quick splash bath over the sink. He sprayed some deodorant on and combed his hair back and he was pretty much ready to go.

Sam sat with his mum for a bit while he ate the sandwich she'd made him. She had put a slice of tomato on a cheese sandwich, for reasons he couldn't fathom. Even at sixteen, Sam's mum was still trying to get him to eat tomatoes, which he had always hated. He ate it anyway, tomato and all, so as not to offend, although making a very obvious disgusted face when doing so. He washed it down with a cold glass of Ribena and he was now itching to leave, even though he still had a little time. Just then, there was a knock on the door. They weren't expecting anyone but they both went to the door to see who it was. It was Derek Paton at his door in his 'uniform'… standard black heavy metal t-shirt, Ozzy on this occasion, black jeans, black leather jacket and black doc martins. Derek is tall and thin, and, along with his long dark hair parted in the middle, he looked somewhat of the rocker stereotype. "I'm looking for Sam Hamill, security guard?" Said Derek to a bemused Sam. The penny dropping that Derek the van driver was Derek Paton. He had assumed Derek would be someone he didn't know but he knew Derek to nod to around the village. Derek was a few years older than him, Sam reckoned maybe eighteen/nineteen, so they had operated in different circles, but they were on friendly terms, much to Sam's relief.

Sam remembered that this wasn't the pickup point, saying. "Oh, wait a minute." Wasn't I supposed to meet you at the Miners' Welfare?".

"Don't worry, must have been crossed wires. I'm happy to get you here." Derek confirmed.

Sam shrugged his shoulders and headed out, turning back around to ask his mum, who was still standing in the doorway, to call Tommo's mum to say thanks for the job recommendation and to tell the boys not to expect him tonight, which she nodded in agreement to do. As they continued down the front path, Sam almost stopped in his tracks as his eyes met the ancient looking brown Ford van parked outside. Derek smiled and rubbed his hands together with excitement as they approached.

They climbed into the van, Derek into the driver's seat and Sam into the passenger seat, Sam toeing the empty bottles and crumpled up paper bags in the foot well out of the way as he moved into position. Looking behind him, Sam took a quick scan of the interior of the van and wondered how he was a going to spend two evenings a week in a portable rubbish bin. Two front seats, a radio, a carpeted floor, what appeared to be an old couch in the back, and the smell of rotting food – what's not to like?

Derek chimed in "Great, eh?"

"What?" Sam queried, genuinely puzzled.

"The van, the *vannn*." Derek said, while attempting to present the van in a positive fashion, with the use of accompanying hand gestures.

"Oh, yeah, magic." Sam said, trying to sound sincere.

"This job is the best" said Derek enthusiastically. "Not only do I get to use the van all week, the petrol's free as well! If you ever need a lift anywhere just let me know."

Sam nodded rapidly at him, attempting to look appreciative. "They let you keep the van even though you only do two shifts a week?" he asked.

"No, I also do the money drops as well as switch out the machines sometimes, and some other odds and ends. It's not quite a full-time gig but sometimes seems like it is." replied Derek. Sam nodded.

The only area of the van which wasn't strewn with discarded crisp packets, fish and chip wrappers and juice bottles was the very back by the doors where around a dozen or more white bags were sitting. Derek saw Sam spot them.

"Those are the cash bags. That's basically the job right there. And don't get any ideas about pinching any of the money, as you can't." Derek exclaimed with a smirk.

Sam stammered "I... I wouldn't." and started to shake his head slightly. It hadn't even entered his head, to be fair.

"You wouldn't? *I* would. I genuinely mean you can't. The machines tally the money on a paper receipt. and they provide specifically marked bags to empty into, so it all has to be accounted for. And if it isn't, we're toast" Derek explained with the most serious look on his face. "Who cares about that though? We get to cruise around in this mean machine and that's all that matters." said Derek, showcasing his serious face again. Sam gave the merest of smiles in acknowledgement before Derek finished with. "So, Dunfermline first and finish back here is the plan."

Sam agreed, although there didn't appear to be much of a choice.

"Also, you get paid for 3 hours but we can do it in 2, sometimes an hour and a half if the conditions are right." Sam nodded again, although was thinking this gig could be very good if it's £10 for 90 minutes' work.

They turned left out of Hill View onto Station Road and then immediately right, adjacent to the Miners' Welfare, where Sam was originally to be picked up, onto Carnock Road. The road was busy, but they made good time going into Dunfermline. The van was extremely loud, rattling and creaking the whole way in. Sam didn't want to ask on his first time out, but he was thinking some music would help disguise the noise. Sam then had second thoughts, as God only knows what kind of tunes Derek would be playing.

"Big cheese mansion." Said Derek, breaking the silence.

"Sorry?"

"Big cheese mansion." repeated Derek, this time nodding across to his left towards a large house set a good distance back from the road, as they approached the outskirts of Dunfermline. "Clint Westwood's house."

"Oh" replied Sam, nodding in acknowledgement.

"Yep. The pub king of Fife has done well for himself." added Derek. "The publican game has been good for him, among other things."

Sam hadn't heard anything much about Clint Westwood so just nodded again while looking over at the house, which was a large, modern looking detached villa surrounded by small trees and privacy fencing.

Their territory was not *all* of Dunfermline, just the western part of town and the villages further to the west of that and, just as Derek had described, each cloth cash bag had the name of the establishment written on it in permanent marker. Their first stop was The Wander Inn which meant parking right outside on the yellow line with the hazard lights flashing, grabbing the designated cloth cash bag, the keys for that particular machine, walking in and emptying the cash into the bag along with the printed record of the takings. Easy. It didn't take more than a few minutes, and they were off again to the next place. The full bag was put against the side of the van wall and when they arrived outside of The Wine Bar, they grabbed that bag and so on. Derek had this gig down to a fine art. Into town via the high road and back out on the low road going through Crossford and Cairneyhill and looping back up into Oakley via Station Road.

"Do you ever get any hassle?" asked Sam.

"I can handle myself, if that's what you're asking?" Derek said in response.

It wasn't. "I meant punters playing the machines getting annoyed. Do they complain when you have to shift them?"

"No. we don't really interfere too much. They might have to pause for a minute but that's about it." Derek explained, and that was good enough for Sam.

By the time they arrived back in Oakley they only had three bags left. "Where do the bags go once we're done?" Sam inquired.

"The vending company has a lock-up near the bowling club" replied Derek.

They went to The Black Dog, the Miners' Welfare and finished at The Railway Tavern. They then drove towards the lock-up so Sam could see where it was. As they approached, he could see it was dark and deserted and didn't look all that secure.

"Aren't they worried about theft?" Sam asked.

"They don't seem to be. To be honest, I don't think it's all that much money, plus it's all in shrapnel so any thief would need a vehicle themselves. Plus, it's only here for a day or two at most and it's picked up and banked anyway." explained Derek.

Derek opened the door of the lock-up with one of a multitude of keys he had on a keyring in his pocket and stood at the door. Sam positioned himself at the back of the van, and as he passed each bag to Derek, he tossed them inside the lock-up. In very short order, all the bags were inside and that was it, the job was over. Derek locked the lock-up door and asked where Sam wanted to go. Sam asked to be dropped off on Wardlaw Way, i.e. Tommo's house.

"What are you guys up to?" Derek asked.

"Just watching a video," replied Sam.

"Oh, sounds good. Any chance I can join?"

But Sam explained that he didn't think that would be fair as Tommo wasn't even expecting *him*, never mind Derek as well. Derek accepted this and bid Sam farewell as he slowed to a halt outside Tommo's.

"See you on Sunday!" he shouted to Sam out the open van window as he screeched off. The van leaving behind a cloud of white smoke that was reminiscent of a plume from one of the colliery's steam locomotives.

Tommo's mum let Sam in. He made sure to thank her for the job referral before running upstairs to join the video viewers.

"Alright?" Gub said as Sam walked in to see the lads scattered around Tommo's room. Tommo was sitting upright on his bed, Gub was sitting in the chair in front of the bedroom window, and Shug on the end of the ottoman that was situated at the end of Tommo's bed.

"I see you rented Fletch again" said Sam, noticing they were already halfway through one of their regular rentals. What else did you get?"

"Weird Science" Gub and Shug replied in unison.

"Nice" Sam said, nodding in appreciation.

It was fortunate that Mr Das's shop had a small video library at the back of the store, but it was usually slim pickings on the rental front, especially over the weekend. Even still, the ritual of choosing videos to watch for the evening, hoping one of the new releases would still be available, but then realising they never were and picking the best of the rest that were left was always something to look forward to at the end of the week. Sam hoped his new job wouldn't prevent him from partaking in this exercise in future.

"How did you get on with the new gig?" asked Shug, as Sam stood in the open doorway.

"It seems pretty good, so far anyway. It's really easy. It looks like it'll be much the same every time, so I think it'll be fine. Money's good, so no complaints." replied Sam. "I said thanks your mum on the way up." He continued, as he turned to face Tommo "that was really good of her."

Tommo asked "Who's your boss?"

"Wouldn't say boss, exactly, but the van driver is Derek Paton."

Tommo spat out some of his Orangeade. "Ha, ha. That tube? That is priceless. I didn't know he worked there."

"Well, he can drive, other than that we seem to have the same job. Plus, he seems alright to me. Why do you think he's a tube?" Sam queried.

"He's just a bit of an arse. Harmless but definitely an arse. He'll wear you down in due course, you'll see. I see him racing around the village all the time with his heavy metal tunes blaring." Tommo retorted while mockingly headbanging and playing air guitar.

Sam laughed. Now that the Spanish Inquisition was over, he rummaged around in the white plastic bag resting on the floor in front of him, grabbing a bag of pickled onion Monster Munch and a bottle of Irn Bru and sat down beside Shug to lose himself in the film, for a short while at least.

Chapter Six
Blowing Smoke

The next morning Sam was up with the lark again and repeated his previous Saturday effort of dog searching, although this time he decided to get a different roll from Mr Das, to mix things up a bit. His choice this time, a bacon and potato scone roll with brown sauce. With his bag of provisions, Sam wandered from the shop down to the railway crossing to see if there was anything of interest there after the body had been found the week before, and, of course, look for any signs of Millie.

He'd polished off his roll by the time he arrived at the railway crossing and had shimmied through the little gap in the gate to gain access to the tracks. He walked for only a minute or so and he could see where the emergency services had cleared a path through the undergrowth to access the body in the burn.

Sam thought about how the old man had met his demise in the water. His mum had told him that it was Mr Leitch, an OAP and long-time Oakley resident they'd known, who'd died. Apparently, he left the pub drunk, falling over the stone wall into the burn as he headed home for the night, ultimately drowning in the shallow water. A terrible way to go but possibly the saddest part was that nobody posted him missing. He lived on his own, had no close family and it took three or four days to recover his wallet, so identification was difficult.

Sam's mum had also told him that the locals who frequent the bar were organising the funeral.

The fact that it was Mr Leitch and not Lauren also meant they were no further forward in solving the mystery around her. Sam did wonder, going by Shug's theory about Lauren having done something to get on the wrong side of Clint Westwood's crew, that maybe old Mr Leitch had gone the same way. As soon as the thought entered his head, he dismissed it, as they surely can't just be killing everyone that crosses them. That would definitely draw attention, especially in a place of Oakley's size. Sam decided an unfortunate accident was much more probable.

Sam continued up the railway line towards the colliery. He wasn't sure if he would quite go as far as the pit today, he would just play it by ear.

It was another pretty day. The sun was out, and it was too warm for a jacket, so Sam took his black Harrington off and tied the sleeves around his waist, so he didn't need to carry it. He whistled and shouted for Millie as he went but he'd already been up this way weeks ago so was not hopeful of success. He was compelled to keep looking though, and he had nothing else to do in any case.

Sam continued on for about half a mile and then decided to change direction, cutting east through a field then across the Saline Road towards the Bluebell Woods. Once in the woods, he started following a little dirt path beside the Blair Burn which continued out of the woods and onto a farmer's field which ran behind the football ground. He regretted going this direction as it was muddy and was far too exposed for Millie to be hiding out here in any case. He was grateful, however, that he hadn't worn his good trainers as he trudged through the soaking wet field. He stopped for a second and looked downhill towards the village. He had a great view from up here. It wasn't particularly elevated, but it was high enough to see much of the village. He could see his grandparents' house behind Blairwood Park, Oakley United's football ground, and wondered if there was a home game today. He could also see all the way to his street, although his house was obscured by other homes. Sam was impressed at how many houses he could see from his vantage point and even on this mild morning there were smoking chimneys as far as the eye could see.

Sam carried on walking until he met the farm road that would take him back down to the village. It started off as a dirt road, but, as he neared the village, it turned from dirt to gravel and then to tarmac. He continued downhill heading in the direction of the village, reaching the small collection of commercial businesses on the other side of the football ground as he got closer to the main road. The car repair shop, the tile store, the joiner's office. Sam glanced to his left as he walked by and stopped in his tracks… Derek's rusting heap of a van was sitting on the little gravel side road outside of the lock-up where they stored the cash bags last night. Curiosity got the better of him and he decided to investigate.

The lock-up door was closed and locked, so Sam knocked, hard. After what seemed like a few minutes Derek opened the door from the inside. This particular lock up was one in a row of three and were all basically just standard car garages by another name. In fact, the door handle was identical to the one on his Uncle Tam's garage and it looked like, just like with his, that the door was being pulled up from the inside via a short rope. As the door slid upwards Sam could see Derek's black boots, then black jeans appear under the door and before he knew it, there he was standing there looking bemused.

"What the fuck are *you* doing here?" Derek demanded to know, albeit with a wry smile on his face.

"I suppose I could ask the same." retorted Sam. "I saw the van so was curious. I thought the pickups were just Fridays and Sundays?"

"Aye, but that's money in. Money out can be anytime." Derek explained."

"Oh", Sam said with surprise. "So, they're picking up this morning?"

"Sure are. Sometimes I take the cash to them, sometimes they come here, sometimes they wait, and we do it during the week. But keep that to yourself. It's why I have twenty-four-hour access and can come here any time I want, so sometimes I'll be here even when they're not coming. Another perk of the job."

"Oh" said Sam again, wondering what could possibly be interesting about hanging out at a damp, windowless lock-up. There was a faint sound of music coming from a small radio sitting on top of a pile of cardboard boxes which were stacked against the rear wall. This would have been Derek's 'entertainment' while he waited for whoever was coming to pick up the money bags.

Sam looked around the inside of the lock up. There was nothing very exciting about it. One large front door and a standard wooden rear exit door up the back. and what he saw confirmed what he was thinking. The small space was basically a breezeblock and mortar replica of the van with discarded food wrappers and cans laying around on the floor, as well as all over the one and only table inside. The main difference from the back of the van was this place had no natural light whatsoever and, by necessity, had a buzzing, strobing fluorescent strip light in the middle, directly above the table, which shone its artificial glare on the white cloth cash bags they had deposited last night.

"How long do you need to wait?" asked Sam.

"Hopefully not much longer, the pickup is already late. What are you doing later?" Derek inquired.

"Probably looking for my dog." Sam answered quickly, hoping that his response would sound convincing.

"Oh, ok, no problem. If you ever need help looking, let me know. I'd love to have a dog, but my mum and dad won't let me get one." Explained Derek, pretending to cry and wiping non-existent tears from his eyes with his knuckles.

"Thanks, I'll keep that in mind. See you tomorrow night." said Sam, heading off having narrowly avoided a request to hang out with Derek, again. He wondered how long he would be able to keep him at bay. This will be what Tommo was getting at, he thought to himself.

Sam cut through the lane next to Mrs Young's house again and she was outside checking on her plants.

"Oh, hiya son. What have you been up to? She asked.

"Just looking for Millie, Mrs Young."

"Still no sign, son? I'm not really a big fan of dogs usually but as long as they're nice I'm ok with them. I used to see your dad with her a lot, she seemed a friendly dog." She asked.

"Yes, she is. She's too friendly, if you know what I mean." Which Sam wished he hadn't said as it made Millie sound overtly amorous.

"Sorry you haven't found her yet." She said as she turned to look across at her next-door neighbour's house, her face suddenly conveying a pained expression. As she turned back towards Sam, her mouth opened as if she was about to say something about her neighbour, but, after a short pause, she didn't, just looking back at him, saying. "See you later then, son."

As Sam arrived back home, he noticed a strange black car parked outside. When he walked up to the front door, he could see through the living room window that the new police inspector was sitting on the edge of the couch having a cup of tea. He should have recognised the car. It was a plain, but now very obvious, Ford Sierra, which he should have known is the standard unmarked police car around here. He walked in to see what was going on.

Standing up to shake Sam's hand, the Inspector was tall and thin with short dark hair. He also seemed young for an Inspector. "Hello Sam. I'm Inspector Paterson, nice to properly meet you. The lads at the station have told me a lot about you. As you know, we have been continuing our enquiries into the disappearance of Lauren Smith and have now broadened out our investigation to include Michelle Polson, who recently went missing from Dunfermline."

"Your dad was instrumental in putting Lauren's case file together which was a very difficult job, given there is so little hard evidence to go on. We have now transposed all of his meticulous notes so we thought it might be nice if we gave his old notebooks to his family. We only ask that we keep them handy in case we need to refer to the original notes in the future. Very unlikely but possible." Sam took the stack of eight or nine notebooks, saying thank you, before temporarily departing the room to put them on the shelf above the kitchen table, stopping for a moment to open one of the books and seeing his dad's version of shorthand inside. It was strange seeing his dad's writing in this way, and it gave Sam goosebumps as he thought about his dad doing the job he loved.

When Sam returned, the Inspector and his mum were discussing Michelle Polson's disappearance. "We have no option but to assume the two disappearances are connected, Mrs Hamill, given cases of this nature are so rare and taking into account the geographic closeness of the locations." explained the Inspector. And, with that, the inspector was standing up and ready to go. Sam walked the inspector to the door. "Feel free to swing by the station any time, the lads would like that." Sam nodding to convey that he would.

Once the Inspector was away, Sam went through to the kitchen, leafing through another of his dad's old notebooks. Not much by the way of interesting stuff was to be found; details of speeding drivers, the description of a missing black cat, a report on missing tools from someone's hut were the highlights of the first few pages, which told its own rather dull story about life in the village.

Sam was hungry and had a look to see what they had in for lunch. There was a scotch pie in the fridge and that would hit the spot, so he turned on the grill to heat it up. Sam felt like he'd been neglecting his mum of late, so he sat through in the sitting room with the pie and an accompanying cup of tea. She had been doing better lately but, since his dad's death, she had been different.

It was totally understandable after a huge shock like that, but she had started sleeping a lot during the day and didn't seem to want to socialise like she used to. She was the social butterfly of the family, or certainly used to be, more than making up for his dad's reserved demeanour, but these days she was becoming more reclusive. Sam wasn't sure what to do to help and keeping his mum company this afternoon was the best he could offer right now.

"What are you up to today, mum?"
"Nothing much" she replied, "but later this afternoon I've arranged to go and see your Granny Agnes and Grandad Bob."
"Oh, do you want me to come?"
"That would be lovely. I feel like I've neglected them since your dad's death. Aside from your dad's service, I haven't seen much of them recently. They would love to see you too." She added.
"Ok, I'll come as well, then, it'll be great to see them." said Sam.

After a few hours hanging around the house and listening to the Dunfermline game on the radio, in which they triumphed away from home over local rivals Cowdenbeath, they were ready to go. It was a dry evening, so his mum's lack of a driving licence wasn't an issue, and they strolled up through the heart of the village, past the shops, towards Erskine Wynd. His dad's parents lived in the bottom flat in a two flat building. They had a larger front garden than his other grandparents, which some neighbours had turned into a driveway, and a decent sized back garden, which was split in half between them and their upstairs neighbours. Both were entirely covered in grass, the front looking impressive with neatly mowed rows going left to right and vice versa.

Both of Sam's dad's parents were heavy smokers and, as the front door opened, he could already spy the ever-present cloud of stoor behind his grandad in the hallway. This cloud would undoubtedly be present in the living room and the kitchen too. His grandad was all smiles as he showed them through to the back room. Sam's Granny Agnes was sitting in her big armchair and rose to her feet as they walked in, giving both Sam and his mum a big hug. Sam scanned around the room, getting an instant reminder that his grandparents' entire lounge was a shrine to smoking. In this house it was more of an occupation than a pastime. Giant table lighters made of metal and semi-precious stone rubbed shoulders with crystal ashtrays. Smoking paraphernalia adorned every surface, including the coffee table, side tables, the mantlepiece and the top of the tv, which could occasionally be seen clearly when the cloud of smoke dissipated.

Incredibly, or maybe this was the very reason why they weren't smokers, neither his dad nor his Uncle Tam had taken up the habit. Probably having second-hand smoked a pack a day in their younger years was what kept them from becoming smokers themselves.

Sam followed his granny through to the kitchen where dinner was bubbling away on the stove. "What's cooking, gran?"

"Goulash, son"

"Goulash?" Sam wondered out loud.

"It's Hungarian stew. I promise you'll like it." She replied.

Sam loved spending time with both sets of grandparents, but he found it difficult to see as much of his dad's parents because they both worked full time. His grandad worked as a security guard for Dunfermline District Council and his gran was a secretary for the owner of a large furniture store, both were located in Dunfermline. When he did see them, however, he was always well looked after. This side of the family were more subdued than his mum's side, with them both leading a pretty quiet existence, with his dad and Uncle Tam both being fairly quiet too.

Sam helped his gran move the kitchen table out from against the wall and set it for dinner. His gran had also bought good bread from the shop. It was a pretty simple dinner, stew with buttered bread, but this was the perfect family meal, and his granny was right, Sam *did* like the Goulash.

"I see Dunfermline won, Sammy." said his Grandad.

"I know, grandad, terrific result. I listened on the radio." Replied Sam.

"The pressure doesn't seem to be showing... yet. That's twice we've beaten them there in a few weeks." His grandad said enthusiastically.

Sam nodded vigourously. "I just wish we could get there, grandad, it would be so good for the club to get back into the first division."

"It would, son. It would." opined his grandad, while nodding in agreement.

"Have you seen any of your dad's police colleagues lately?" Sam's granny asked him.

"Yes, gran. I have been in to see them a few times. They've been really busy on the Lauren Smith case."

"Oh, aye. Terrible, that. I see her mum along at the shops every now and then, poor thing." Sam's gran responded.

"I don't suppose they're any closer to finding her?"

"No, they have very little to go on." Sam explained, solemnly.

"Your dad said the same." She replied, her voice wobbling a bit. "He so dearly wanted to find out what happened to that girl."

"He really did" added Sam's mum.

Everyone sat in silence for a minute after that.

Sam's granny went through to the kitchen to clear the table and bring dessert through. It was Baked Alaska, which was her speciality. It was a triumph, as usual. They sat and enjoyed their dessert and reminisced about Sam's dad. It had been a long overdue visit, but it was just like old times. The sign to depart was when Sam's grandparents started getting their cigarette packets out for a post-meal smoke. The smoke clouds had been

97

absent for a while as they all ate their dinner, but Sam and his mum knew to leave before they returned, so they said their thankyous and goodbyes and headed back down the road.

Chapter Seven
There Will Be Blood

Uncharacteristically, Sam had slept in, but, despite the later hour, he decided to do another futile shift looking for Millie anyway. He made himself some toast and a cup of tea and sat in the kitchen wondering where his mum could be? Usually, she'd leave him a note, but he couldn't see one, so he left one for her instead.

For today's adventure, Sam decided to search near the bottom end of the village, an area known colloquially as the flat roofs, which bumps up against some farmers' fields and a large private estate called Pitgarvie. He walked out of Hill View and onto Station Road, then along Wardlaw Way past Tommo's and then took a right turn down the lane which leads to Sir George Bruce Road. He had considered chapping on Tommo's and/or Shug's doors, as the lane was very close to their houses, but decided to go solo since he hadn't given them any warning. He was about halfway down the lane when he heard Tommo shouting for him.

"Sam! *Sam*!! I saw you walking past my window." Tommo said, out of breath, as he caught up to where Sam was. "Where you off to? Looking for Millie, I am guessing?"
"Yeah, over to Pitgarvie Estate today, I reckon." answered Sam.
"What about the gamekeeper? I've heard stories about him shooting people who trespass."

"I think that was a long time ago, plus I heard that it was with salt pellets so not exactly lethal."

"Can I chum you, then?" Tommo asked, seemingly unperturbed by the prospect of being shot at. And, with Sam answering in the affirmative, they set off downhill towards the Carnock Burn.

On their right was The Black Dog, where Sam had just been on his cash collecting duties only a couple of days earlier and would be again tonight. Next, they wandered past the little row of shops next to the pub. There was the paper shop, the Ironworks Café and the hairdresser where Lauren used to work. "Let's get some juice for our travels" suggested Tommo, so they went into the newsagent to get supplies.

With their newly purchased cans of Red Kola in hand, they continued their quest towards the Pitgarvie Estate, heading up the hill towards the flat roofed houses. They cut up Lindsay's Wynd, in order to get to the walking path at the end of the street which would take them out of the residential area and into the fields behind. Once again, Sam saw the now iconic brown van. "Is this where Derek lives?" he asked Tommo. "Yep, that's his mum and dad's house." He replied. They continued on, half expecting Derek to come bounding out to greet them, but he never did.

Sam and Tommo walked further on to where the path narrowed significantly then disappeared altogether as they crossed from the playing field into a farmer's field. There were gorse bushes marking the outskirts of the farm property and the field itself had what looked like potato seedlings growing in it.

The pair carried on walking along the side of the field, being careful not to stand on any of the future crops. Soon enough, they reached the fence at the end of the field which separated it from the railway line and walked around the back end until they came to the stone bridge which took them over the track. As they walked over the bridge. the vast woodland which covered most of the estate was visible as far as their eyes could see. Now that they were on the other side of the railway line, they only had the short walk down to Sunnyside Road and they'd be standing at the small stone dyke which marked the boundary of the estate.

As they walked down the hill towards the road, they cracked open their cans of Red Kola and clunked them together as a mock toast to celebrate nearing their target. "Do you have any clues about Millie at all?" Tommo asked.
"Absolutely nothing at all. It's bizarre." offered Sam. All I can do is keep on looking until I find her, or at least find out what happened to her. I hate to think that somebody took her but that's looking more and more likely."
Tommo nodded solemnly. "As long as they're taking care of her." he added.

They looked both ways and crossed the road arriving at the little stone wall. It wasn't so much that they were assiduously following the Green Cross Code, more that they didn't want anyone seeing them entering the estate. The wall was low enough that they could easily climb up onto the top and hop down the other side, and with one small leap they were now on private land. They had been here many times over the years, always without incident, but the fact that it was a private estate, and they were now officially trespassing, always resulted in a little lift in excitement levels.

Pitgarvie Estate was basically all forest with a large mansion within, located close to the intersection of Station Road and Sunnyside Road. The official entrance was probably a good half mile or more from where they were. The estate used to have very active deer and grouse hunting seasons but that all seemed to be done with now. When the boys were younger, it was a common sight to see Land Rovers and other 4x4s, laden with their haul from a day's hunt, drive through the village. Now it was only lorries loaded up with fresh cut estate timber which rolled through Oakley these days.

The two explorers were planning on steering well clear of the house and road, as they would prefer to stay undetected on this mission. They walked into the almost pitch-dark forest but, once they were in, they could see well enough. They made their way further in along a makeshift path which consisted of well-trodden grass and ferns. They weren't sure if it was deer or humans who had created this route, but they were grateful that they didn't have to contend with foliage the whole way.

Sam and Tommo had only been walking for around five minutes, calling for Millie as they went, when they arrived at a clearing. A large number of trees had been chopped down here, not recently though, judging by the weathering on the stumps, with the thick carpet of ferns benefitting from the little bit of extra light in this open area. There was something which made the boys uneasy here. Perhaps it was because they had lost the protection of the woodland and were now out in the open, or perhaps it was something else.

Already on edge, they continued walking towards the centre of the clearing, until they saw something which made both boys abruptly arrest their progress. A large stump, which was directly ahead of them, was awash with what looked like dried blood. It took them a few seconds to gather themselves, as blood was not exactly what they were expecting to see here. There was no other conclusion to arrive at since also scattered around the base of the stump were some tufts of fur and what looked like animal bones. The fur was black and white, and Sam's heart suddenly dropped to his stomach. 'Oh god, this can't be Millie, can it?' he thought to himself. The evidence, for a few seconds at least, seemed to be telling him that, but, on closer inspection, it appeared to be the remains of a small black and white cat. There were pieces of fur and body parts strewn around the area next to the stump as well as on top of it. Could it have been an animal or raptor attack?

They shuddered to think what animal could have done this, but the cat looked like it had died some time ago,

103

and it was hard to fathom what had happened to it. Then, just as they were about to walk further on, they noticed another part of the gruesome scene, directly behind an adjacent tree stump.

There was more blood and much more fur, ginger and white this time. It was what they would see next that would change their view of the scene entirely. Tucked behind the stump was metal wire, pliers, a hunting knife, a hammer, a saw, and some nails, and next to them was the worst thing of all; two cat bodies with no heads. It was obvious, despite what people in the village had been suggesting, that no wild animal had done this. And with that realisation, the hairs on the back of their necks tingled and a heavy feeling consumed them.

Their hearts were now racing. The two boys suddenly feeling very unsafe and insecure. The woods around Oakley always had an element of local folklore about things that had happened to animals and people in the past. They were old enough to know that this was probably mostly the older generations winding the younger ones up, as well as parents scaring their kids into not exploring these areas. However, their grisly discovery had resulted in the departure of rational thought and the cold embrace of fear.

Sam and Tommo were now gripped by the inexplicable and uncomfortable feeling that they were potentially being monitored from the woods. Without speaking, they knew they could both feel it. The boys immediately stood up straight, looking around the clearing, gazing into the dark woods which surrounded them for signs of anyone watching them. While Sam, with his brown hair, would be somewhat camouflaged against the treeline, he did suddenly consider that Tommo would be far more noticeable with his thick mass of bright red hair, if anyone was indeed watching.

Their gruesome discovery, as well as the possibility that someone was watching them, creeped them out to such an extent that they decided to cut short their wander through the woods, immediately heading back the way they came, out of the estate and, ultimately, back up the road to the village. With adrenaline still pumping from their recent scare, they decided to walk along the road this time, connecting with Station Road after about ten minutes.

Neither of them had uttered a word since they departed the clearing, Tommo breaking the silence. "What the fuck did we just find?
A shellshocked Sam replying with "I think we just discovered what's been happening to the local cat population!"
"So, someone is taking cats into the woods just to butcher them? There's no other explanation. unless you think it's some sort of ritual animal sacrifice?"
Sam whipped his head around to look at Tommo. "I honestly don't know! Whatever it is that's going on, it's evil and sick." Their discovery had really shaken them up.

Just as they were about to turn right, to head up the hill towards the railway bridge, a white works' van pulled up beside them. The window rolled down and old Slater, the gamekeeper from the estate poked his bald, sun-dried head out. His arm now resting on the window frame as his visibly smoke-stained fingers held a smouldering cigarette.

"Hello ladies, what have you been up to?" He said in his trademark gravelly voice, as a cloud of cigarette smoke escaped from his open mouth and, when it dissipated, his scrabble-tile-coloured teeth could be seen, probably from space.

"Nothing much, Mr Slater, just out for a wee wander." replied Tommo.
"Are you sure that you two haven't been for a wee romantic rendezvous up in the woods?" Slater said while laughing a clearly fake but still obnoxious laugh.

The boys chose to ignore Slater's teasing, simply forcing a little smile and shaking their heads at him, then turning to continue their walk. Unperturbed, Slater continued "It looks like rain, do you want a lift up the hill? I'm away up there anyway to grab some food" he responded. But they both shook their heads.
"We're fine, thanks, Mr Slater." Sam answered. And with that, he drove off flicking his cigarette across to the curb as he departed, leaving the two boys standing at the road end.

"Do you think he knew we'd been in there?" asked Tommo.

Sam shrugged his shoulders saying. "No, I don't think so. If he saw us from the woods, there's no way he'd have been able to get back to his van and intercept us on the main road. Plus, I think he just would have come out and said something, he's not known for his subtlety."

Having just turned down a lift, the pair were overjoyed to see Mr Slater's weather prediction proved correct after only a matter of seconds, as large droplets of rain were now landing on their hair and faces. They had the whole length of Station Road to cover before they would find shelter. There was only one thing for it, so they immediately started a brisk jog up the hill to the shops before they got too soaked.

The boys had managed to dodge most of the rain, but it was getting heavier, so they ducked into Mr Das's to wait it out. They browsed the video library for about as long as they could possibly get away with before buying a sausage roll each from the hot food counter, deciding they'd need to brave the weather at some point, or they'd be stuck in the shop all day. "Ok, we better make a run for it. Want to get the lads together tonight so we can tell them about the cat butcher?" asked Tommo.

"Sounds good. I should be done by about half six. I'll come to yours when I'm finished my shift." Sam replied. They headed off home in different directions, both raising a hand to each other to say goodbye. A sausage roll and a bath would sort everything out, for the rest of the afternoon at any rate.

A few hours later, Sam was standing in his doorway, sheltering from the rain, which was still coming down, when the rusty brown heap pulled up outside. Another night of roving around West Fife collecting the hard earned, quickly spent cash of the fruit machine addicts. Unfortunately for Sam, Derek had brought a tape with him this time. He should have known something was up when Derek didn't screech off as soon as Sam had closed the van door behind him. Looking at Sam square on, he thrust his hand towards Sam's face, like a football referee brandishing a red card, to reveal… a tape with 'New Rock' written on the outside in marker. "This good?" Asked Derek. "Erm, sure" replied Sam, somewhat unconvincingly.

The entirety of their drive to Dunfermline was taken up by Derek's insistence on, firstly, finding Why Can't This Be Love on the tape by constantly fast-forwarding and rewinding, and then, once he found it, playing, rewinding and playing again. When the track *was* playing, Derek sang every word and played every instrument, frequently performing guitar solos, often while letting go of the steering wheel, all in dreadful driving conditions. "What do you think?" Derek inquired. "Not bad." Sam said, not being entirely truthful. "Good, just taped it off the radio last night." Derek, rather unnecessarily, explained. Sam was relieved when they arrived at the first pub.

Luckily the gaps between collection points were not long enough for Derek to keep messing with the cassette player so Sam got some respite from Sammy Hagar and co, and it wasn't until they left the town to head back to Oakley that the music made a comeback. When they finished at the last pub and dumped the cash at the lock-up, Derek asked if Sam had any plans. He was tempted to say no, but he had fobbed Derek off a few times already, so he was honest and said he was meeting up with the boys, but they didn't have any fixed plans.

"I have an idea" Derek said, "let's take the van for a run through the beautiful Fife countryside." Sam didn't really know what to say but offered to see if it was ok with the boys. After all, it was Sunday, and they had school the next day. They pulled up outside Tommo's where the three friends had congregated. Sam ran over to them, posing the question as they all stood in Tommo's doorway, Sam's friends looking out at Derek and the van, appearing rather nonplussed.

Despite none of them seeming particularly enthusiastic for this evening's drive, they all hopped in the van against their better judgement. Sam in his usual seat and the three additional passengers jumping in the back via the side door. The combination of street illumination and the dim lighting provided by the door light inside, showcased everything that the van had to offer. Wall to wall carpeting, a free-standing couch and numerous pieces of rubbish strewn across the floor. Derek observed their concern. "Don't worry lads, you'll be safe as houses with me at the wheel!" The boys just looked at each other with expressionless faces.

Sam suggested that they listen to Radio 1 for the drive as he was also trying desperately to avoid a repeat of his recent Van Halen experience. It was coming up to 7pm so they caught the end of the Top 40 chart show. Derek groaned, as if he had just been punched in the stomach, as The Bangles' Manic Monday came on, although the rest of them seemed fine with it. Tommo singing along to rub it in. Derek put his foot down on the accelerator as if to underscore his disdain.

The next song, at number two, was Absolute Beginners by David Bowie and Derek's stony face told its own story. They were all given a brief reprieve from Derek's unhappiness as the DJ then read out the whole Top 40 before announcing this week's number one. Unfortunately for all the travellers, it was Chain Reaction by Diana Ross, and this was finally a step too far for Derek. "Right, that's it! A bloody tape's going in", as he fumbled in the compartment under his tape deck for a cassette. The rest of the guys were laughing uncontrollably at this point. Nobody would disagree that a tape would be preferable to this.

They waited with bated breath for Derek's music selection. Sam was surprised, if not a little impressed, at Derek's choice, which was the album Love by The Cult. Not directly in Sam's wheelhouse but he could listen to this. The good laugh they'd all been having had cut through the initial awkwardness and everyone was chatting away merrily about football, music and films by the time they reached the Golden Chip in Dunfermline, as the cassette deck blared in the background.

Derek somewhat assumed they'd all be getting something to eat, starving as he was, and they all piled into the chip shop to order. As they'd already had their tea, Tommo and Gub just ordered a small bag of chips each but the rest of them ordered suppers. Derek got a fish supper, his eyes on stalks at the huge piece of fried haddock they laid on top of the bed of steaming hot chips underneath. Sam and Shug got black pudding suppers. "Salt and Sauce?" the rotund, greasy-haired girl behind the counter asked, looking at the five piping hot meals in front of her. They all nodded in unison as she smothered their food with a liberal amount of both. They all bought a can of juice to accompany their meals and jumped back in the van. There was no talking, for a few minutes anyway. Only the sounds of fried food being devoured, and cold, fizzy drinks being guzzled.

"Just chuck your rubbish back there, lads." Derek announced, as they were all finishing up. Given the already disgusting state of the van, none of the passengers queried his request at all. The van rolled out of the parking space outside of the chip shop, heading further along Pilmuir Street before turning left onto Carnegie Drive. After a few minutes they drove past East End Park, which was deserted on this Sunday evening. but the Main Stand was looking resplendent, towering above the surrounding houses on Halbeath Road.

They continued east for another twenty minutes, winding their way around the undulating back roads of West Fife,

111

driving past farmland and heavy industry as they went, finally arriving in the small coastal village of Aberdour.

Aberdour is a pretty place. An abundance of large houses, public parks and well to do shops. After driving along the main street and passing by the charming train station, Derek manoeuvred the van off of the main road, turning slowly down the narrow lane towards Silver Sands Beach. There would be no skimming stones on the water or playing in the sand, they were only going as far as the car park.

The car park was entirely deserted and, as he slowly drove from the road end onto the parking area's gravel surface, Derek cut the van's lights and rolled along slowly in darkness for what seemed like an age before coming to a complete stop, the engine still running. "What's happening Derek?" Sam inquired, somewhat puzzled at Derek's antics.
"Wait until I fling the lights back on." Derek replied, as he floored the accelerator and the van screeched back into life. As promised, he switched the lights back on as the van thundered onto the manicured grass behind the car park. Before them were dozens and dozens of rabbits who were either standing stock still or running for their lives, their terrified eyes reflecting the light from the van's headlights. Derek let out a maniacal laugh as he zig-zagged across the grass ahead of him causing the poor little bunnies to flee in panic, and the contents of the van to slide around the floor.

The rabbits weren't the only ones in a panic as the guys were all hanging on for dear life but, after a short time, the initial panic turned to hilarity as the comedy of the situation hit home. Derek then slowed down, announcing in a poor action film voiceover style accent "no animals were hurt during the making of this movie." Much to the great amusement of everyone in the van.

The younger boys, much to their collective surprise, had enjoyed hanging out with Derek, and, if it was usually this much of a laugh, they would definitely do it again. However, as it was a Sunday night and everyone bar Derek had school the next day, they decided to pack in the fun and drive back home. As they turned onto Aberdour Main Street to head back home, Tommo asked if they wanted to hear about his and Sam's creepy discovery from earlier in the day. They all nodded, eyes wide in anticipation. Derek responding, "oh yes, we certainly do!" while banging his hands on the steering wheel in excitement.
"You know how there are missing cat posters all over the village?
"Yeah?" Shug piped up, slightly confused.
"Well, Sam and I think we know what's been happening to them. The cats, I mean. Someone is butchering them in Pitgarvie Estate."
"No way!" Gub exclaimed.
"Yep, there was a pretty gruesome scene a few hundred yards inside the stone wall with all sorts of body parts and blood all over the place" added Sam.
"Jesus! Really? How do you know it's a person and not an animal?" responded Gub.

There was a short pause before Tommo explained
"Because there were tools there too."
"Tools? Fucking hell! Who do you think is doing that?"
asked Shug.
"God knows." Sam added.
"It's probably Mr Pitgarvie himself, creepy Slater."
suggested Derek.
They all laughed.
"He actually drove up to us as we were leaving." Sam
said.
"There you go!" shouted Derek, laughing.
"Nah, he was just asking if we needed a lift." Tommo
chimed in.
"Are you going to tell the police?" asked Shug.
"I'll tell them about the cats and leave it up to them."
replied Sam.
The topic of conversation had made the journey home
pass really quickly, and they were back in Oakley in no
time. The boys thanked Derek as he dropped them off
back outside Tommo's and, as he reached his final drop
off, Sam's house, he pulled up and gave Sam an
unsealed envelope with his £20 in.
"If I don't catch you through the week, I'll see you
Friday." Derek said, as Sam departed the van. Sam
waved as Derek drove off, then looked down with pride
at his first wage packet. He smiled to himself as he
walked to the door.

Mrs Hamill was already upstairs in bed when Sam got
in. He went through to the kitchen and ran the cold tap
for a second and then filled a glass to the brim with
freezing water, drinking about half before pouring the

rest down the sink. It had been an interesting day and, as he climbed the stairs, he thought ahead to his upcoming visit to the police station to tell them what he and Tommo had found.

He knocked lightly on his mum's bedroom door to check on her before he went to bed. There was no answer, so he poked his head around the door. She was fast asleep, so he walked quietly over to her nightstand and turned her bedside lamp off before stealthily retreating back out and heading to bed himself. Sam hoped he'd dream of his hard-earned money, football or something else nice, but he had a horrible feeling those poor cats would be visiting him in his nightmares.

Sam had gone the whole school day thinking about little else than the cat murder scene, and he was planning to do something about it as soon as the bus dropped him off. He'd told the boys that he was jumping on the earlier bus again.

Sam was sad to forego one leg of the twice daily school commute with his pals, but such was his enthusiasm to get to the police station and tell them about his findings, he was willing to make that sacrifice. As the bus navigated its way through the countryside towards home, Sam was looking out the large upstairs front window and becoming slightly concerned that the skies would open again. He imagined a miserable time in the not-too-distant future, trudging through the saturated woods and newly created mud, but he was hopeful the cloudy but dry day would stay that way.

Sam jumped off the bus and bounded the short distance from the bus stop to the police station, desperately eager to tell his story. Constable Redpath was at the front desk and pretended, initially, that Sam was a stranger, flipping open his notepad and formally asking for his name and address while pretending to jot down details. However, Redpath really *did* have to take down his particulars once Sam he was given the opportunity to explain that he wasn't at the station on a social visit and had sinister news to spill.

Sam explained what he'd found at Pitgarvie Estate and, given the scene that he'd described, Constable Redpath immediately suggested that they jump in one of the two police vehicles parked outside and go down there so Sam could show him where the gruesome scene he'd described was.

They rolled out of the small parking area in front of the station and turned right down Station Road, heading down the hill towards the vast estate. The journey only took a few minutes by car. Sam had been a frequent passenger in squad cars during his dad's long tenure as sergeant, so this drive was nothing new and not particularly exciting for him. His heart was racing, though, for other reasons.

"Sorry to add to your workload with this, especially when you're already snowed under with the Lauren Smith investigation, but I felt it needed reporting." Sam explained to Redpath.
"No, It's fine. We've have had so many calls about missing cats, even before Lauren disappeared, and it would be good to close that down, if possible. We haven't had the resources to properly investigate, beyond keeping our eyes open for a fox or some other predator." answered Redpath.
How well do you know Mr Slater? Sam asked.
"Pretty well. I can introduce you now if you don't know him." Redpath offered.
"Oh, we need to see him? I was hoping not, as I was pretty much trespassing when I found the site."

"Looking for Millie? Redpath asked. Sam nodded. "Ok, you show me the place, and I can drop you off before going to see Slater officially afterwards. I'll say it was an anonymous tip."

"Thanks", Sam said, breathing a sigh of relief, as he didn't want to be caught having lied to Slater's face the day before. Sam got on well with all the police officers at the station, but he got on best with Redpath. Maybe it's because he was the youngest at the station that they got along so well? Sam had known all of them as long as he could remember but he has a distinct memory of when Redpath started and his dad showing him the ropes. If he had to guess his age, he'd probably say mid-twenties, but, from Sam's perspective anyway, seemed more mature than his years.

They pulled off the road and onto the grass verge immediately across from the wall where Sam and Tommo had entered the woods the day before. Redpath making sure to tuck the car away from the road, as best he could. Sam and Redpath crossed the road and jumped over the wall. They were walking at a brisk pace and, thanks to the dry ground and therefore lack of mud, in a matter of minutes they were at the clearing, but the view was very different today. Instantly, Sam could see that the site had been interfered with. In fact, so much so that there didn't seem to be much evidence of anything at all. Everything Sam and Tommo had seen the day before had been removed including most of the fur, the body parts and, most importantly, the tools.

The only sign that anything sinister had happened here was that bloodstains remained on the tree stump and there were a few tufts of fur nearby. Constable Redpath knew Sam too well to think he'd have invented this story, and the blood proved that there was something to it. However, this was a very peculiar development and clearly the perpetrator must have seen Sam and Tommo going to the site, was watching them while they were there, or spotted them when they were leaving the estate after their discovery and put two and two together. Whenever it was, someone had attempted to clear the scene of anything incriminating and had been highly successful in that regard.

"What do we do now?" asked Sam raising both his voice and his hands in obvious frustration.

Redpath said "Well, Sam, your report has made us look at this in a different way and we now know it was a person not an animal. Let's head back up to the station and I'll take some further notes. This isn't over."

As they walked back to the car, Sam thought of the run in with Mr Slater the day before, and wondered if it *was* actually just a coincidence or something more?

Sam finished up at the police station, deciding to walk over to Tommo's to tell him about what had transpired. Tommo answered the door.

Before speaking, Sam had a quick look over Tommo's shoulder to check if his mum was close by. "You'll not fucking believe it!!"

"What happened?" asked Tommo, as he invited Sam into his front room, where they sat.

"I took Redpath to the tree stump and everything except the blood stains had been removed. No tools, no cats, nothing!"

"No fucking way!" exclaimed Tommo, standing back up. "Someone must have seen us. We both had that same creepy feeling we were being watched, right? I was hoping that was just our imagination playing tricks on us, but I believe it now."

"That's exactly what I was thinking." replied Sam. "But who?"

"Slater?" pondered Tommo.

Sam thought for a second, but he shook his head. "I don't see it. He's an old creep but cat murders? Seems a bit of a stretch. Plus, like I said at the time, how could he be watching us in the clearing and get back to his van in time to intercept us on the road? Anyway, I need to go now as I've got my Co-op shift changed to tonight. Still on for tomorrow?"

"Half ten outside Mr Das's?" replied Tommo, pointing a finger gun at Sam while winking and making a clicking sound with his cheek.

Sam laughed as he departed, heading the few hundred yards along the road for his evening of stacking shelves.

It was a typically uneventful shift, with the latter half of it far more bearable as the shop was closed to the public. It didn't make a huge difference, but it could be a little annoying when customers would try to take items from the new stock, he was filling the shelves with, or just generally getting in the way of him doing his job. No customers also meant he could wear his portable cassette player, and it went without saying that stacking shelves

120

to some of his top tunes was far preferable to in store muzak and dithering customers.

Having slid Tears for Fears' Songs from the Big Chair into the cassette player before he left for school and choosing not to listen on the bus journey home, Sam made full use of his loaded device as he covered the last hour of his shift. The album was about twenty minutes shy of a full hour, so he rewound his favourite track, Head over Heels, a few times to fill the gap. It was a nice distraction from thinking about the cat murderer, but it was only partially successful, with thoughts of both the animal murder scene and the potential suspect filling his head at times. The whole thing had him feeling uneasy and he felt his heart race at times when his mind returned to the subject.

Given Sam was now feeling more than a little on edge about the fact there was *definitely* a cat murderer in the village, as well as running through in his head was who that might be, the upshot was that he didn't feel like he was in his typical comfort zone in his usually safe little fiefdom. It was just after 8pm when he left the shop, but he did what he always did when he felt this way, and that was run as fast as he could between his present location to the safety of his house.

It was pitch dark, the roads were wet from rain, which must have occurred while he was busy working inside, and it was quite windy, which added to the sense of foreboding. He quickly checked the road was clear for crossing before setting off at full sprint speed towards home. He made it past the entrance to the swing park before he saw anyone, quickly crossing to the other side of the road to avoid them. He couldn't tell who it was in any case and was past them in a flash, so onward he dashed. If it had been someone who was out to get him, for whatever reason, he would have ducked through the nearby houses to get away, possibly entertaining some hedgehopping to make his escape. That's what he was telling himself, in any case.

In a matter of a few minutes, he was at his front gate, which he swiftly opened and closed again behind him, continuing up the path to his front door. As he turned the door key in the lock, he glanced behind him to have a quick look around. The coast was completely clear. He was probably overthinking things, but he felt better for it. Once inside, he snibbed the door lock and looked in the sitting room to see if his mum was in there, but the only sign of life in there was the table lamp which had purposefully been left on. His mum had been going to bed noticeably early the last few months and it looked like she was having an early night again. It was still too early for Sam to follow suit, and he had no homework to do, so he turned on the tv to see what was on.

Sam had been afforded a late night and a long lie the next morning, because of a teacher 'in service' day tomorrow, which, in actuality, meant a day off for Sam and his pals. An 'in service' day also usually means raiding the drinks' cabinet at whichever one of his pal's houses was sans parents that day, and generally larking about. Unfortunately for the fab four, none of their houses was free tomorrow so another plan would have to be hatched. They could have asked Derek, who would have undoubtedly bought them some drink, but that would have required an element of pre-planning and Sam's friend group weren't renowned for thinking ahead.

After surfing through the few channels available to find nothing worth watching, Sam decided to shove a video in the machine instead. In his house, they didn't have all that many tapes to choose from, but he knew exactly which film to watch. He remembered when Raiders of the Lost Ark was shown for the first time on British TV a few years earlier. It was Christmas Day, and the house was filled with excitement in anticipation of the film being shown. It was also one of the first tests for their new video recorder in taping this momentous event, and it passed with flying colours.

Between Sam and his dad, the tape had been watched so many times it must have been almost worn out. The film itself always made him think of his dad… One of his favourite memories was when they had gone to the cinema to watch it when it first came out. Sam was ten, and they had originally gone into Dunfermline to see Clash of the Titans but, when they arrived at the cinema, it was already sold out. Raiders of the Lost Ark was the only realistic alternative, but their initial disappointment turned to joy as Raiders turned out to be the best thing they'd ever seen. A late evening viewing of his favourite film was exactly what the doctor ordered, taking him up to bedtime. It still wasn't too late, and he thought better of staying up later, just for the sake, instead opting for a good night's sleep before tomorrow's activities.

Chapter Nine
In Service

After a solid ten hours of sleep, Sam awoke, ate breakfast and got dressed, thereafter wandering up to the rendezvous point. The gang had agreed to meet outside Mr Das's to see who could come up with the best idea. They also weren't alone. Margaret Stafford and her pal were hanging around looking for something to do and walked over to the group, who were idling outside the shop. Of course, the girls knew the boys would be planning something and were already set to tag along.

It always seemed like a bit of a random day, a Tuesday, to have a day off from school. It was never a Monday or a Friday, which would have been much more useful in extending the weekend, but they welcomed the extra day off, nonetheless. It was a beautiful spring day, so being outside was at least a good option, for once. What could a group of fifteen and sixteen-year-olds do with themselves? After some discussion, they decided to head along the railway line and see what trouble they could get into.

The group cut downhill towards the sawmill, walking past their old primary school on the way. The chat was mostly about music, tv programmes and teachers at the high school they didn't like. Inevitably, though, the discussion turned from day-to-day trivia to the missing girls, and particularly Lauren. Margaret's pal, who they eventually discovered was called Dawn, and was from the neighbouring village of Carnock, was, like Margaret, a year below them at school. She was visibly upset talking about Lauren, explaining that her parents and Lauren's parents were close friends and, understandably, it had been an extremely difficult time for them all. This reminded Sam of the Hairy Mary bus debacle and further explained why Margaret was probably unhappy with him, given her best pal's family were close friends with Lauren's family.

They were heading in the direction of the woods where Sam had to take his enforced dip in the pond, when a coal train made itself known in the distance with its loud engine, screeching metal wheels and, the most obvious sign of all, the clouds of white steam billowing from the smokestack.

At this point, the group made a snap decision to jump on the train and take a free ride up towards the colliery instead of going to the woods. The guard's van, at the train's rear, had wooden planks running along each side which allowed standing while holding onto the side of the wagon, and they all knew from experience to jog alongside and then hop on. They were all trying to hitch a lift in covert fashion, but they all knew that the guard could probably see them and was simply choosing to ignore.

Once on board, they rattled along at a fair old pace only slowing down briefly as the steam train passed through the level crossing. As the train sped up again their excitement heightened. They weren't sure how fast the train was travelling, and it probably wasn't actually going as fast as it seemed, but it felt like they were hanging on for dear life as the train powered its way up to Comrie Pit. The hissing of the steam engine, the speed which the large metal rods drove the wheels, the locomotive creating its own wind, which blew their hair back and filled their eyes with tears. All of these things, coupled with overgrown foliage by the rail side occasionally thrashing them, made for a thrilling ride and they screamed with joy as the locomotive ate up the track ahead.

After about ten minutes, the train started to ease off. The tell-tale sign that the train was nearing the entrance to the colliery, which consisted of a vast open area with a multitude of rail sidings and mine personnel milling around. As the locomotive slowed down further, they knew this was when they had to make their exit, otherwise they'd be inside the colliery property, and in trouble.

Knowing it was now or never, they all piled off, standing to the sides of the tracks as the train rolled past them, all of them standing to watch as the metal marvel left them behind. Adrenalin was still through the roof for the illicit train passengers as they cut up from the tracks through a thicket to a farmer's field on the other side.

The group were in very high spirits and singing, laughing, climbing on each other's backs as they walked across the field towards Porterfield and the next stop on their travels.

"Slag!" shouted Shug. But before anyone could take offence, he could be seen smirking as he pointed at the distant Blairhall Bing, a colossal slag heap to their right as they continued their climb up towards the main Porterfield. "Oh, very funny." said Dawn, with a smile, who did seem to appreciate the joke.

It was no more than a ten-minute walk from the farmer's field to the football pitches, which were at the top end of Porterfield – the posh part of Comrie. They had no ball and no plan, but they would find something to do. The weather was glorious which made it a very pleasant walk through a field containing a mystery crop. It was too early in the season for most insects and there was plenty of floral scents being carried on the breeze. They crossed the main road and walked up the gravel path to the fields. There was no one else around, which was surprising as all the local schools were off today. As they walked around the perimeter of the fields, they found a ball which was almost entirely deflated. The ball was no use for kicking, given its deflated state, but they could throw it at each other and made up a derivative of dodge ball, which kept them going for a bit.

As the game started to wind down, the sound of police sirens could be heard in the distance. It sounded like another big event with numerous vehicles, but they didn't seem to be coming any closer, so they stopped their game and started walking towards where the noise seemed to be emanating from. As they reached the edge of Porterfield housing estate, the sirens had stopped but they could see multiple police vehicles with flashing lights sitting outside The Railway Tavern. This was only steps from last week's incident with the body in the burn. Had the police found someone else? Naturally, they walked down the hill to investigate.

As the group arrived outside the pub, they were just in time to see a handcuffed Steven Morrison, aka Bairn, being escorted from the premises and into one of the three waiting police cars. Constables Seton and Sneddon walked Bairn out, a strange sight given how much larger Bairn was than his two handlers. Seton pushed Bairn's shorn head down and manoeuvred him into the back of the car before departing. Sneddon peeling out in another vehicle a few seconds later. Just as the group were about to leave, Redpath appeared from inside the pub carrying a large clear bag which contained what looked like a pair of white women's high-heeled shoes and a similarly coloured handbag. He placed the items in the boot of the car and went back inside.

The group looked at each other, with the others noticing that the two girls immediately looking upset.

"What's wrong?" Sam asked.

"I think that stuff might be Lauren's." advised Dawn. "I didn't get a close enough look but it really seemed like that could have been her shoes and handbag."

Suddenly the boys realised what this could mean. Had the police finally found some clues related to Lauren's disappearance?

"Wait a minute, wouldn't they have searched the pub already, though?" inquired Shug.

"They did, my dad told me they did." Sam answered.

"Maybe they missed some evidence?" suggested Gub.

"Possibly. But I know they went through this place with a fine-toothed comb" Sam countered. "A few times, I think."

Just then, Redpath reappeared and gave a nod in their direction as he climbed into his vehicle.

"What's happening?" asked Sam.

"Sorry folks, I can't comment right now but we'll hopefully know more later." replied Redpath. And with that, he drove off.

After engaging in idle speculation about the items in the bag for a few more minutes, they decided to walk up to the Miners' Welfare. There was a chance that the recovered items were nothing to do with Lauren, but it seemed significant, the police obviously thought so. They all knew about Bairn by reputation. When he was younger, he was constantly in trouble with the police, and it seemed like he was always getting arrested. In a village of Oakley's size, this gets you a reputation that is difficult to shake off. As far as they all knew, Bairn had

130

been staying out of trouble for the last few years, but it's possible he just wasn't getting caught.

After their relatively short walk, the group wandered into the club and headed towards the games room. Nobody else was in there and they all sat down for a minute to gather their thoughts.

They decided to hang there a while and got a couple of pool games going. One game of doubles, featuring Sam and Margaret versus Dawn and Tommo, Shug and Gub playing a more traditional 1 v 1 on the other table. The losing doubles' team switching with the boys who would then pair up to play the winners, and so it went on. They started a kitty, putting a pound in each. Sam and Tommo took a (soft) drinks order and walked through to the bar to grab them, adding a selection of KP Nuts and various flavours of crisps to the haul which they carried back on a couple of trays. The drink of choice was a pint of Coke with ice, with the girls both opting for fresh orange and lemonade. It felt very grown up even though it was just juice and snacks.

They played pool for a couple of hours, switching sides a few times but mostly in their original pairings. Sam was impressed at Margaret's pool skills, with their team winning the most games. They were starting to get a little bored of pool so they agreed that Sam would head up to the police station and see if there was any update. The others stayed behind while Sam ran around the corner to the police station to see what he could find out.

The station was alive with activity, phones ringing, multiple conversations competing and overlapping. Constable Redpath spotted Sam and came over to the front desk.

"You guys are making a habit of hanging around at crime scenes" Redpath said wryly. Sam gave an uncomfortable smile, while nodding. "I know you probably can't say, but I've been asked to find out if the items you found are Lauren's."

"We have asked Lauren's parents to identify the items. They're heading up here shortly. If they are positively identified we'll brief the media and do another canvass of the surrounding villages and here, calling for anyone who knows anything to come forward."

Sam nodded. "Do you think Bairn was involved?"

"Keep this to yourself, but my personal view is no. We have checked the pub a few times before and there was nothing there, now potential evidence suddenly appears. Also, Bairn had a pretty strong alibi for the night that was confirmed by half a dozen folk who stayed behind with him in the pub."

Redpath continued "It's definitely peculiar, though, and we're treating this as a proper lead in the investigation into Lauren's disappearance. Assuming Lauren's parents confirm that these items are hers, we will be going all out to get as much information about this potential suspect as we possibly can, despite our reservations about the way this evidence has been discovered."

And with that, Sam left and headed back to the club to meet the rest of the group. They were all ears, but Sam didn't really have the news they were looking for, which was the answer to whether or not the handbag and shoes belonged to Lauren. Sam told them what Redpath had said about them all speaking to their parents about whether or not they'd seen anyone.

It had been a busy day so far and, now that it was mid-afternoon, the sustenance previously provided by the crisps, nuts and juice had worn off. They needed to get something more filling, otherwise they would have to leave and potentially miss out on the news from next door. After a short-lived debate on the subject, they decided that they'd see what hot food they could get in the club. The food was not of a high standard there, but they would take their chances. Tommo and Dawn were tasked with finding out what options were available and returned with the news that the kitchen was actually closed, *but* there were some scotch pies left over from lunchtime and the cook would make some chips and beans to go with. They couldn't have hoped for much better, so this offer was quickly snapped up.

Once all the food was polished off, and their strength restored, the group immediately went back to discussing the items in the bag and whether or not they were Lauren's. Gub and Dawn were pushing quite hard for Sam to go back to the station to see if Lauren's parents had been in to verify the items, but Sam thought this was premature, having not long come back from there. Nobody wanted to leave, however, until they had confirmation either way so, reluctantly, Sam trudged back around the corner to see if anyone in the police station would tell him the news.

As he neared the station he stopped in his tracks as he saw Lauren's parents departing the station. He could tell from their demeanour that the items must have been hers. They both looking visibly upset, her mum in particular shaking and sobbing, as Mr Smith helped her into the car. The answer was obvious, so he immediately returned to the club to tell the rest of the guys. He walked into the pool room where everyone was waiting, open mouthed. Sam looked at the ground as they looked at him, uttering only two words… "they're hers".

Chapter Ten
Suspicious Minds

Margaret had decided to walk across the football field to join Sam at the bus stop outside the co-op, instead of her usual stop on Wardlaw Way. She joined Sam outside Mr Das's, where neither of them could help but see the newspaper front pages on display reflecting the dreadful news they heard yesterday afternoon. One such example was The Courier.

'Items Belonging to Lauren Smith Recovered by Police. Fresh Appeal to Public in Hunt for Abductor'

The word 'abductor' was what really brought the new development home to them. There was always hope that Lauren had left the village of her own accord, and there was some remote possibility of an innocent explanation for her disappearance. But the discovery of some of Lauren's belongings had changed the way everyone thought about what happened, they now knew for sure it was a deliberate act, and definitely someone from around here.

The one-time village of innocents was now a place where the cloud of suspicion hung over almost everyone. Neighbour now mistrusted neighbour, and the title of friend had to be earned again. They could all feel it. It was almost a relief when the bus hissed to a stop in front of them. Sam and Margaret both climbed on for the short drive along to Wardlaw Way where Gub, Tommo and Shug would get on. When they did, everyone sat in silence until Sam eventually spoke. "Did anyone hear anything else?"

"No, nothing at all." said Margaret. "It does seem strange that they arrested a member of staff at the pub."

"I don't think they can name him if he's not been charged, but I'm not sure they think it's him anyway". replied Sam. "When I spoke to Redpath yesterday afternoon, he didn't seem to think it was Bairn at all. Kept saying the discovery was weird. Also, according to the papers, the police have made a fresh appeal for information. That sounds to me like they don't know who it is."

Tommo chimed in "Isn't it strange that the items just suddenly appeared?"

"Yeah, whatever is going on at least it's a clue to who did it, as there hasn't been much up until now." added Shug.

"Who or what are the police looking for, if it isn't Bairn?" asked Margaret.

"I think they're just looking for anything strange that people might have seen." Sam responded. "Hopefully people will call in with some new leads now."

At this point, the bus stopped in Carnock and Dawn climbed on, finding her way to where they were sitting, and joining the rest of them. "Hi" they all said together. "We're just talking about the papers, have you seen them?" asked Margaret.

Dawn nodded solemnly.

"We're just saying that we hope the find gives the police something new to go on." offered Tommo.

Dawn nodded again, and looked down at the bus floor, clearly still upset from yesterday's developments.
The rest of the drive was spent in silence.

As they arrived at the school, they all jumped off, Sam walking alongside Margaret. Before they got too far, Sam spotted Derek sitting in his van at the school gates, so he said bye to Margaret and walked over to see what was going on.
"Oh, good" said Derek, seeing Sam walking up to his open window. "I was hoping to grab you at the bus stop before you got on, but I obviously missed you, so I thought I'd get you here."
"Oh, yeah?" queried Sam.
"Yep, I need you tonight as we need to swap out a broken machine for a working one, so I overtook the bus so I could intercept you before school. You in? There's an extra tenner in it for you."
"Err, yeah. I think so." said Sam trying to think on the spot if he had anything on after school. It was a Wednesday so no Co-op.
"Magic! Just as well really, as I can't move the machines on my own anymore. I'll get you right here after school."
And with that Derek screeched away leaving Sam to wander in through the school gates to start another no doubt uneventful school day.

As he walked towards his first class, Colin Walsh jogged up to him and started walking alongside.
"Got any fags on you?"
"None on me, pal. Sorry," replied Sam. Of course, Sam didn't actually smoke, but for reasons he couldn't

fathom, he wanted to give Walshy the impression that he did and was somehow cooler because of it. Walshy wasn't cool either, but he definitely carried himself like he thought he was. Heavily built but always trying to be trendy through various haircuts and fashionable clothing. He had been trying hard to project a Curt Smith vibe for the last few years but, unfortunately for him, he had only succeeded in looking more like Roland Orzabal.

As they walked into the main building, Walshy asked Sam if he was going to East End Park for any of the games before the end of the season. "If you are, there's a few of us who meet at half two at the bus station and walk along Halbeath Road to the ground together." He added.
"Sounds good. Will need to check what I've got on, but I would like that. Will let you know."
Sam was quite flattered by Walshy's offer and would definitely see if he could make any of the next few home games. And with that they nodded at each other and went their separate ways to class.

As expected, the brown van was idling at the front of the school at close of play. Sam could hear the rattle from the engine from a hundred yards away. There was definitely zero street cred to be gained by being seen getting into the rusting heap, so he did a half speed walk, half jog over to the van, quickly jumping in. Derek nodding his approval at Sam with a big cheesy grin.
"I bet they'd love to see me back here." Derek said, laughing. "I was the star student here."

Not wanting to delay their departure in case anyone saw him, Sam quickly responded "When did you leave?" inquired Sam.

"At the end of 4th year, for an apprenticeship at the dockyard."

"How come that didn't work out? asked Sam.

"It was too far, and I had no wheels then. It was a good laugh for a while, but I couldn't hack the return bus journey every day." Derek answered. "And now that I have the mean machine, who cares anyway!" and with that they screeched off down the hill towards Dunfermline town centre, leaving a small cloud of smoke in their wake.

Not much else was said for the first few minutes of the drive, until Derek broke the silence. "So, any luck finding your dog?" He inquired as they rumbled past Carnegie Swimming Baths.

Sam shook his head in response, also feeling a little guilty as, with his new busier schedule, his search for Millie had somewhat wound down lately. Not that he cared any less about finding Millie, it was just that he had pretty much exhausted every place she could possibly be. "No, no sign so far."

"Nightmare. Hopefully she'll still turn up."

"Hope so" Sam replied, rather disconsolately.

"She will." Derek offered. "I'm staying positive. Dogs are the best."

"Did you hear about Bairn?" Sam inquired.

"No, what's that giant idiot done now?" Derek retorted.

"You really didn't hear? They found some of Lauren's belongings at The Railway Tavern and it's all over the news today." Sam explained.

Derek looked surprised. "Haven't heard a peep, although I don't watch the news, or read the paper, and you're the first person I've spoken to today. I'm always the last to know anything. They really mentioned Bairn on the news?"

"No. sorry, I didn't mean to make it sound that way. The police just confirmed the items have been found. Bairn's involvement is only known village wide as the police didn't go public with that."

They didn't say too much for a while, just travelling along with their own thoughts. Sam thinking again about Walshy's invite as they drove past East End. They had made good time, as traffic was light. After a few more minutes, Derek reduced his speed so they could turn into a bleak looking industrial estate off Halbeath Road, just beyond the railway bridge.

Derek rolled the van slowly through the open metal gates, then reversed up to the raised concrete loading platform in front of the lock-up. Sam could see immediately that the raised concrete platform was level with the bottom of the van doors. This building was much bigger than the one Sam had previously visited in Oakley, although it would have been a surprise if it wasn't.

They climbed the short set of concrete steps that were set into the raised platform towards the door, Derek rummaging for a set of keys before unlocking the padlock and sliding the metal door upwards so they could see inside. There was quite a bit of equipment in this lock-up, which was very different to the one in Oakley. Also, it seemed organised and very clean, which was a little surprising. Clearly, Derek was not in charge of this facility. Right at the front, a lone machine was standing with a cover on it. On the cover was a small white piece of paper being held on by a strip of Sellotape which said Shooters Pool Hall. Sam recognised this as one of their usual stops on their Friday/Sunday rounds.

Derek grabbed a dolly, which was propped against a wall immediately inside of the lock-up, before wheeling it over to where the machine was. "Sam, if you could tip the machine forward so I can get this under it." Sam duly obliged and Derek slid the bottom of the dolly under and then they both pushed the machine backwards, so it was sitting flush with the back of the dolly. They then rolled it into the van and secured the dolly and machine to the van wall with some straps, which were laying on the floor of the lock-up, so it wouldn't topple over or roll away. They shut the lock-up doors, as well as the rear van door, and slowly trundled out of the industrial estate. Sam thought to himself that Derek takes this job very seriously for someone who clowns around so much the rest of the time.

They made the trip back along Halbeath Road to the town centre and were now nearing their destination. A few extra careful manoeuvres around the giant roundabout outside the police HQ and a couple of sharp

141

bends later and they were pulling up in the alley behind
Shooters, Derek enthusiastically pushing the button on
the dashboard to activate the van's hazard lights. They
opened up the back of the van and rolled the new
machine to the edge of the van. Derek asked Sam if he
could help lift the dolly and machine out of the van and
onto the ground. This was the tricky part. The machine
was heavy, but between the two of them they were able
to carefully place the machine safely on the alley floor.
Next was to wheel the dolly through the service door of
the pool hall and into the service lift.

The job had been much easier than Sam had anticipated,
although they weren't all the way done. They rolled the
new machine alongside the broken machine, which was
easy to find as it had a huge out of order sticker on the
front. With a bit of teamwork, Sam and Derek were able
to guide the old machine out of its designated space and
jockeyed the new one in its place. They rocked the
broken machine onto the dolly and used the straps to
secure it, just like they did with its replacement. Then
Derek had an idea. "The hall is completely empty. Fancy
a quick game of pool?"
"What about the van?" asked Sam.
"I've never had any hassle before and I have the hazards
on, which is van speak for 'we'll be right back'"
responded Derek with a grin.

Sam was in no position to question this and took his
word for it. And with that, Sam walked over to the bar
and paid for 30 minutes' game time. The place was
indeed dead. The good citizens of Dunfermline clearly

did not play pool at 4pm on a Wednesday. Derek, meanwhile, had his back to Sam on the other side of the room. He was hovering over the jukebox, Sam shuddered to think what his choices would be. Sam racked up the balls looking back over to the jukebox as Livin' on a Prayer started playing over the speakers. Derek grabbed a pool cue from the rack on the far wall, striding back towards the table acting as if the cue was a lead guitar, then flipping it vertically to use as a microphone when Jon Bon Jovi started to sing. Sam found it impossible not to laugh as Derek strutted around.

The pool playing adversaries fought their battle on billiard cloth, managing three games in their thirty-minute time slot. Derek winning 2-1, before the bright light above the table flickered on and off a few times to alert them their time was up. The barman was no doubt delighted that the array of rock songs would be over. Sam and Derek made sure the pool balls were re-racked and put their cues away, subsequently rolling the broken machine to the lift and then outside to the parked van, which, as Derek had predicted, was just as they left it. They weren't nearly as careful with the machine this time, rushing it outside, roughly hoisting it up onto the flat bed of the van, and quickly belting it in place against the wall. Once it was secured on the van wall, they speedily drove the short distance back around to the lock-up, where they wheeled it inside before pulling the lockup door shut.

As they departed to head home, it was clear Derek was still on a high from their pool hall antics and had selected more of his music for the drive back to Oakley. Sam was being subjected to Queen now.

Derek rattled off a couple of quick questions. "Do you have any homework? Working tonight?"

"No and no." answered Sam, wondering why he was asking.

"If you're up for it, we should do something."

Sam thought for a second and agreed. "Ok. What though?"

"We can go somewhere in the trusty van, maybe? I need to nip home first though."

Sam nodded his approval.

They pulled up outside Derek's house. Sam was all set to wait in the van, but Derek insisted that he come inside. As they walked in the front door, Sam couldn't believe his eyes. Instead of carpet, the hallway and stairs were covered in light green linoleum, as was the living room, which he could partially see to his right. He wondered if the house had been decorated in reverse and the kitchen and bathrooms were carpeted.

Nobody appeared to be in, so Derek showed Sam upstairs to his room, while he went into the bathroom to freshen up. Incredibly, the upstairs landing and Derek's bedroom floor were *also* light green linoleum, so it was virtually guaranteed the whole house was. Aside from the novel floor covering, Derek's room was painted entirely black and was adorned with various posters representing his penchant for heavy metal music. Above his bed was a Motorhead poster, featuring some sort of rock beast with tusks. Other prominent posters featured Iron Maiden, Judas Priest and Def Leppard. If Sam had shared Derek's passion for heavy metal music, he imagined it would be quite cool, but it wasn't his thing at all. Derek had certainly gone all in on the theme with matching black duvet, stacking stereo and furniture. His room was the opposite of his van, and the Oakley lock up, however. It was spotless, from what Sam could see. The bed was made and there was literally nothing on the floor or on his chest of drawers, or any of the various other flat surfaces. On his bed, a small stack of folded black clothing was sitting on the bottom end of his duvet. They were the only items that weren't put away.

Derek reappeared and they headed back downstairs towards the front door, only to hear Derek's mum call out to them. "Boys, can you come in here for a minute before you go?" This was a surprise to Sam, given it seemed that nobody was home. Derek's mum must have been sitting quietly in the living room with the tv off when they came in. They both went through, Derek introducing Sam to his mum, who was sitting in a large, old brown armchair. Sam suspected Mrs Paton was much younger than she looked. She had long greying hair, which rested on her shoulders. She also looked unhealthily thin. Her face drained of any colour. Her appearance was striking but she also looked a bit like a creepy character from a horror film.
"Hello Sam, I haven't seen you much since you were wee. I used to see you and your mum all the time when I worked in the Co-op."

145

Not sure what to say, mainly because he had no memory of this, Sam just said "Oh, right." while nodding, then saying "nice to meet you" even though they had clearly already met before. "I work in the Co-op now, myself." he added, a bit pointlessly.

"Where are you heading off to, boys?" Derek's mum asked. "Off to paint the town red?"

Derek replied. "Not sure, mum. We might just take the van for a wee drive, see where it takes us."

"I don't know if your mum thinks you're never in, Sam, but I feel like I hardly see this one these days. Especially since he started this job of his. If it wasn't for occasionally hearing him in the bathroom or running upstairs to change his clothes, I wouldn't know I had a son." Mrs Paton commented, sounding half serious. Sam smiled. "Anyway, watch yourselves out there, there seems to be nothing but bad news around at the moment."

"We'll be fine, mum. Don't worry." responded Derek. Sam nodded in apparent agreement, but he wasn't really listening. His attention had been grabbed by the room decor. Obviously, the floor was the most eye-catching element, but the large Crying Boy painting above the fireplace also stood out to him. There had been a series of recent stories in the newspapers about those paintings being cursed, as a number of them had been found untouched after devastating house fires, which some in the media claimed the paintings had somehow caused. The more realistic explanation was that they had been treated with a fire-retardant varnish which protected them from the flames. Derek's mum's demeanour, coupled with the rather strange surroundings had Sam a

146

bit off kilter. She seemed nice enough though, and they bid her farewell as they walked back out to the van.

"Can we just nip past my house, so I can dump my bag and tell my mum what I'm doing?" Sam asked. Derek nodded and off they went, pulling up in front of Sam's house in short order. He said he'd only be two minutes and leapt out of the van and ran in the front door. He was probably even quicker than he said, coming bouncing back down his front path before Derek had time to decide on the music for the upcoming adventure.
"Where we off to, then?" wondered Sam.
"Let's head west and see where we end up." replied Derek.

Sam was surprised to note that the musical selection for this drive wasn't too bad. As was typical, not exactly Sam's cup of tea, but Derek had found a Masters of Rock compilation tape, which featured a broader selection of music than his usual fare, such as Jimi Hendrix, Steppenwolf and even E.L.O.

From the Miners' Welfare, they took a left towards Comrie and continued in that direction for a few minutes towards Blairhall.
"Have you looked for your dog around here?" inquired Derek.
"No. I haven't come this far along. I've been as far as Porterfield and I've done a fair bit of the railway line, but never this far along." Sam explained.
"Well, let's remedy that, shall we?" Derek said, taking sharp left turn into the village of Blairhall.

Derek drove for a short time, which took them down to the bottom end of the small village, parking the van where the houses ended, and farmland began.

They both hopped out, walking from the residential street into the adjacent farmers field and on across the barren land towards a group of trees in the distance. As soon as they neared the treeline, and therefore the first area of the surrounding landscape where they couldn't see everything ahead of them, they started to shout and whistle for the dog.

Having traversed the field, Derek and Sam stepped across a small dirt path on the edge of the farmer's field, and were then able to climb a small embankment, stepping through a thin line of small trees and shrubs onto the railway tracks.

Even though this was only a couple of miles from Oakley Station, it seemed completely alien to Sam, even though he had been along here a few times before. Maybe it was because he always walked from the Oakley end, and they were entering the tracks from Blairhall? He couldn't put his finger on it, but it definitely felt strange.

The two of them walked along the tracks making quite a racket with all their yelling for Millie, although, for all their efforts, there was no sign of the dog. As they walked, the land adjacent to the tracks became more wooded and there was also a noticeable change as the tracks seemed to be much more elevated in this area, with the fields now a significant drop down from where they were. After around ten minutes walking the tracks, they came to a stop atop the Dean Viaduct, naturally leaning over the stone walls at either side to peer down to the woods and burn below.

"I think it's amazing that this is here." Sam said, gesturing at the huge engineering marvel that they were standing on.
"I think you're right. It does seem pretty fancy for our neck of the woods, but I don't think most folk realise it's here. They would never build anything that nice now, it would just be some concrete and metal monstrosity." Derek pontificated.
Sam was doing his best to count the numerous sandstone arches under their feet by leaning as far over the upper wall as possible. "I think there are eight, it's hard to see from up here but I don't fancy climbing down to the bottom to see for sure."
"Don't lean over too far, that would be the last we'd see of you." Derek said, laughing.

They continued on for another fifteen minutes but there was no sign of Millie, or anything else that would have held their interest. They decided to cut back down from the track, this time into a different field and followed the perimeter until they looped back around towards the bottom end of Blairhall, and back to the van. it hadn't been a complete waste of time as Sam hadn't paid much attention to the viaduct before, and he was now a convert to its charm.

Derek started up the van again and, after turning out of Blairhall, they continued on their journey west on the Alloa Road before turning off and meandering around some back roads. The evening had somewhat turned into a tour of mining areas, the next on their journey was fairly new Castlebridge Colliery followed quickly by the entrance to the defunct Solsgirth Mine.

If the van wasn't so decrepit, it would actually have been a lot of fun racing around the narrow, winding roads of West Fife. It was still enjoyable, but with the added fear of wondering if the van was going to hold together on tight bends. Sam hadn't been out this way for ages, but he had fond memories of his gran and grandad taking him for a drive on a Sunday for a change of scene. Sometimes they would stop at Powmill, as they had a nice café there. Not today, though, as they quickly passed by the entrance, carrying on past Dollar and on towards Tillicoultry. Sam could see there was still some snow on the Ochil Hills on his right, which was currently being illuminated by the last remnants of today's sunshine.

Derek had been mainly just singing along to his tape up this point but took a break to ask Sam if he was hungry. "Fancy some chips?" he said.
Sam was famished and agreed to this immediately. "Yes! Great idea. I'm Hank Marvin. Where were you thinking?"
"There's a magic chippy in Kincardine." replied Derek. "That should hit the spot. Oh, I also owe you a tenner for

helping me today." And with that he opened the glove box and took out an envelope, sliding a ten pound note out, then passing it to Sam as they idled at a red light.

"I'll get the chips then." offered Sam.

Derek liked this idea, immediately banging out a drum solo on the steering wheel while smiling and nodding in deranged fashion. "So, when are you going to ask?"

"Ask about what?" Sam asked, in puzzlement.

"The linoleum."

Sam didn't know what to say.

"Don't worry, I know it's weird. My dad... my dad happened upon a supply of linoleum and, hey presto, it's all over the house now.

"Oh."

"Yup. And, when I say 'happened upon', I mean stole." Derek continued, grinning like a buffoon.

Sam didn't know what to say, again.

"He got away with that one. Usually he doesn't though." explained Derek.

"Doesn't what?" queried Sam

"Get away with it."

"He's been caught stealing?" Sam asked in a surprised tone.

"Yup. All the fucking time! When I was a kid, I didn't know if he was going to be there from one week to the next." Derek explained, while pretty much laughing at the same time. "Sorry for laughing but he's a really terrible thief. He got away with the linoleum and the patio pavers out the back, and that's about it. In fact, he could be away just now. I never know. Also, sorry about the way my mum is. I wouldn't say she's exactly moody, just that she has one mood and that's sombre – I try to

151

stay out of her way as much as I can, as she brings me down."

Sam acknowledged this with a nod and a wry smile.

As they drove, Derek continued to tell Sam stories of stupid things his dad had done, and they were both laughing about them as they pulled up outside the chip shop.

Sam jumped out the idling van to grab their food. He was starving so had decided on a double fish supper and Derek had requested a white pudding supper. Luckily for them, there were chips ready, so he didn't have to wait for ten or so minutes for them to cook. He was in and out with the suppers and cans of Irn Bru in no time. They sat in the van to eat their chips, the hot food immediately steaming up the windows with condensation. There was a fairly long period of silence, aside from munching, as well as some slurping of the Irn Bru. Eventually Sam decided to break the silence.

"How come we only empty the fruit machines on a Friday and Sunday, and what would happen if we missed a pickup?"

Derek took a second to finish chewing, holding a sauce covered finger up in the air to signify that he had heard the question and that a response would be forthcoming.

"They worked out the optimum days for pick up. The Friday pickup catches all the late Sunday to early Friday cash, and the Sunday pickup captures the late Friday through Saturday and Sunday until early evening, which is a much busier time period. I only know because I asked the same question. If we missed a pickup, it would probably be fine but DLB Vending like the clubs and pubs to know we operate like clockwork."

Derek wound his window down and asked Sam to do the same. Their suppers were almost gone, the windows needing clearing before they could head back to Oakley. They both crumpled up their wrappers and threw them in the back, followed soon after by two empty Irn Bru cans. Derek set off with now clear windows while Sam had a sneaky peek back there, as the refuse slid around on the floor, and it was even dirtier than the last time he'd paid it any attention. Luckily nobody at DLB seems to care about any of that.

It had been a nice wee change, going for a drive, and Sam had enjoyed hanging out with Derek. They were now coming up to Longannet Power Station, it was quite a sight at night. Its array of gold lights emanating from the turbine hall looked almost like it was glowing against the now dark night sky. Sam wished he had brought The Man Machine for this moment, as Neon Lights would have been a perfect accompaniment. Even Spacelab would have worked as the building had a celestial quality to it. The song playing happened to be Smoke on the Water from Derek's compilation. Not ideal but not terrible either, it would have to do.

"What is it that you like best about this gig?" asked Sam. Derek answered instantly "The van, *has* to be the van. I love roaming around in it. DLB don't care if I use it for personal use, so I am always on the go and I enjoy driving to new places to check them out. Villages and

153

towns I haven't been to before, the countryside, even new housing developments."

"I get the visiting new places part, but what's interesting about new housing developments?" asked Sam.

"I've only done it a few times, but it's a laugh to pretend I'm interested in buying a new house and touring around the properties before anyone has bought them."

"They just let you check them out on your own?" Sam queried.

"Yep. If the salespeople think you're interested, they take you around the showhouse and, if you still seem keen, they let you walk around a few of the other houses on your own. They let *me*, anyway."

Sam wondered what sort of idiots thought Derek, with his greasy long hair, heavy metal threads and rust bucket on wheels would be able to buy a house, but he didn't query. He simply said "Cool."

They were on the home stretch now, with the houses at the top end of High Valleyfield on their right. This was their moment to turn left towards Oakley via the skinniest, darkest backwater road he knew of; Clinkum Bank. Naturally, Derek picked this road to start acting like the rally driving stalwart Jimmy McRae, going extremely fast and screeching around bends. Sam didn't want to let on he was scared so tried to appear unfazed by looking out the side window and fiddling with the radio volume. Derek had been trying to kill them both for a few minutes when Sam turned to look out of the front window and let out a high-pitched scream. "DEER!"

The van screeched to an abrupt halt with the contents of the mobile rubbish receptacle, i.e. everything in the back of the van, sliding forwards at high speed, with multiple bottles, plastic bags and other detritus sliding and rolling under Sam's seat to the front. It was pitch black with only the headlights ahead of the giving any light, but Sam could feel the mounds of discarded rubbish against his trainers. He was sure some were leaking juice onto the worn carpet under his feet. He really wished he could see something. A large stag with an impressive set of antlers stood looking at them, them likewise looking at him, the deer appearing to be a bit non-plussed. A literal deer in the headlights. Derek leaned heavily on the van's horn, startling the large beast so much that he dropped his front legs and launched himself up the roadside banking with his hind legs, disappearing into the night.

Derek smirked, looking down at the mess around Sam's feet. "I suppose I need to tidy up now."
"I am happy to help." offered Sam, desperately hoping Derek that would actually let him tidy up the van.
"Ok, let's go". Derek said, as he drove the rest of the way at a much safer speed. Having avoided any mishaps for the rest of the drive, they pulled up behind The Black Dog. There were two large metal open-topped rubbish bins on wheels in the car park behind the pub. Derek pulled the van up alongside.

It wasn't very well lit with just one large rectangular light beaming down from the pub's rear wall, but it would have to do. Sam hopped out and took a look down inside the bins, as best he could. One was for bottles and

the other seemed to be for everything else. Derek opened
the rear doors while Sam shuttled back and forward
taking an armful of debris with every trip from where he
had been sitting. Empty juice bottles, chip and crisp
wrappers, a half-eaten Mars Bar, it was pretty disgusting.
Once Sam had cleared the passenger seat area, he moved
to the back to help Derek. Yet more juice bottles and
other paper wrappings of differing sizes, with a
smattering of plastic bags. "Hold it!" said Derek,
sharply. "Don't touch that one."
Sam turned to look at Derek who was pointing at a
medium sized white plastic bag, which was tied in a knot
at the top. Derek stepped forward, grabbing two empty
cola bottles and lifted the bag, using the two bottles in a
pincer type fashion, and walked carefully over to the
metal bin, dropping it in with a light thud. Sam
wondered what the hell was in that bag, since Derek was
acting like it was a bomb.

Sam looked at what remained inside the van, the only
items left that hadn't been thrown out were an old dust
sheet, a ripped t-shirt, a dented can of cream of chicken
soup, and a cardboard box. Sam was desperate to know
what the van's brown carpet looked like, now that
mostly everything had been thrown away.
"Ever had this carpet cleaned?" he asked.
"Nope." Derek said dryly, almost sounding proud.
"What do you want done with the remaining stuff? asked
Sam.
"Just chuck it all in the cardboard box, cheers. I'll go
through it later." replied Derek.

"I've got to know, what on earth was in that white plastic bag?"

Derek paused and then took a long intake of breath. "So, you know how I was telling you about the new housing developments?"

Sam nodded, not having a clue where this story was going to go.

"I was on my own and walking around upstairs in a brand-new house when, I suddenly realised I needed to go to the bathroom."

"A number one?" Sam asked in a hopeful tone.

Derek sheepishly shook his head.

Sam listened on, open mouthed.

"So, I thought, there's nobody around, why not? Nobody would ever know. The bathrooms were all fully decorated, towels were on towel rails, fancy soaps by the sinks and, most importantly of all, toilet paper was on its bespoke holder next to the shiny convenience. It was only after I had, ahem, done my business, that I realised that there was one detail I hadn't checked. There was no water in the toilet!"

Sam burst out laughing. "Why was there no water in the toilet?"

Derek answered, turning all serious for a moment "Thinking back, I believe it's because it was winter and they didn't want the pipes to freeze, as nobody was occupying the house, therefore no central heating."

"What did you do?"

"There was a small rubbish bin in the bathroom, with a white plastic liner inside, so I was able to use that to dispense with any toilet paper I used. But I still had the challenge of disposing of what I left in the toilet.

Sam, both intrigued and disgusted, asked what happened next, his hand now partly covering his shocked face.

"I ran downstairs and saw that they had a set of kitchen utensils hanging from hooks next to the cooker. I grabbed a slotted spoon and transferred the offending item to the bin, putting everything in and then tying the bag shut."

Sam was still laughing at this but was also in awe at the way Derek dealt with his predicament. "When was this?" Oh, a couple of months ago." Derek retorted.

"A couple of months ago?!?" Sam almost shouting his response. "Why the fuck would you keep it in the van all that time?"

"I kept meaning to dispose of it." Derek said, laughing. "I just got busy."

After they had both stopped laughing at Derek's story, it was time to finish the job and head home. The inside of the van was noticeably cleaner, but did it make a huge difference? Not really, no. It might not smell as bad now, but Sam did feel better about not riding around in a sea of filth, especially now that he knew what some of that filth was. "Thanks for your help with cleaning the van, I appreciate it. It was long overdue."

"No problem" replied Sam.

"It seemed like you actually enjoyed it." Derek suggested.

"I wouldn't say enjoyed the cleaning part, but it'll be nice to have a clean van for a wee while."

"You're a good egg, Sam. Do you, or your pals for that matter, ever do anything bad?"

"I'm sure we have done our fair share." said Sam, trying
to think of something and failing.
"Hmm, nowt that I've ever heard about." Derek scoffed.
"That's usually a good thing; we have enough toerags
around here."
Sam didn't reply but it did make him ponder the fact that
he and his friends weren't exactly troublemakers. It just
never occurred to him. Maybe he needed to change that?

Derek drove Sam the rest of the way home, which only
took a few minutes. "See you Friday. And thanks again
for the help tonight, and for the chips."
Sam offered a thumbs up as he walked away from the
van, then saying hi to his mum, who was watching tv,
when he got in.
"Did you get something to eat?" she asked.
"Yes, I'm all good thanks."
Sam grabbed his school bag from the bottom of the stairs
and took it up to his bedroom. He had a quick shuffle
through his books to make sure he had everything for the
next day, and then leaned the bag against the wall next to
his bedroom door. As his mum was still up and about, he
decided to play his Man Machine tape on his stereo,
since it was still front of mind from earlier. He lay face
up on top of his duvet, closing his eyes and listening to
Kraftwerk while picturing the glowing gold cuboid of
Longannet in his head. It had been a long and eventful
day.

Chapter Eleven
Slater

After the excitement earlier in the week, the last few days had been very uneventful. There was nothing new to report on the police investigation, school had been quite dull and there was no drama during either his Co-op shift or the fruit machine emptying last night. In fact, afterwards, Derek said he was "busy, busy" and, after his explanation of his 'dirty protest' in the van earlier in the week, Sam knew better than to ask with what. It had been a fairly dreich Friday night, with neither Sam, nor any of his pals angling to do anything much in the rain, so Sam just opted for a quiet night at home with his mum after work.

It was now Saturday, and Sam was up early doors, as he had a couple of things he needed to do. The first of which would be to seed the bare patch in Mrs Young's garden with the grass seed he'd 'borrowed' from his grandad yesterday afternoon before work. The second was to bring breakfast to his grandparents, to say thanks for the seed, but he wanted to get the first job out the way first.

He was up and out before his mum was awake, jogging along the pavement towards the swing park, breathing the crisp morning air as he went, plastic bag of seed in his jacket pocket. He was almost there in a matter of minutes, cutting through the paved area with the lockups to the swing park and down to the cut through path which ran along the side of Mrs Young's back garden.

He saw Mr Slater walking up the hill toward him with his dogs and they nodded at each other as Sam ran past. As he glanced at the back of Mrs Young's house while running along the lane, he noticed immediately that there was a gaping black hole where her light blue back door used to be. Her door was wide open. Sam assumed Mrs Young was pottering around with her plants somewhere around her property in the early hours of the morning.

When he arrived at the back of the house, he still hadn't seen Mrs Young, so he placed the bag of seed on the bench under her window and ran up the steps, rapping on the open door a few times, shouting inside for her. When he didn't hear anything in response, he then walked inside to see where she was. Through her kitchen, past her pantry, turning left into her living room, where, again, there was no sign of life.

He checked her front reception room, walked back through the hallway to the living room and looked out the window to the back garden and hut, just to make sure that he hadn't somehow missed her as he was coming in. Nothing. He continued to call out for her but, just like before, there was no response. He was becoming concerned as he walked around the rest of the house, knocking on every door, shouting her name before he went into each room. When he'd exhausted the ground floor, Sam then climbed up the stairs to search more rooms, starting with the bathroom directly ahead of him at the top of the landing. The door was slightly ajar, and he knocked lightly, called Mrs Young's name, and attempted to walk in. He knew instantly something was wrong as the door wouldn't open all the way, it was clear something was blocking it on the other side. He pushed on the door just enough so he could squeeze his upper body through only to discover a horrifying sight.

Mrs. Young lay lifeless on the floor, lying face down in her dressing gown. He assumed she had hurt her head as there was a small amount of blood on her temple. Sam squeezed all the way through the gap in the door and bent over Mrs Young to check her jugular vein. He was relieved to find a pulse, albeit an extremely weak one. He could now see that her back was rising up and down ever so slightly as she breathed in and out.

Sam immediately ran back downstairs to call for an ambulance from the phone on the small hallway table. He also called the local police station number so that one of the officers would come to help while the ambulance travelled out from Dunfermline. He got Seton, so he explained about finding her door open and then, subsequently finding her prone upstairs. Seton said they'd be there imminently. After Sam finished the call, he unlocked the front door, leaving it ajar, and ran back up to the bathroom to try and help Mrs Young as best he could. He badly wanted to do something to comfort her. He moved her slightly so he could open the door all the way, and rolled up a hand towel, wet it under the tap, and carefully dabbed the wound on her head. Sam held Mrs Young's hand while they waited.

Hanging on for Constable Seton to arrive seemed to take forever, even though it was probably only a few minutes

162

and Mrs Young's laboured wheezing had Sam checking his watch. He had a high regard for her, naturally hoping whatever was wrong with her could be easily fixed, even though it didn't seem very likely just now. Finally, the footsteps of one of the officers could be heard coming up the stairs, so Sam stood back to give them some space to work. It was constable Redpath, who immediately felt for a pulse and checked out her vital signs. As Redpath kneeled over Mrs Young, he motioned with his head that Sam should go downstairs. This was fine with Sam as he felt completely useless in any case. He decided to wait in the kitchen at the back of the house, Seton was already in there on his radio talking to the ambulance, Sam assumed. It sounded like he was relaying specific details of Mrs Young's injuries in order that the ambulance crew could be as prepared as possible.

As the ambulance arrived, Seton ran along the hallway to the front of the house to hold the front door open so the crew could come straight in. Sam was watching from the hallway as two paramedics ran in and disappeared upstairs with a stretcher. They seemed to be taking their time, so Sam started looking around at the table in the hallway which was adorned with various pictures and ornaments. There was also a barometer next to it, mounted on the wall. Sam tapped the glass lightly and noted that the arrow was pointing to low pressure/rain – shocker. That was actually good news, for once, as he wanted the seeds to get a good watering once he had put them on the ground.

The pantry door was still open from earlier so Sam had a quick nose inside to see if there was anything he could eat, having been delayed getting to his grandparents' house for breakfast. At first glance he could see that Mrs Young was a big fan of soup! He scanned around what else she had… some Fray Bentos tins, loose potatoes in a box on the floor, Knorr stock cubes, cans of peas and carrots, and numerous jars of preserves. Nothing too exciting, and nothing he could eat right now. He wondered why there were no crisps. There were a few half-empty bottles of various Mitchell's Soft Drinks on a low shelf, which he was tempted to sample for a second but thought twice about it. Just like at his grandparents' house, the contents would be room temperature and almost certainly flat. He could hear them coming downstairs directly above his head now, so he ducked back out of his broth-filled hidey hole to get a better look.

Sam stood in the hallway watching as they carried Mrs Young out to the ambulance. She looked so frail. Seton asked Sam if he knew of any family that they could inform about her condition.

Sam shook his head. "My mum might know. I'll ask her to give you a call."

Seton nodded in acknowledgement. "Tell your mum she's being taken to Milesmark Hospital."

"Is she going to be ok?" Sam inquired, more than a note of concern in his voice.

"We think so. It looks like she hit her head on the sink or on the bathroom floor when she fell." Seton said. We're not sure how she did it but that seems to be the main concern."

"You don't think she was attacked, do you?" inquired Sam.

"No. Even though we can't rule anything out, it doesn't look like it was a break in. You said that the door was open, but it seems intact, and, most of all, nothing appears to be missing or disturbed." explained Seton. Looking around at items that might be worth something but are clearly still there, Sam had to agree. It didn't seem like a robbery.

Redpath and Seton were looking to leave, so Sam duly showed them out, thanking them for their help and making sure the front door was locked behind them. He quickly gave his mum a quick call to tell her the news and to get her to put the police in touch with Mrs Young's family. Despite the circumstances, he decided to complete the job he had come to do. He still had his seeding to do and felt it was right he finished that before heading to his grandparents'. He exited via the back door, which he left open for now, and stepped into Mrs Young's hut to grab a pitchfork.

Sam then walked down to the bottom of the garden and inspected the bare patch he was going to reseed. He couldn't help but think back to why the patch was bare in the first place and his episode with the cat carcass. He popped his seed bag down next to the bare patch. His granddad had shown him how to reseed and that it wasn't just a case or sprinkling seeds on top of the ground. He took the pitchfork and started spearing and

165

scraping the ground with it, making holes around 2-3 inches deep across the bare patch, as well as the adjacent healthy grass. When he was done it was probably an area around the size of a small coffee table he needed to seed. He grabbed his plastic bag and began sprinkling a liberal amount of grass seed across the whole area. Once the bag was empty, he grabbed a watering can from the hut and jogged up to the kitchen to fill it. He returned through the back door, using the outside of his leg to help support the now full can as he cut across Mrs Young's healthy grass towards the thirsty seeds. Sam then grabbed a few handfuls of soil from her plant beds and sprinkled that over the seeds He made sure that the whole area got another really thorough watering which should help get them started, Scotland's rainy climate being relied on to do the rest.

Glad to be finished, Sam looked back at Mrs Young's house from the foot of her garden just as Mr Slater appeared with his two dogs and disappeared inside his back door. Sam hadn't connected that Slater was Mrs Young's neighbour until now. He had probably seen him coming and going many times, but the penny had finally dropped that this was where he lived. Sam recalled that recent morning when Mrs Young looked across at Slater's house with disdain or fear, or perhaps a bit of both. He knew she didn't seem to like him, and he was curious to find out why.

It did make Sam wonder how it was that Mr Slater managed to leave from his own back door without noticing that Mrs Young's was wide open. The houses were part of the same structure, and the back doors were almost side by side. Curious. His mind then took him further down that rabbit hole... what if Mrs Young wasn't robbed but *was* attacked in her house for another reason, and what if the perpetrator was Slater? She had suggested before that she had issues with him. Did she suspect him of having something to do with her cat's disappearance? Slater did have easy access to her garden. He seemed an unlikely cat killer, in truth, but Sam didn't really know much about him at all. He is the common denominator with the cat killings, the first having been right next door to his house as well as being the manager of the estate where the main killing site was. Sam was convinced he was onto something.

Sam put his thoughts to the back of his mind for a bit, putting all the tools away and going inside. He called his gran and grandad from the hallway phone, to make sure they were still expecting him to bring some breakfast rolls over, and to explain why he was running late. He checked around Mrs Young's ground floor again, making sure nothing was left on, closing the back door behind him as he left. He didn't see any more of Slater as he departed Mrs Young's garden, but he thought some more about him as he walked towards the shop. Slater could well have been the person that Sam, Tommo and Constable Redpath suspected of cleaning up the cat murder site, and he had easy access there too and he saw them leave the estate after their discovery.

He arrived at Mr Das's where he ordered a selection of bacon and square sausage rolls to take away. He refused any sauce as he knew his grandparents would have both HP and ketchup in the house, plus he couldn't remember who'd ordered what combination in any case. It was only a few minutes to his grandparents' house from the shop. As he walked in the back door, he could already hear the electric kettle rumbling away as the water neared boiling point, his gran standing over the tea tray, at the ready. She gave Sam a hug and the two of them sorted the rolls, the condiments and the teas and Sam carried the tray with everything on through to the sitting room where his grandad was sitting in front of the tv. Sam's gran allocating the correct tea, rolls and condiments to the right recipient.

"All alright with you and Mrs Young, son?" His grandad asked, taking a sip from his piping hot tea.
"I'm fine grandad, all a bit of a shock but I'm hoping she's going to be ok."
"What do you think happened?" his gran inquired.
Not wanting to start in on his conspiracy theory with his grandparents, Sam stuck to the facts. "The police think she might have fallen and hit her head. They're not sure yet if it was last night or earlier this morning. The one thing that was a bit odd was her back door was wide open when I got there."
"How strange." responded his gran. "Maybe she had just nipped upstairs when it happened, having been outside before? Anyway, it's as well you were there."
"It is, gran. I did wonder how Mr Slater never saw her door open."
"Maybe he did?" his grandad interjected "but maybe he didn't think anything of it. Like your gran says, maybe

she leaves her door open all the time? It's not that strange at this time of year as there are not many beasties flying around yet, and the weather's been mild."

That's true, thought Sam, even though that put a hole in his thinking. "What do you think of him?" Sam asked his grandad.

"Scabby Slater? He's always been a bit of a strange one, ever since I've known him.

"Scabby? He was a scab during the strike?" queried Sam.

Sam's grandad explained "Yep, he was one of the few volunteers who crossed the picket line and helped keep the mine open when the rest were on strike. He was threatened by the union and some of the striking miners, and he couldn't have cared less. He virtually egged them on to do something, which, of course, nobody did. Once the strike was over, he went right back to his gamekeeper gig. I'm not sure if he has any friends in the village, and that episode certainly wouldn't help, but it doesn't seem to bother him. I've seen him around, always on his own. I'm not sure if he was ever married but I've never seen him with anyone and he's definitely not welcome in the Welfare. He's always walking his dogs and is always friendly enough, to me anyway, but I've heard there's a few folk that don't like him."

Sam nodded.

Sam and his grandparents had polished off their tea and breakfast rolls, so Sam headed through to the kitchen with the empty cups and plates on the tea tray. His gran wouldn't let him do the dishes, even if he wanted to. His current thinking on Slater needed to be shared, so he said his goodbyes and headed up the road to Tommo's.

Tommo's mum answered the door and invited Sam in. "He's still in his bed but I'll wake him up and tell him you're here, son." Mrs Thomson advised.
Sam sat on the couch to wait. The TV was loudly blasting Saturday Superstore at him. Sam looked for the remote control, but he couldn't see it so had to make do with the high volume.
Tommo's mum re-entered the room. "Would you like a cup of tea, Sam?"
"No thanks, Mrs Thomson. I just had one at my gran and grandad's house."
"Just let me know if you change your mind." she said as she exited the room.
Just then, Tommo appeared looking extremely dishevelled, clearly having just woken up. His trademark Celtic shorts accompanied with a Bunnymen t-shirt were his clothes of choice for this mid-morning meeting. His already curly ginger hair was somehow even curlier than usual, and his pasty white face had even less colour than his standard washed out look.

"I think I might know who the cat killer is."
"Mmh?" said Tommo, groggily.
"I think I know who the cat killer is" repeated Sam.
"No way!" exclaimed Tommo, clearly having now awoken from his groggy state. "Who?"
"Slater."
Slater? Really?" said Tommo, in a doubtful tone. "What makes you think that?"

"Ok, here goes." Sam then laid everything out. The cat murder locations, Slater's proximity to those locations and, the most recent development, his theory about the attack on Mrs Young.

"Hmmm, I can't see it. And why do you think he would attack Mrs Young?" asked Tommo.

Sam thought for a moment and then said "That's the bit I don't fully understand but she didn't like him, and I don't think he liked her. Maybe she confronted him about her dead cat? It's also very weird he just ignored her door being wide open, for quite a while too. He'd have seen it when leaving *and* coming back about 40 minutes later."

"Ok, I have my doubts but he's the biggest prick in the village, so who knows what he's capable of. Have you said anything to the police?"

"No, I only just came up with this and they have the murder inquiry to focus on. It's just a theory, so I don't think I can bother them yet." Sam stated.

"What do you suggest we do then? Follow him to see what he does?" suggested Tommo.

"Yep, we definitely need to find out more about him. We should tell the others."

Tommo called Shug, and then Gub, from the kitchen phone and they agreed to meet at the swing park in half an hour, giving him time to get changed.

They assembled at the roundabout and spun slowly around, as per usual, as they discussed Sam's theory.

"What do we know about old Slater?" Tommo asked, as they all took turns saying what they knew.

'Face like a walnut'

'Yellow teeth'
'Not funny'
'Bald'
'Scab'
'Dislikes Mrs Young'
'Heavy smoker'
'Irksome'
'Mongrelmonger'
"Wait, isn't monger a seller of something?" asked Sam pedantically.
"Not necessarily" Gub chimed in "fearmonger and warmonger don't fit with that."
"Ok, fair enough." acknowledged Sam "we're straying off track a bit."
"In his 60s." added Tommo.
"He might not be as old as you think. He just looks old." reasoned Sam.
"Let's just agree that he looks old, whatever his age might be" suggested Tommo, which seemed reasonable.

The group agreed that there was undoubtedly something strange about Slater, but they were not as convinced about him being the cat butcher. The gang decided it merited further investigation, though, so they set about keeping tabs on him, as much as they could.
They were all familiar with Slater's white van and they now knew where he lived. They could keep an eye on him when he was walking his dogs, which they knew was usually first thing in the morning or last thing at night – because they had seen him doing so numerous times. If his van was parked outside his house, he was either at home or dog walking. If the van wasn't outside

his house, it would likely be that he was either at Pitgarvie or around the shops in the village. They were at a disadvantage if he was going around by van as they didn't have any wheels themselves. "Could we ask Derek to help?" inquired Gub.

"I thought about that. He can sometimes be busy with his job, but I will find out if he can help." Sam replied. For now, they would see if they could pinpoint Slater's whereabouts, hoping his actions might provide some sort of confirmation of Sam's theory.

The foursome walked down to the bottom of the park, where the lane cuts through past Mrs Young's house. As they emerged from the path into the cul-de-sac, they could see Slater's white van was parked right outside the front of his house. But was he in?

"You guys stay here. I'm going to pop into Mrs Young's and see if I can see any sign of life on the way." offered Sam.

The rest of his crew nodded and stayed where they were as Sam walked around the outside of Mrs Young's front garden to her steps. He climbed the few steps that took him from the street to the front path, turning as he approached her front door to walk around the side of the property towards her back door. He figured there would be a much better chance of the back door being unlocked, especially since he had ensured the front door was locked just this morning. Sam knew, from her telling him so, that Mrs Young always kept the back door unlocked so he was hoping her family hadn't subsequently locked it, assuming they'd been over by now to check on the place. He turned the corner from the path she shared with Mr Slater to the rear of the property where the back doors were located side by side. He had to walk past Slater's back door to get to hers and had a quick glance to his right, trying to peer into the kitchen window, as he did so but was none the wiser.

Sam didn't want to make it obvious what he was really doing so he thought it would be a good idea to water the seeds again. He checked Mrs Young's back door, and it was indeed unlocked. Sam walked out to the hut to get a watering can, which was also always unlocked, and then back into the house to fill it, watching Slater's back door like a hawk the whole way. Again, there was no sign of life. Even though the grass got a good watering earlier that day, he figured another soaking would do no harm. Sam filled the can about halfway and walked back down to the newly seeded area, giving the dirt patch a good dousing. He walked back up to the back of the house, returning the watering can and shutting the shed door behind him. Once again, Sam peered at Mr Slater's house for any activity. There was none.

After popping his head back inside the kitchen to make sure he hadn't left the tap running, Sam pulled the door shut and jumped down the couple of steps from her back door to her rear path. As he turned the corner onto the shared side path, he let out a high-pitched squeal. Slater was right in front of him.

"Back again? Aww, how nice." said Slater in a mocking tone.

"Yes, Mr Slater. Just watering the grass seeds."

"Some service you offer, son." Slater said with a cheesy grin.

"What do you mean?"

"You were only here a few hours ago, and you're back already."

Sam thought about a sarcastic reply but decided to just play along. "My grandad said he wasn't sure I had given the seeds enough water before, so I am just making absolutely sure now." and decided to wave cheerio instead of prolonging the discussion, heading along the shared path to the cul-de-sac.

Sam walked around the corner where the rest of the gang were idling beside the chain link fences which marked the cut through path.

"Well?" said Tommo.

"Oh, he was there. It was almost like he was watching me, instead of the other way around." Sam advised.

"Did you speak to him?" asked Shug.

"I didn't have a choice. He basically ambushed me as I was leaving."

"No way!" Do you think he knows we've started to watch him?" asked Gub.

"I don't think so, I think he's just an annoying wank and can't help himself. At least we know where he is now and can keep an eye open for when he's on the move."

With that, the collective gaze of the group was drawn to Slater's garden and, there he was, looking right back at them with his two dogs at his side. It was extremely creepy and completely bizarre. He just stood staring across Mrs Young's back garden directly at them. It was akin to something from Hammer House of Horror or

175

Tales of the Unexpected. He just stood there, motionless and sinister. Sam and his pals felt a bit exposed and uneasy, so they ambled back up to the roundabout. This was a fairly decent observation post anyway, with the added bonus of being far enough away from Slater for them not to feel so uncomfortable.

Having adjusted his position to match where the boys now were, Slater kept his one-man staring contest going for another five minutes, or so, then eventually went back inside with his dogs, much to the relief of Sam and co.

"Thank fuck for that! What is he on?" said Shug.

"He's just messing with us. He's a warped wee man." said Sam.

"I can honestly say that I wasn't sure about your theory before, but I am now! That was truly bizarre." added Gub. "Do you think he's gone mental?"

"Maybe he's always like this and we just weren't on his radar?" opined Tommo.

"I don't know, but the more we keep an eye on him, the more we'll find out." said Sam.

There had been no activity for some time. Undeterred, the lads slowly rotated on the roundabout, while continuing to keep all eyes on Slater's back door. Then, movement. The door swung open, and Slater was exiting his house by himself. Slater locked the door behind him and turned the corner, presumably towards his van since he only walks when he has his dogs with him. The novice surveillance team's attention moved to the only part of the cul-de-sac they could see from their vantage

176

point. The back end of the white van was currently visible beside the hedge which ran along in front of Slater's and Mrs Young's property. As the gang homed in on their target, the van started to slowly roll out of sight.

They all looked at each other and nodded. They had previously agreed that Shug and Gub would jog up to the shops through the top gate of the swing park. The weakness in their plan was that if Slater didn't go that way and was, say, heading towards Dunfermline or Comrie, then the stakeout was over. As the two joggers were nearing the road end on Station Road, near to the Co-op, they saw his tell-tale white beast zip by. The bad news now was they would have to keep jogging to see if he turned up Wardlaw Way or continued down Station Road towards Pitgarvie. Again, their day would be done if he had taken the latter option. As they turned the corner, they could see the van sitting outside Vincenzo's.

In the meantime, Tommo and Sam were standing at the wire fence at the bottom end of Slater's garden looking in his hut window. The window was covered in dirt and dust so they couldn't see much at all. Tommo wiped the window with the sleeve of his jumper. It didn't really help as most of the dirt seemed to be on the inside and it was too dark inside to see in, in any case. They looked up the garden from the shed and Slater's van hadn't made a speedy reappearance, so they felt confident enough to step over the small fence and check the perimeter of the hut. His garden wasn't as tidy as Mrs Young's but there was nothing obvious by the way of

clues. They weren't actually too sure what they were looking for but fur, bones, blood etc would be handy if they wanted to prove their theory and report Slater to the police. They walked up towards the rear of the property, continuing to scan over the ground as they went, focusing on avoiding dog mess land mines as they went. "Doesn't look like there's much to go on here." commented Tommo.
"Nope, nothing. At least we can say we've checked this property over and can rule out the outside."
"The outside? You mean we need to get inside?" replied Tommo in a somewhat shocked tone.
"I'd like to, but I've not got a clue how we'd do that. For now, we need to stick to outside." answered Sam.

Since they were here, again, they popped into Mrs Young's house via the back door. They walked through the hall to her front room and parted her lace curtains so they could see out the window to the street. Still no sign of Slater. There wasn't much else to do for now, so they went back into the kitchen for a glass of water and nosed around her kitchen. They drank their waters and looked up to the swings to see if Shug and Gub had returned but they hadn't, which they assumed meant that Slater was otherwise engaged in the village somewhere.
"Why do you think Mrs Young still has all that pet food?" Asked Tommo staring at a stack of cans on the floor of her larder.
"She probably just hasn't had a chance to throw it away." Said Sam
"I thought she had a cat though?"

Sam looked down at where Tommo was looking and, sure enough, there was a case of Pedigree under the Whiskas. "Had is right. I don't know about a dog though. She must have at some time, I suppose." said Sam shrugging his shoulders.

They finished their waters and rinsed the glasses, carefully putting them back in the cupboard before they left. Sam ran through to the front room and double-checked that the white van hadn't returned. It hadn't, so they decided to make their move, pulling the door closed behind them on the way out. They walked down to the bottom of Mrs Young's garden, this time, scissor jumping over the low fence before walking up to the swings and roundabout. Not that their mission really achieved anything, but they made it back to the swings without incident, which was something at least.

Sam and Tommo hung out for another ten minutes before Shug and Gub returned to the park, sitting upright as the two of them approached out of breath. As the two joggers were about to spill the beans, Tommo aimed a single nod in the direction of Mr Slater's house. They all turned to watch as the white van eased into the gap in front of his house. A few seconds later Slater emerged swinging a white plastic bag as he turned the corner, again looking at the boys and sticking his middle finger up to them before heading inside.
"Chips." said Shug.
Tommo and Sam turned to look at Shug.
"He was getting chips." Shug further explained, with additional 'eating chips' hand gestures.

"Was that it?" Sam asked.

"Yep, nothing too exciting." added Gub "Did you guys find anything?"

"Nothing." Tommo said. "But we've only just started, I suppose."

They all nodded in unison.

"What now?" asked Tommo

"I think we need Derek to help us." replied Sam "If Slater goes anywhere in the van, then he will lose us, and it's more likely we find out something useful if he is heading further afield. I'll try and get hold of him this afternoon and see if he can help us tonight. Slater is likely settled for the afternoon now."

They agreed.

With Slater seemingly ensconced for the time being, they all went to their respective homes for lunch with Sam planning to head to Derek's house after he'd eaten his. He decided he'd take a walk down there after his food had digested, which would allow him to drop a note through Derek's letterbox. Sam used the notepad next to the phone to write a message to Derek about meeting up later, in case he had gone out by the time Sam got to his house. Sam didn't say why, as they needed to keep their observation of Mr Slater to as small a group as possible and there was no need for Derek's mum or dad to know.

The day had turned out quite nicely, so it was something of a pleasure for Sam to stroll down to the bottom end of the village. Given the lovely weather, he decided to walk along the railway line instead of around the road. Pollen and flower petals were blowing around in the breeze and there were numerous insects going about their business. He breathed in long and hard, and it smelled of spring. There was enough warmth in the air for him to take his tracksuit top off, so he did and tied it around his waist.

Sam knew what was coming ahead of him... the scene of his dad's death once again. As he got closer, he began to have second thoughts, but he needed to lance this particular boil, once and for all. He had seen it from a distance on the tick/black hole day, and that now he was up close, had convinced himself that there would be some obvious sign that his dad had died here. But, in reality, there was nothing which would have made anyone think anything of note had happened here at all.

Sam looked up at the coal trucks which towered over him. Why did one of the doors suddenly open just as his dad was passing? Why couldn't it have been a close call or a lucky escape. It seemed highly improbable for the door to drop at the exact moment his dad was walking by, but unfortunately it did.

Sam felt both happy and sad at the same time. Happy that he had pushed himself past his fears about the site of the accident but all the memories of the night his dad died had come flooding back. There was no point hanging around here anymore. The mini assignment had been successfully completed, even though there was effectively nothing there to see. His mind cleansed and catharsis achieved, he decided to walk on. After leaving the coal trucks behind, he navigated over the combination of tracks and stones to the fence beside the sawmill and pushed through the small gap. The sawmill was eerily quiet. Sam was now inhaling the smell of recently cut wood, once again, as he walked through the grounds.

As he carefully weaved his way through the piles of discarded machine parts and stacks of timber which littered the property, Sam heard a noise close by which made him stop in his tracks. He listened intently for another sound so he could pinpoint what it was and where it was coming from. There it was again, a noise not unlike one of Millie's squeaky toys. It sounded as if it was on his right, and he turned his head to see. It was a tiny fawn. A smile appeared on Sam's face as he watched as the tiny deer walked closer to him. Without any predators in the vicinity, and the absence of hunting around these parts, the deer approached him entirely without fear. Sam knelt down, putting his hand out to stroke the fawn on the head. Sam wasn't particularly spiritual, but he couldn't help but connect the baby deer with the scene of his dad's death, which was only a few steps away. He had heard people swear that dead relatives had reappeared to them in other forms. Could this be what he was experiencing?

"BANG!"
Sam jumped out of his skin, falling backwards into the long grass behind him, the deer bolting off in the other direction. Momentarily discombobulated, Sam realised that someone had shouted bang, as opposed to something mechanical or combustible making the noise.

When Sam gathered himself, he saw Slater guffawing with laughter to his left, seemingly having entered the sawmill property from the Station Road end.

"Ha, ha, haaa!" Slater laughed loudly, bent nearly double as he slapped his knee with his spare hand, the other holding his now excited dogs' leashes. "Now that was priceless." Slater teased.

"Yeah, very good." replied Sam dryly, his face showing his unhappiness at the practical joke.

"Aww, did I spoil your Kodak moment?"

"No, just gave me a fright, that's all." Sam couldn't believe that, of all people, Slater bumped into him on his walk. He'd only been following him for half a day, and he'd gone from ambivalence about Slater to despising him.

Slater walked past with his two mutts, heading for the railway line, still chuckling away.

Sam gathered himself to soldier on. There was no further sign of the wee deer.

Sam walked for another ten or so minutes, crossing over Station Road and cutting through the sports fields at the catholic school, eventually appearing at Link Road which would lead him up to Derek's house. He was still smarting from Slater's foray into slapstick as he walked up the steep hill to Lindsay's Wynd. As he approached the house, there was no sign of Derek's van, nor did Derek's mum answer when Sam knocked, so a note it would have to be. He pushed it through the letterbox, the note simply asking Derek to call Sam's house when he was able. He had no option but to head back down the hill, as he was lift-less. He also knew where Slater was, having just seen him on his dog walk, and he'd be too far gone by now, so there wasn't a lot of point of trying to follow him.

He wandered back towards the centre of the village, heading for Tommo's, passing over the burn and up the smaller hill towards The Black Dog. As he passed the entrance to the pub, Lauren's parents were coming out. Mr Smith had his arm around his wife. She seemed upset. Sam didn't know what else to do so he said hello. Much to his surprise, they stopped to talk to him.
"How are you doing, son?"
"I'm fine thanks, Mr Smith. Is everything ok?"
Thanks, Sam. We just got some upsetting news from the police."
"Oh, really sorry to hear that." replied Sam.
 Mr Smith nodded in response as they headed back the way Sam had just come from.

Sam decided to swing by the police station instead of going to Tommo's. The Smiths already knew about Lauren's clothing being found, as they were the ones who had to identify it. This must be something new, and he needed to find out what it was.

After a swift five-minute walk, Sam was standing at the front desk of the station, having caught the eye of Redpath who was on the phone at his desk taking down information in his notebook, but had made the exaggerated nod gesture, so Sam knew he had spotted him. As soon as he was off his call, Redpath walked over to greet Sam.

"What's new?" he asked.

"I was hoping you could tell me." said Sam.

"Do you fancy a cup of tea?" asked Redpath.

Sam nodded and they walked over to the break room and sat down, facing each other at an old kitchen table with flaking veneer. Redpath poured them two teas, which were completely stewed, as always.

"Well, we have decided to officially rule out Bairn as a suspect." Redpath using air quotes when saying suspect, to convey that he didn't believe there was ever a realistic chance that Bairn had been involved. "We had statements from customers in the pub that Bairn was in the pub well after Lauren left, and this type of crime isn't exactly his modus operandi. *And* we believe the real perpetrator returned to the scene of the crime to plant the items in the pub in a poorly executed attempt to frame him, because he had a criminal record."

"How would the perpetrator know that Bairn had a record?"

"Very perceptive, young Mr Hamill." Redpath responded. "That's why we believe the person responsible for Lauren's disappearance is likely from the village or the wider local area."

Sam was surprised at this, his eyes widening in disbelief. People in the village couldn't fathom this being done by someone from here, or near here. He knew his dad had scoured the village for clues but never truly considered the culprit to be from here.

"I can't believe that it could be someone from the village." replied Sam.

"Neither can we but it's what the evidence is telling us. And there's more."

185

Sam's eyes widened further.

Redpath continued "We are still working on the basis that the two girls' disappearances are connected but there are some major differences."

"Are you able to further explain, or is it confidential?" asked Sam.

"This is all for your ears only. As you know, Lauren was a homebody. A quiet girl from a nice family who, for the most part, spent her time partaking in activities around the village. You could describe her as a good girl who was very locally focused. Michelle, on the other hand, was pretty much never at school, came from a broken home and had been in trouble with the police numerous times. She had even been arrested for suspected prostitution." Redpath explained.

"What do you think connects them then?" asked Sam.

Redpath continued "Well, not too much actually, but it's significant that both disappearances were only seven miles and a few months apart. Abductions are extremely rare in Scotland, never mind Fife, and these are the first we've had for a while. There were also no clues or witnesses to either disappearance. The girls were just spirited away."

"Don't you think Michelle Polson could have just run away?"

"Definitely more of a possibility than Lauren having done that. And we considered that, even before Lauren's items of clothing were recovered, but Michelle's mother and friends say definitely not. Even though she was troubled, they don't think she would have run away." Redpath looked at his empty cup and stood up. "I better be getting back to the grindstone. Did you have anything for me?"

Sam considered unloading his Slater cat butcher theory on Redpath but thought better of it with all this going on. "No, nothing new." Sam replied.

Sam said his goodbyes and wandered back to his house for a bit. His mum was in the kitchen, and he went through to see what was new with her.

His mum was reading a magazine. "Where have you been since the early morning drama?" she queried.

Sam almost asked what she was on about as it had seemed days ago since he found Mrs Young.

"Oh, I was talking to Redpath and following up on a theory."

"Theory? What theory?"

Sam didn't really want to get into the whole cat murder thing with his mum, but he also realised that he had already made a mistake by saying it out loud which would only result in even more questions, so he decided to confide in his mum.

"Well, you know all those cats that have been missing for a while?"

His mum looked up from her magazine, clearly somewhat surprised by Sam's answer. "The cats? Yes, I know about some being missing, there's posters all over the village. Your dad said they were looking for a wild animal."

"Well, a wild animal isn't far from the truth, mum. I found a clearing in Pitgarvie Woods where there were quite a few dead cats along with a whole load of tools."

"What? What do you mean dead cats and tools? You mean a person has been killing them?" his mum's voice becoming louder and higher in pitch.

"Yes, that's how it looked anyway."

She was clearly concerned with what Sam was telling her "Did you report it to the police?"

"Yes, but when I showed them the place, it had been cleared up."

"Did they not believe you then? She asked.

"It was Redpath, so he knew I was telling the truth. There were a few bloodstains left behind, so it wasn't a huge leap for him."

"Did you see anyone?"

"No, not there. But when we were leaving, we saw Mr Slater, the gamekeeper."

"Mr Slater? Nooo. Even if someone is killing cats on purpose, surely, you're not thinking of him? He works there, for goodness' sake! Which actually gives him a better reason to be there than you. What makes you think he has anything to do with it?" inquired his mum.

Sam explained about Mrs Young's cat's remains being right next door to his house, plus the Pitgarvie connection. But, most of all, he was animated about this morning's events, with Mrs Young's incident and his thinking that Mr Slater has possibly attacked her.

"I thought you said Mrs Young's cat had been killed by a fox. And you don't know what happened to Mrs Young. I think you're getting carried away, son. I mean, he can be a bit strange at times, but him, really?" said Sam's mum, getting louder and still not convinced. "Just doesn't seem to me like he's capable of something like that. Your dad always had a good word to say about him, and I always got on with him. Even though he can be odd he can also be quite funny. In fact, when I was waving to your dad from the bedroom window on the night of his accident,

188

Mr Slater was walking by at the same time and waved up at me too. It made me laugh."

"You saw him the night dad died? Where?"

"Right across the street." As she nodded to the other side of the road with her head. "He was walking in the other direction to your dad, heading up toward the swing park." Mrs Hamill responded.

"Wait. What? "Did he turn around and follow dad?"

"What difference does that make? Sam, you're not suggesting he had anything to do with your dad's death, are you? As you well know, it was ruled an accident. Anyway, no, I didn't see him turn back."

Sam's mind was now racing. Could his dad have thought the same thing about Slater? Could Slater have realised and killed him?

Sam's mum could see the wheels turning in Sam's head. "Sam, I would get off this train of thought right now! You don't know if any of this is remotely true! This is how malicious rumours get started."

Sam could see his mum was getting annoyed, so he dropped it. "It's nothing more than a theory." he said softly and departed the room. He needed to clear his head and went upstairs to think and play some music. He didn't like arguing with his mum at all, but her comment about seeing Slater the night his dad died had really got him thinking. Had his dad got too close to finding out what Slater had been up to? Again, there was no real evidence of this, but it was another little piece of information that, when added to everything else in Sam's little bag of theories, started to paint a picture for him. He would think further on this in the morning.

As soon as Sam woke up, he immediately felt a pang of anxiety from his quarrel with his mum the night before. He had sneaked downstairs before she was up, as he didn't want to face her again, just yet. Sam didn't like fighting with his mum at all, and also knew she was probably right, but something was nagging away at him that he had to stick to his instincts regarding Slater. He had reconsidered his hunch about Slater having something to do with his dad's death, but there was just too much going on to dismiss his theory altogether, and he fully intended to continue to monitor him for the time being. There was something suspect about him and Sam intended to find out what.

Sam was also acutely aware that his mum was not the same as she had been when his dad was alive. She was quick to temper these days, and generally operated in a fairly sombre state these last few months. Sam knew she had had every reason to be short with him, worrying about what he was up to wouldn't help her and he regretted bringing up the Slater theory at all. He also knew she continued to carry the weight of the world on her shoulders, what with missing her partner and also with money being tight. He didn't want to add to the heavy load she was already carrying so he opted for the utmost secrecy from now on.

Sam determined that continuing his herculean effort to avoid his mum was imperative, so he got dressed and flew out the door in record time. He decided to walk down to the railway crossing for a change of breakfast option, foregoing Mr Das's for the wee newsagent/sweet shop across from The Railway Tavern. This place was run by the other Italian family in the village, the Baresis, and was more of the place to go for a quarter of Soor Plooms or Kola Cubes, or some of their homemade ice cream. It was far too early for that though, so he would see what hot food options they had today.

Mr Baresi was behind the counter this morning and seemed his usual cheery self. A jovial heavy-set man, the top of his head completely hairless and extremely shiny, sandwiched by thick brown hair on the sides, with a large, full moustache being the final flourish. Sam thought Mr Baresi reminded him of Super Mario, albeit with a strong West Fife accent. His small talk would typically consist of asking all the younger crowd who they were going out with, which always made things a bit awkward. He had also been known to boast about how generous he was at Christmas time, when Sam delivered to him on his old paper round. Ironically, being the only customer who never tipped him at all.

"Who are you winching these days, son?" were the first words out of his mouth.
"Oh, nobody Mr B." replied Sam.
"Well, that's not very good, is it? You need to get your act together." Mr Baresi retorted with a smile.
At this point, Mrs Baresi came through from the back saying something in Italian to her husband and then walking back out. After this, the personal intrusion

immediately ended and Mr Baresi gave Sam the hot sausage roll he had asked for, in a white paper bag.

Sam said his thankyous and walked out to the street just as Steven Morrison, aka Bairn, was about to walk in. Before Sam could say hello, Bairn grabbed Sam by the front of his jacket with one hand and lifted him up off the ground and against the shop window, shouting.

"Fancy seeing you here, ya wee dick."

Sam was frozen in fear and couldn't understand what was happening. He couldn't generate any words, just a spluttered attempt at speaking. Bairn was huge compared to him and Sam could do little other than squirm.

"Thanks to your prick of a dad, the police are always blaming me for anything that happens around here." Bairn continued.

Sam shook his head. "My dad's dead, how is it his fault?"

"Because he always had it in for me, I went to jail because of him." shouted Bairn.

Even in his terrified and helpless state, Sam thought 'you went to jail because you kept getting caught breaking into cars and houses', but he just said "sorry".

And with that, Bairn relinquished his grip on Sam's jacket, placed him back on terra firma, and took a step back. Sam was now able to get a proper look at his assailant.

It was no surprise that, in addition to working as the bar manager at The Railway Tavern, Bairn was sometimes a bouncer for other venues in Clint Westwood's empire, and, if rumours were true, a violent enforcer when necessary. He looked every bit the henchthug he was. He

192

was massive. Tall and broad shouldered with shaved blond hair and, despite the frigid temperatures this morning, his bulky upper body and forearm tattoos were visible, since he was sporting only a t-shirt. He was the sort of person you crossed the road to avoid, even if he wasn't after you for no apparent reason. Bairn seemed to have calmed down somewhat although concluded his salvo by saying. "If the police come back to talk to me again, I'll be looking for you."

Bairn seemed to have forgotten about whatever he was going into the shop for, turning to cross the road towards The Railway Tavern. Sam swallowed deeply and let out a huge breath of air, waiting a minute for Bairn to disappear inside the pub. He was a bit shaken up so went back into Mr Baresi's shop to grab a bottle of Irn Bru. Sam wasn't sure if Mr Baresi had seen any of the altercation, but he appeared from the back when the little bell above the shop door tinkled, so probably not. There was no chit chat to speak of this time, so Sam grabbed his juice and left the shop with a wave of acknowledgement to Mr Baresi. Immediately on exiting the shop, Sam guzzled down his cold Irn Bru, pretty much in one go.

Sam was somewhat shocked, when he had regained his composure, to discover that his sausage roll was still intact. It wasn't particularly hot anymore, but he was starving, so he walked over the level crossing and climbed up on the wall on the opposite side from the signal box to eat his food. Sam liked sitting up here. It was typically a great place to watch the traffic heading along the Dunfermline to Alloa road, as well as cars coming and going to Saline, but it was quiet so far today.

With the lack of vehicles to ogle at, Sam's eyes were drawn in the opposite direction to a distant figure walking along the railway tracks. It looked, although he couldn't be sure, like Slater with his dogs. Could it be? Even when Sam wasn't trying to follow Slater, he still appears. Or at least that's how it seemed.

Sam munched down the last of the sausage roll and jumped off the wall. If it was indeed Slater, Sam wanted to avoid being spotted, so he ran up the hill, along the stepped path, to the banking near his house. This was so he could sneak down to the railway line using the adjacent trees as a screen.

As he reached the tree line, Sam tried to find a section of the woods which he could see through to the tracks and locate Slater. It was tough to see since the trees were starting to bud and the bushes below had begun to thicken. Sam spent a few minutes peering through the trees as best he could, looking for Slater and his dogs. He wondered if he'd missed him as it was hard to tell where exactly on the railway line Slater was from the brick wall back at the level crossing. But there he was, almost directly down below him on the tracks.

Now that Sam had located his target, he was fairly easy to track. The sheen from the top of Slater's bald head, occasionally catching the light from the morning sun, acted like a beacon of sorts. However, Sam couldn't really keep a keen enough eye on Slater from up in the woods, so he decided to creep down to the tracks for a closer look at what he was up to. As he was working his way downhill towards the railway, Sam noticed that as well as the dogs' leashes in one hand, Slater had something tucked under his arm. It appeared to be a large bag or sack of some sort.

As Sam continued his stealthy journey through the woods, a thought entered his head. The operation to catch Slater doing something criminal or even mildly suspicious hadn't really turned up anything worthwhile so far. He was hopeful whatever Slater was up to now would be significant. Sam continued carefully, walking down the slope towards the tracks, trying not to make a sound. As he reached the bottom part of the woods where the dirt path was, Sam laid low making sure not to be spotted. The fence ahead of him had been consumed by bramble bushes, which acted as another layer of defence against the prying eyes of Slater. Sam stayed quiet and listened carefully for movement on the other side of the fence/bushes, but it was eerily quiet. He moved a little further down to where the gap in the fence was and still nothing.

Sam poked his head through the fence gap, looking both ways along the tracks but there was no sign of Slater or his dogs. Slater had only been out of sight for a matter of seconds, but he and his dogs had completely disappeared. Where could they have gone? Could they have cut through onto the same dirt path Sam had just been on? Almost certainly they would have bumped into each other if that was the case?

Sam couldn't really move until he knew which way to go. He contemplated taking a 50/50 chance and heading in one direction when, right in front of him, across the railway line, the bushes started to move. Sam jumped back behind the bushes and waited with bated breath to see what this was. Just then, Slater appeared. He had dog leashes in one hand, pulling his faithful pooches behind him, and a cloth sack, like the type for carrying potatoes, in the other. Notably, the bag looked like it had something in it now. Nothing too big, but big enough that there was a bulge in the bottom of the bag.

Slater was walking back towards where Sam had just been at the level crossing, so he followed him at a distance, staying on the dirt path behind the brambles so he would remain unseen. What was Slater up to? There was nothing down in the woods on that side of the tracks, except the burn and a couple of areas Sam and the boys used to play at. This seemed very mysterious. Suddenly, Sam remembered that there was a back way up to Porterfield down by the burn. There was a large pipe which was easy enough to walk over to reach the other side and a worn path which took you into Porterfield estate. The boys had a rope swing down there for a good while.

Sam tried to make sense of what he was seeing. Was this how Slater would access people's gardens to snatch the cats? How would the dogs get over the pipe though? No sooner had Sam pondered that thought, Slater was back again. It looked like the sack now had something else weighing it down. Again, didn't seem very big. Could it be a cat? Where would the cat have been? A few minutes later, after having walked further down the tracks, Slater was back in the woods. This was very peculiar. After what seemed like only a few minutes he was back out again, and this time the bag seemed fuller still. One thing was certain, there was no chance Slater was going over to Porterfield, given how quickly he was coming back out. Slater did this a few more times, then hoisted the now very full looking sack over his shoulder and walked further down the tracks towards the level crossing.

Sam gave him some space but continued to follow Slater at a good distance behind, so as to stay hidden from view. It had been quite easy to follow discreetly alongside the railway line, but it would be harder out in the open of the main road. Slater nipped through the gap in the fence by the level crossing and turned up the hill towards the football ground, and ultimately, Sam assumed, his house. It was not going to be possible to follow Slater going this way as it was too exposed, so Sam had an idea.

He walked from the dirt path onto the access road which runs along beside this part of the railway line, Slater was now out of view. Sam was taking a gamble that Slater was indeed heading home and, if so, he could follow him by walking along the path which cut through the field behind the houses on Blairwood Terrace, which ran parallel to the street. Instead of using the trees as cover, he could now use the row of houses, including his gran and grandad's. The only difference this time was that he wouldn't be able to see Slater, even intermittently, and Sam was working purely on his hunch that Slater was heading back to his house.

As Sam thought more about how he would get close enough to Slater to potentially see what he had in the bag, he decided to change tact. He started jogging along the cut through path, his thinking was that if he could get into Mrs Young's kitchen, he might be able to see Slater arrive back home at close quarters. He had thought about idling on the roundabout, but it was too far away to get a good look. Sam's jog turned into a sprint as he pushed hard to make it to Mrs Young's before Slater appeared at the top of the cul-de-sac. Slater had been a good bit ahead of Sam, but was walking compared to Sam's running, so Sam guessed they were about level as they passed his gran and grandad's back garden. No sign of anyone outside there, which was good, as he didn't have time to stop and chat.

Sam continued along the path, sure that he was in the lead now with about half of the way to go. Slater the unwitting competitor in this race was surely far behind now and, as Sam entered the cul-de-sac from the cut through path, he was certain he would make it to Mrs Young's without being seen. He sprinted along the front of Mrs Young's house, up the front steps and along the side of the house, only slowing down when he reached the back garden. He walked past Slater's back door and jumped up the rear steps to try Mrs Young's back door handle. Just as he was about to turn the handle, Sam suddenly panicked, wondering if Mrs Young was back home now, so he knocked lightly and, with no response, entered her kitchen and pulled the door shut behind him. He was sure his mum would have mentioned it, if so, but she hadn't so he was sure the house was empty.

Sam stood, catching his breath, in the kitchen for a minute or two until it dawned on him that Slater could be some time yet, given how fast Sam had been running. He decided to monitor from the front window, first of all, and would run through to the back once Slater had passed him. As he looked out the front window there was no sign of Slater, but Sam's heart was still racing. Sam tried some deep breaths to calm himself down, and it seemed to be working. Not for long though, as soon as he saw Mr Slater turn from Blairwood Terrace into the cul-de-sac his heartbeat was elevated again.

As Slater and his dogs approached the bottom of the cul-de-sac, Sam tried to home in on what was in the sack, but it was impossible to see, and he was stuck with guesswork. Even when they passed almost right in from of him it could have been almost anything in there. Undeterred, Sam ran through to the sitting room at the back of the house just in time for Slater to turn the corner. Sam had positioned himself in the far-right corner, looking left along the back path, to give him the best angle possible. Slater stopped right outside his back door but facing the away from it. He stepped forward and opened the hatch to his coal bunker and placed the entire bag inside. Once it was inside, he turned back towards his back door and went inside. Sam was puzzled. He needed to find out what was in that bag.

Sam was left pondering how he would be able to leave Mrs Young's house without being spotted. His best chance was if Slater went back out again, but he wouldn't know if he was planning to do so anytime soon. If Slater does leave, maybe Sam could check the coal bunker, but this was all proving quite a challenge. Sam decided to sit and wait for a bit to see if an opportunity presented itself. He walked through to Mrs Young's kitchen and looked out the window. There was no sign of life outside so he decided he would sit down for a minute or two until he could decide what to do. The kitchen had a small table against the wall, not unlike the one he and his mum used at home, so he sat down and looked around. Obviously, nothing had changed since Mrs Young's accident, everything was in its place and the kitchen was very neat and tidy. Sam didn't know if Mrs Young's daughter or anyone else in her family had been coming in, but he was glad he was able to hide out here for the time being.

Having scanned around the room a few times and drummed his fingers on the table, Sam was out of things to do. His options were to wait it out, bored, or make a run for it, but Slater would likely see him. Just then, he heard the door shut through the wall, Sam leapt up and looked out the window again. No sign of Slater, so he ran around the to the front room, just in time to see the white van peel away from its parking spot and head towards the road end. The van then turned right along towards the Miners' Welfare, so Sam jumped at his chance to check the coal bunker. He ran out of Mrs Young's house and pulled the back door shut behind him. Mr Slater's coal bunker was right next to his back door, so Sam had a quick look along the side of the property, to see if the van had unexpectedly returned, but the coast was clear.

Sam stood in front of the bunker wondering what on earth was in the bag. He lifted the heavy metal lid to the bunker and looked in. Slater clearly knew that there was plenty of coal in his bunker, otherwise the bag would have dropped down too far to reach without a major effort. Sam could see the bag sitting inside near to the top of the bunker and reached in to grab it.

"Excuse me!" came a shout from close by, Sam almost dying from fright. "What do you think *you're* doing?" it was an old lady standing at the back door of the house across the shared path, on the other side of Slater's and Mrs Young's property.

"Oh, I'm looking for something." responded Sam.

"I can see that, son." The old lady answered with more than a hint of snark.

"I look after Mrs Young's garden, and I mislaid a trowel." said Sam.

"Well, I don't know what it would be doing in Mr Slater's coal bunker" scowled the old lady.

"I thought Mr Slater might have picked it up." responded Sam.

"And you thought that's where he would have put it?" The old lady shouted back clearly not convinced whatsoever by Sam's reasoning.

And with that Sam decided to give up. He nodded at the old lady and replaced the lid to the bunker. "I suppose you're right" he said to end the conversation. "Just out of places to look." And with that he walked down through Mrs Young's back garden, stepping over her bottom fence and walked back home via the lock ups.

When he arrived home, his mum was in the living room, so he popped his head around the door to say hello, immediately heading upstairs to his room before she could engage him in conversation. He sat on his bed feeling more than a little disconsolate. So far today, he had been assaulted by Bairn, spent the best part of an hour following his prime suspect in the cat murders, only to have his hopes of finding any evidence against him gone, and it was only lunchtime. Sam let out a long sigh and laid back on his bed, looking up at his ceiling he wondered if he would he ever catch a break. How would he find out what was in the bag?

It had been a long time since his early morning sausage roll, so Sam ventured downstairs to see what he could eat. He felt slightly awkward as he had been avoiding his mum since their argument the night before, but his stomach was ruling over his head at this point so he went through to the kitchen in full knowledge that his mum would probably follow soon after.

Sam was proved correct in under a minute as his mum, presumably having heard him go through to kitchen followed him through a few moments later. "Hi, son. What have you been up to today?"

Sam didn't want to tell her about Bairn, and he *definitely* didn't want to mention Slater. "I was just up early and did a bit of scouting around for Millie." replied Sam, while looking over at the little hook beside the pantry door which still had her backup leash and old collar hanging on it.

"Oh, I know it won't make a difference to you, son, but I don't think she's coming back." said his mum.

"You're probably right, mum, but I can't settle until I know for sure."

"I know, it's nice you're still trying. Do you want some tomato soup for lunch?" she asked.

Sam nodded with a smile and went through to see what was on TV while his mum was busy in the kitchen. As he was passing the hallway phone table, the phone rang so he answered. "Hello" Sam said.

"Wellllll, howdy Sam." said Derek using a pretty terrible fake southern American accent. "Wanna mosey on out and round up some cash with me tonight?"

Sam just laughed.

Derek, using his traditional voice now, asked "Sorry I missed you yesterday, me and my mum were out seeing my gran. I just wanted to make sure you were good for the usual shift.

"Yep, that's good with me." replied Sam, which Derek acknowledged before hanging up.

Sam knew he had his soup and a relaxing afternoon to look forward to before he started work in the evening. With the security of that knowledge, Sam settled down to see what was on tv, Sunday afternoons were not renowned for good viewing options, but he would make do and frittered away a few hours channel hopping.

It was a nice, warm afternoon as Sam stood outside waiting for Derek and the now mythical brown van. He was a little early so was standing on the other side of the road from his house, admiring, as he always did, the light brown Ford Granada belonging to Mr and Mrs Robinson. Even through the owners were elderly and used it for towing a caravan, Sam always felt the car was a little bit gangster. It was the sort of car he could see Arthur Daley, or Bob Hoskins in the Long Good Friday, driving. Unlike every other neighbour, the Robinsons had dug out their grass along the side of their end unit and made a driveway with paving stones and red stone chips.

Both car and caravan were parked along the side of the house inside a black metal gate, which, again, was unique for this street. The car was cherished, always gleaming. Another notable feature was that the shining chrome front grille had both AA and RAC badges attached to it. Surely, they wouldn't be members of both breakdown organisations, but given the care given to this vehicle it was entirely possible they were.

Sam felt good. His afternoon had been relaxing, especially after his rough morning. He was enjoying his job, especially making the money he was making, and driving around with Derek collecting turned out to be fun and somewhat lucrative. Derek had turned out to be good company and, despite his musical tastes, it felt liberating to drive around Fife in the van. The tranquillity of the street was soon shattered as the increasingly loud noise emitting from the van's engine was becoming more audible. Once Sam could really hear the engine, he started to also hear the initially faint but growing noise of some heavy metal racket too. Sam looked up the road as Derek turned onto the straight part of Hill View and directly towards where Sam stood.

In a matter of seconds, the van was screeching to a halt in front of Sam, shattering the peace of the neighbourhood. With Sam being across the street, he was on the correct side of the van to simply walk over and climb into the passenger's side which is exactly what he did. Sam was met with an "alright?" from Derek and, with a quick nod from Sam in response, the two set off to undertake their collection duties. Derek threw out a surprise by playing Mr Mister's Broken Wings, which Sam was embarrassed to admit he liked.

"Nice one." said Sam.

"We'll make a rocker of you yet." laughed Derek. As they set off, Derek asked "what have you been up to since Friday night?

"Well." Sam said, taking a pause before unloading about Slater. "You know how we were joking about Slater being involved in the cat killings at Pitgarvie?" Derek nodded. "I now think he might actually be involved."

"Seriously?" Derek replied sounding a tad shocked. Sam replied "yeah, I won't bore you with all the details but there's something very off about him, so we've been following him."

"Following him? Who, where?" asked Derek sounding even more surprised.

"Me and the boys. Just around the village when we've been able. Watching his house too. I saw him earlier with a bag of something which he'd collected from the woods beside the railway line."

"No way!" Derek said loudly. "I wish I could have helped. You couldn't see what it was in the bag? Are you saying it was a cat?"

"Yep, I know it's weird, but I honestly don't know what was in it. He kept diving in and out of the woods down the hill from my house and coming out with more and more stuff in the bag. I followed him to see if I could see anything, but I couldn't. Then, when he left the bag in his coal bunker, I tried to look but some old wifey next door chased me away." answered Sam.

Derek said "Well, now that I know, I can definitely help you guys."

Sam was delighted. "That would be amazing," he said. "We can only follow him so far on foot so it would be good to have wheels when needed."

The chat about Slater had taken them pretty much all the way to the first pub, so they got to work collecting the fruit machine cash. They had developed a good working partnership, not that there was too much to the job. Sam knew exactly where he was needed at each stop on their route and, as a result, they were getting through their shift even faster than before. Even though Sam knew he wasn't exactly the 'muscle' the insurance company had demanded, he was always vigilant and made sure he was ready for any scenario, not that anyone in and around the pubs seemed to care.

Before too long, Derek and Sam were on the way out of Dunfermline towards Crossford.

"How's your love life?" Derek asked with a wry smile.

This was not an area Sam wanted to discuss, particularly, not that he had much of a love life. "I'm not seeing anyone, if that's what you mean?"

"You must have someone in your sights though?"

Sam didn't want to get into it but, against his better judgement, he decided to tell Derek something he hadn't officially told his friends. "I like Margaret... Stafford. She's a year below me at school and she's nice."

"I knew it!" said Derek, momentarily lifting his hand off the sterling wheel to rub them together.

"You knew it?" Sam queried.

"No, I don't mean I knew you liked her, but I knew you had your eye on someone. I'll say no more."

Sam was relieved that it ended there.

"So, are you going to ask her out?" Derek added.

Sam whipped around to look at Derek and Derek just laughed.

"I'm winding you up." Derek said smiling again. "You should be getting my sense of humour by now." Sam smiled back, although it was a bit put on, since he wasn't at all happy discussing who he fancied.

"If you ever want to take her out for the night, I'd be happy to give you a lift into Dunfermline, or I can wait for you at the school."

Sam gave a minimal nod in faux appreciation. He didn't see himself taking Derek up on his offer at all. While a trip into Dunfermline with Margaret would be wonderful, the thought of Derek chauffeuring them around town in the brown heap made Sam shudder.

Derek suddenly veered right into the Cairneyhill Petrol Station. "I need to fill her up."

Sam sat tight while Derek filled up the van and then went inside to pay. The bonus was Derek had bought some snacks at the garage shop and threw Sam a bag of cheese and onion Square Crisps, a packet of Minstrels and gave him a can of Top Deck shandy. This was unexpected but warmly received.

They sat where they were to eat their snacks, before rolling out to stop only a few hundred yards further down at their last non-Oakley stop, the Main Street Hotel, to empty the machine. It seemed more like a pub than a hotel to Sam, but he assumed there were rooms upstairs - they had only ever seen the bar.

After only a few minutes, the white bag was thrown in the back of the van, and they were on their way again. Three stops to go and another shift over, and, more importantly, another pay packet for Sam. They were coming quick and fast which was a good thing.

"So, back to Slater. What can I do to help?" asked Derek.
"You could see if you can keep an eye on him tomorrow while we're all at school?"
"No worries. I can do that." said Derek. "I can either pop round tomorrow evening or call and update you."
That seemed ideal to Sam. "Perfect." he replied.

Chapter Twelve
Stock Boy Syndrome

Getting up for school on Mondays was always difficult for Sam and, since he'd started doing his Sunday night shifts, it was even more of a struggle. He and Derek hadn't stayed out too late, but it was late enough. They had been chatting at the lock up as they deposited the cash from last night's collection and time had gotten away from them somewhat.

It was probably around 10.30pm when Derek dropped Sam off at home and he still had to wash up, check his bag and lay his clothes out for school before he got to bed, so it was well after 11pm when he fell asleep. It wasn't a long enough rest after his weekend of work and reconnaissance.

The next morning, Sam stumbled out of bed in silence and got himself to the bathroom to clean his teeth and have a good wash. He had forgotten to set his stereo to come on and he was all the worse for it. He looked at the clock, he was running late. This meant he would not have enough time to make breakfast, but, if he got his skates on, he might be able to grab something from Mr Das's before jumping on the bus.

Sam got himself together and ran out the door. He shouted bye to his mum as he pulled the door shut but he had no idea if she heard him, and it was too late for him to check.

It was a pretty ugly day. The wind was blowing and there was some rain mixed in, the dark morning sky had contributed to his accidental long lie. On days like today, a door-to-door school bus service would have been preferable, but Sam had to get up the main road to catch his bus. The only way to have a chance of squeezing a quick visit to the shop was if Sam jogged the whole way so that's what he did. It also meant less time facing the elements.

Sam was covering ground at a good pace and, as he reached Station Road, there was no sign of the bus, so he bolted across the road and into Mr Das's to see what he could grab. Worried that the bus would appear imminently, Sam decided that a prepared roll would take too long so he saw a pre-made cheese and pickle sandwich in the display cabinet and grabbed a can of Coke and a packet of Discos to accompany it. A swift exchange of goods for money followed and Sam was back outside ready for the school bus.

Standing now at the deserted bus stop Sam briefly became concerned that he had arrived at the main road after the bus had already been but, no sooner had that thought had entered his head, the bus turned around the corner. He was always one of the first on, so looked for a decent spread of available seating in advance of the other three of his crew getting on. He was also aware that Margaret had not been at his stop. This didn't mean she wasn't getting on, as her house was behind the football fields, so it was not much difference for her to get on at the same stop as the boys. She could have also got the earlier bus.

No sign of Margaret at the next stop either but the boys were all there and climbed aboard and scattered themselves around where Sam was sitting.

"What's this? Extra breakfast?" asked Shug.
"My only breakfast." answered Sam.
"Late night, last night?" Tommo inquired.
"Sort of. Wasn't really up to anything." replied Sam. "Just lost track of time talking to Derek at the lock up, and then I slept in this morning."
Gub added "Talking of Derek, is he going to help us keep an eye on you know who?"
"Yep, spoke to him last night and he says he's going to follow him today."
"Great." Gub said enthusiastically, while clapping his hands together in excited fashion.
"I did some yesterday and it got interesting." added Sam.
"Oh yeah? Tommo inquired.
"I saw him on the railway line with his dogs and decided to see what he was up to, while hiding. It was really strange. He kept disappearing into the woods on the Porterfield side and reappearing a few minutes later with an ever-growing bag of something."
"A bag?" Gub asked "And what do you mean 'ever-growing?"
"Just that. He started with an empty bag, and every time he reappeared from the trees, it was fuller."
"With what? asked Shug

"Well, that's the thing. I have no clue. I followed him via the cut through path behind Blairwood Terrace and he put the bag in his coal bunker. When he left, I tried to see, I was chased away by the old wife from next door."
"How weird." stated Tommo.
"Yep. Very." added Sam.
"Hopefully Derek has some info for us later." said Gub. The rest of the journey was spent talking about non-cat related subjects.

As the bus pulled up in front of school, Walshy was waiting and signalled to Sam he wanted a word.
The four walked over.
"Would you guys have any interest in going to the Dunfermline game on Saturday? We're at home to Stranraer.
"Not me." said Tommo, instantly. This was no surprise as he was a Celtic fan.
The others stood quietly pondering until Sam said, "what would the arrangements be?"
Walshy explained "We're all going to meet outside the fire station at half two and walk along to the game. There should be loads of us."
"Ok, I'll check what I'm doing and let you know." said Sam, with Shug and Gub nodding in agreement, indicating that they would do the same. As they left this little rendezvous, Sam asked if the other two were interested and they seemed to be to a reasonable degree, so they arranged to reconvene this discussion on the bus after school and headed off to their different classes.

213

The school day was dull, as per usual, and the bell to signify the end of the day couldn't come quick enough. When it finally rang, there were a few kids who effectively sprinted for the bus. Sam was one of them and the rest of his friends weren't far behind. They grabbed their favourite seats at the back of the bottom deck and slumped down on the multicoloured upholstery after a hard day's schooling.

"What does everyone think of Walshy's football idea?" asked Sam.
"I am going to think about it." Shug replied. "It's not much of a game, Stranraer, and we'll be gone most of the day. I am tempted though. We *are* closing in on promotion."
"I might be up for it." added Gub. "I reckon there'll be a big crowd given we're on the home stretch.
"Ok, I am definitely thinking about it too. Let's agree to decide before we get to school tomorrow and we can let Walshy know either way."
"Deal." said Shug, and Gub agreed by nodding.

"What are you guys up to tonight?" asked Tommo, who'd been silent during the Dunfermline game chat.
"I am hoping to hear if Derek found anything interesting about Slater today." replied Sam.
"What time?" inquired Gub.
"Hmm, that's the thing, he didn't say. He'll probably just swing by later. Maybe I can call you, or we can get him to pick us up?" offered Sam.
"Sounds good." Tommo said, looking determined.

"If we discover something about Slater, are we going to tell the police?" asked Shug.

"Yes, definitely. I haven't said anything yet, as they're busy on Lauren's case, but if we find something concrete then I will tell them straight away." Sam promised his guys.

The bus journey went quickly as the boys speculated about what Derek might have seen Slater doing today. The gang were convinced that Derek having mobility, and therefore the ability to follow Slater anywhere, meant he would undoubtedly discover some crucial piece of evidence against him. Sam jumped off, raising his arm to bid the others adieu as the bus passed by him on the way to their stop.

Even though he didn't really have to, Sam jogged back down the road to his house. He did have a little homework to do so wanted to knock that out before Derek swung by. There was no specific time agreed for Derek to visit, so it made sense to clear the decks just in case he was early.

Sam spent about an hour doing his homework and then it was time for dinner. His mum had made bangers and mash, which was one of Sam's favourites. No word from Derek, so Sam took his time and relished having an enjoyable dinner and a welcome break from stew or some sort of poached fish.

Still no word from Derek, so Sam and his mum settled down to watch some tv. It was a Monday night, so it was slim pickings on the entertainment front. They sat watching the news and something starring Richard Briers, but Sam wasn't paying attention. He wondered if Derek had been successful in finding anything out about Slater, or had it been a waste of time. Sam decided to be more productive while he was waiting so he decided to go upstairs and make a mix tape. Just as he reached the top of the stairs, the phone rang so he ran back down to answer. It was Derek. "Sorry, Sammy Boy, I've had to change plans. My mum has asked me to help her tonight, but I'm planning to follow Slater again tomorrow and I'll update you after."

"That sounds good." Sam replied. "I'll tell the others."

"I'll tell you what, maybe I can grab you all straight from school tomorrow? I can fill you in then."

"I have my shelf stacking shift at the Co-op tomorrow, but as long as I'm there for 5, I'm good."

"Perfect." said Derek. "I'll be waiting at the gates."

"That's great", Sam responded. "Did you catch him doing anything today?" Unfortunately, there was silence on the end of the line. Derek had already hung up. Sam quickly informed the rest of the gang that tonight was off, and also about tomorrow's after school meet before retiring to his room for the rest of the evening.

The next day at school had actually been decent for a change and Sam passed on to a delighted Walshy in Geography that three more were joining his happy band for the football on Saturday. The only downside was Sam didn't see Margaret again, neither on the bus to school or at lunch. He wondered if she was off sick.

Sam waited by the school gates and watched through the throng of departing teenagers for his pals. No sign of the brown heap yet but he could see the twin red thatches of Tommo and Shug heading his way. He was just about to turn the other way to look to see if Derek was anywhere near when he also spotted Gub join up with the other two heading his way.

Now that Sam knew everyone was going to be there, he focused his efforts on spotting the van. It was hard to miss, so it was clear, at least for now, that Derek wasn't arriving on time.

"Alright." Tommo said as the rest reached the gate. Sam saying 'alright' in response, as was the tradition.

"No Derek, then?" said Tommo, stating the obvious.

"He'll be here." promised Sam.

No sooner had Sam said so, than the rattling roar of the engine could be heard in the distance. The boys all looked downhill towards the town, and they could see a white cloud getting closer to them. The van was creating its own cloaking device, it seemed. The noise became louder as it closed in on them. Luckily, the late arrival of Derek had meant that the crowds of kids had more or less dispersed by now.

Derek brought the brown van to an abrupt stop right in front of them causing the van tyres to make a loud but short-lived screech. "Alright ladyboys, get in." Derek announced from his open window. The boys duly jumped in.

After waiting for Derek to manoeuvre the van around so it was heading back down towards Dunfermline town, Sam couldn't wait any longer. "So, did you follow Slater as planned?"

"I most certainly did. I even participated in some beaking at one point, said Derek.

"Beaking?" asked Shug from the couch in the back.

"You know, like tailing, but when you're in front of who you're following." responded Derek with a smirk.

They all laughed.

"Anything of interest?" asked Sam.

Derek took a deep breath before responding, indicating he might have lots to say, but then not saying very much. "Nothing incriminating, if that's what you mean. But I did follow him around the village and into the town and back."

"Where did he go in the town?" asked Tommo "We haven't seen him leave the village."

"He went into a pub in Abbeyview. The Temple." answered Derek. "I didn't follow him in, I just got a roll from the shop across the road and sat until he came out. He was probably an hour."

"Was there anything happening at the pub?" asked Sam.

"No, not really. Just seemed really rough. Looked like a few druggies and prostitutes hanging around."

"What else did he do?" asked Gub.

"That was it for the town. The rest of the time he was back and forth between his house, Pitgarvie, and the shops around Oakley. He's definitely a dodgy creep, but also boring as fuck."

"Did he show any bizarre behaviour? He was acting really strangely with us. Staring at us for a long time from his back garden." added Sam.

"I'd love to say so, but I didn't see anything. Aside from his trip to Abbeyview, he was just doing what I always see him doing... walking the dogs, driving to work, buying his lunch." replied Derek.

The debrief on Derek's Slater reconnaissance had burned through the journey between Dunfermline and Oakley. They were now driving parallel to Sir George Bruce Road and heading towards the centre of the village. As they turned left at the Miners' Welfare someone was being ushered into the police station, which caught Sam's eye from his passenger seat vantage point. It was Bairn, and Sam's heart sank. He didn't say anything to anyone else, but he immediately remembered what Bairn

219

had told him would happen if the police hauled him in again.

Beyond thanking Derek for the lift, as he jumped out at his house, Sam didn't say anything else the rest of the drive. He needed to have a think about what this might mean for him before he headed back up the road to work.

On Tuesdays and Thursdays, his mum would typically make tea early, so Sam would get a good feed before his Co-op shift. He had about an hour before he needed to get ready, so he went through to the kitchen to see what particular dinner was in store for him. His mum wasn't in the kitchen but there was a pot of beans on the cooker ready for heating and some bread sitting ready for toasting in the toaster, so it was pretty obvious what was on the menu. This was a favourite dinner of Sam's so no complaints there.

Without his mum for conversation, Sam's mind turned back to Bairn and the police station. He considered calling to see if Redpath would tell him why Bairn was being interviewed but he didn't want to be a bother. Instead, he planned his route to and from the Co-op. If Bairn knew anything about him, he would know he worked Tuesday and Thursday from 5-8 stacking shelves. But *would* he know that? He doubted Bairn knew any of it, but he would still have to be careful to avoid bumping into him on Station Road, or on the way there. If he was spotted going in, he would be a veritable sitting duck as customers and shelf stackers mix together until the shop shuts at 6.30pm.

At this point, his mum appeared with a smile and told Sam dinner was coming soon. As she began heating up the beans, he sat himself in readiness at the small kitchen table.

"Mrs Young got home from hospital last night." Sam's mum said. "Her daughter told me on the phone a wee while ago. I'm going to go and see her tomorrow, if I wait until after school do you want to come? "Oh, that's great news. Would love to see her." Sam replied.

After his tasty dinner, which his mum had topped with grated cheese, which was a tremendous addition, it was time for Sam to head to work. He had thought hard about how to avoid running into Bairn, or being seen by him, so he left for work early as he was planning to go an unorthodox route. This would probably be enough to avoid him, but Sam also decided to take his dad's torch which had been given back to the family after his dad's death. He briefly reminisced about how his dad used to joke about it being better than a truncheon, so Sam decided to take his dad at his word.

Instead of turning left towards the top end of Hill View, as he always did, Sam turned right towards his grandparents' house and the field behind it with the footpath which led to Slater's and Mrs Young's cul-de-sac. He walked fast, sometimes breaking into a jog. He was soon out of the street and onto the steps which led down to the level crossing but before going anywhere near as far that, he cut across the grass and down the banking to meet up with the aforementioned path. Sam figured that if Bairn was driving, he'd be going by the main road, and if walking towards The Railway Tavern, he wouldn't cut away from the main road to walk this back way.

Sam was making good time, and he was soon at the entrance to the cul-de-sac. He could have cut through the lane to the swing park but that would take him back the way he usually walked, so he checked the coast was clear and turned left towards the main road. Again, he looked along the road before heading that way to ensure safe passage.

It didn't take him long before getting to the Miners' Welfare. This was arguably the trickiest part of his trek, as this is where he couldn't really avoid being seen by Bairn if he happened to be heading to work in the other direction. Sam had considered this, but there wasn't much he could do since his work was directly across the road from the police station. He would hope that Bairn would still be in there or had possibly left long before.

Sam did have one extra step to take, which was to go directly across the road to the community centre, sneak around the back to the playing fields side, and get as close as he could to the Co-op from the back end before running into the store. As he reached the rear end of the community centre, Sam afforded himself one more glance across to the police station to check the coast was clear. It was, so he ran full pelt across to the corner of the Co-op, quickly switching to a non-suspicious casual saunter to enter the store.

The Co-op didn't require any fancy outfit or special uniform for Sam's stock boy role. Street clothes were fine, so it was simply a case of checking in with the store manager, Mr Kelly, and getting on with it. The job was very straightforward too. Not much more to it than using one of the plethora of Stanley Knives that were strewn around the storeroom to open the various containers stacked back there and get the produce on the shelves.

Sam had learned the best way to transport the products to the shop floor was to use a shopping trolley, which he stacked as high as he could and then whittled it down as he went, and then would start all over again. He had started this shift with soup and canned vegetables, moving through the tall stack of cases until there were none left, and it was time to fill the trolley with another stack.

Cans were easy, they slotted on top of each other, nice and neatly, and the cases were easy to manage. That could not be said of his next tranche of products, sauces and condiments.

Sam had rattled through the first half of his shift. He only had about five minutes to go until the doors are shut to customers and they can play real music over the store speakers. It's the small things in life that make the difference, and the second half of his shift was always more enjoyable, almost entirely because of the music. It was just chart music, but it was better than the piped in Muzak Sam had been forced to endure for the last 90 minutes.

Sam had been doggedly working his way through the stack of ketchup, mustard and Branston Pickle in his shopping trolley and he was near to the bottom now. However, he was saving the worst for last. It had to be tackled at some point but one of the most challenging tasks was dealing with the trays of HP Sauce. For reasons unknown, the condiments in the Co-op were all stacked on shelves above the frozen food section, which meant lifting everything over the chest freezer to their home above. This was fine with most items, if not a slight stretch to reach, but the HP was a different story.

Sam had his technique down to a fine art. He had tried lifting them over with the plastic wrap still on the case, but it was impossible to remove while stretching over the freezer. His tried and tested, albeit slightly awkward method, was to kneel down with the case lying flat on the floor, cut the plastic away and then lift the array of teetering bottles in their bafflingly shallow cardboard tray across to the desired shelf. It wasn't an ideal method, but it was the least troublesome.

Sam was in position. He had cut open the plastic which surrounded the multipack of bottles and their tray, removing and discarding it in readiness for the toughest part. He was on his knees, bent over the case with his hands either side of it, resting on the shop's floor when he suddenly felt a strange pressure on his left hand causing him to look down at it. There was a scuffed work boot pressing down on his hand. Bairn had obviously spotted him before and had now come to pay Sam another visit, he thought.

Sam's eyes slowly wandered upwards, first looking at the boot, which was a black steel-toed Dr Martens style boot, then a cuffed jean leg, a black donkey jacket with bright orange shoulders, and, finally, a pale, wrinkly face, not dissimilar to one of those light-coloured raisins. This wasn't Bairn, it was Slater, and he looked angry.

As Slater pushed his boot down harder on Sam's hand, he said "I've got a fucking bone to pick with you. Why is that big gangly fuckwit pal of yours following me around in his van? It's one thing me playing the pantomime villain with you and your wee bum chums around the village, but I draw the line at that big clown getting involved." exclaimed Slater. As he finished talking, Slater pushed down on Sam's hand one last time before stepping off.

Sam stood up while rubbing the palm of his hand, but before he could say anything Slater added "Do you not think it's a bit strange that he is hanging around with you? Has he got no pals in his own age group. There's something not right about him and you should keep the fuck away."

As Slater turned to walk away, Sam spluttered out his response. "What would you know about pals? I've never seen you with anyone except your dogs." Slater just laughed loudly and walked away.

Luckily for Sam, nobody seemed to have caught this interaction with Slater. It looked as though he was the only customer in the shop and Dave, the other stock boy, was through the back. Sam was a bit shaken up, however, and opened a bottle of coke from the fridge to calm his nerves. Mr Kelly was fine with him and Dave grabbing the odd refreshment or a handful of 'pick n mix' as long as they didn't exploit it. He just marked them down on the inventory as spoiled.

The rest of his shift flew by, which would normally be a good thing, but Sam was in no rush to leave with two people now seemingly after him. He had given it some thought and would go home via an even more circuitous route.

The end of his shift was nigh, and, as Mr Kelly was closing up the store, Sam did his best to have a quick look out from the front door, but he couldn't see much. There didn't seem to be anyone obviously waiting for him, but would they just be standing out in the open? He was going to revert to his tried and trusted method of running full speed as well as going the unorthodox route of cutting through the primary school and running along the railway path behind it to the woods across from his house.

Sam said his goodbyes and immediately broke into a full sprint on leaving the shop. Turning left and bypassing his own road end, heading straight down Station Road towards the school instead. Despite his high-speed running, Sam was keeping an eye out peripherally in case anyone was waiting but it would be odd if they were waiting on him down here, given it wasn't the way to his house – not directly in any case.

As he reached the school gates, he grabbed the top of the metal fence immediately adjacent and swung himself over in one movement. He kept running but was now moving at jogging pace and by the time he reached the woods at the back end of the school playing fields he had slowed down to walking pace.

Sam flicked on his dad's torch and entered the woods via the dirt path. This route was not recommended at night as there was no light at all and, without the torch, he'd be completely blind. Sam shone the light directly ahead of him which created a bright green circle as the beam lit up the leaves.

He was walking quite carefully as it was still completely dark in every direction except ahead of him. He didn't think there was anyone behind him, but he didn't dare look back just in case. It was a blustery night, and he could hear the trees creaking and their branches clacking off each other as the wind knocked them together. As he neared his house, he wondered if either Bairn or Slater would have just waited for him there. He'd have to cross that bridge when he came to it.

Sam had been on the dirt path for five minutes or so and it was now time to climb up the hill through the woods towards his house. There was a thin path which led to the top of the hill, but it was not as obvious as the one Sam had been walking on thus far. As he turned onto the path a muted bird call let out. CAW! Sam, already on edge because of the threats from Bairn and Slater, ducked down thinking that he'd disturbed a nesting bird, but he couldn't see anything. His heart was racing, and he could hear it beating in his ears. He shone the torch down onto the ground and could see that his foot was not resting on a mound of dirt, but rather the chest of a dead crow. It seemed he had inadvertently pushed air out of its lungs, making the dead bird 'call out'.

Sam wasn't superstitious at all, but he couldn't help thinking that there was something ominous about this latest development. He had no choice but to brush it off and continue on to his house, and to safety.

The last few minutes were a blur as Sam just pushed himself up the slope to the edge of the woods. He flicked the torch off and stopped for a moment to see if there was anyone lurking around outside his house but there was no sign of anything or anyone. Compared to the woods, the street was very well lit thanks to the yellow light of the streetlamps, and the coast looked clear. Sam decided he had to just to go for it. He had his breath back now, so ran furiously towards his gate, opening it with urgency and slamming it shut behind him and leaping up the couple of steps to the front door, keys already jingling in his hand by this point. He fiddled with the lock and in he went. Sam had never been happier to get home.

Chapter Thirteen
Mixed Messages

Sam was sitting at the kitchen table as his mum was making him some toast. Of course, he could have easily made it himself, but she insisted, and he wasn't going to argue.

"Remember, we're going to see Mrs Young once you're home from school today. I haven't seen her, but her daughter said she's really frail and would love a visit and maybe some help. I'm going to make her some soup to take round." advised Mrs Hamill.

Sam, now with a mouthful of warm, buttered toast, nodded in an overly obvious way so his mum would see him agree.

For a few minutes, Sam hadn't thought about Slater and Bairn, but they were back in his head now. would they really be up and about to hassle him before school? Probably not, but Sam would adopt his high-speed running defence in any case.

Sam polished off his toast and tea and got ready to sprint up the street. He had decided, erring on the side of caution, to run past his usual stop and wait on the bus outside Tommo's. It would be this sort of genius thinking that would save him from another confrontation.

The moment of truth had arrived, and he sped up the road as fast as he could, which was pretty fast, in Sam's humble opinion. He did do a quick glance either side of his road end at Station Road before continuing on at pace up to the stop on Wardlaw Way.

As he approached the stop, he could see the other three all looking at him. "Can't bear to be without us?" laughed Shug, which really didn't make any sense since Sam would have been on the bus with them in short order anyway. Sam just smiled at the comment, while he caught his breath. "Seriously, why are you up at this stop this morning?" asked Tommo, somewhat puzzled that Sam isn't just getting on at the stop before as usual.

"Half the village is after me." Sam said, exaggerating ever so slightly. "Well, a couple of villagers anyway."

"After you? Who?" Tommo followed up.

"Slater and Bairn." Sam replied. "Bairn threatened me the other day and Slater came after me during my Co-op shift last night."

"Eh? Why? What are you on about?"

"I'm serious. Bairn half throttled me the other morning blaming my dad for getting him in trouble before and now somehow holds me responsible for him getting lifted in connection with Lauren's case. He said if he got lifted again, I'd be in for it."

"No way!" exclaimed Shug.

"Yep, the worst part is I saw him walking into the cop shop yesterday."

"What about Slater?" asked Gub.

Sam reeled off his interaction with Slater. "He came at me when I was doing my shift at the co-op. He stood on my hand when I was stacking the shelves. He was hugely pissed off that Derek was following him around the last couple of days."

"So, we're getting to him? asked Tommo.

"Exactly what I thought." said Sam.

While they were on the subject, Sam had a quick look around to see if there was any sign of either of his two nemeses, but the coast was completely clear. Almost immediately after breathing a small sigh of relief, the bus swung around the corner which meant a break from worrying about his unwelcome followers for a while.

Sam had managed to go through the entire school day without stressing about either Bairn or Slater but, as the school bus was now heading back home, it suddenly dawned on him that he was going to Mrs Young's with his mum after school, which would put him right next door to one of his adversaries. Sam couldn't tell his mum anything about Slater, as she fell out with him for mentioning it before. He could do nothing else but hope that he was able to come and go completely unseen.

Once the bus reached Oakley, Sam again got off at the chippy stop instead of outside the Co-op. He also went another unusual route home to try to avoid being spotted or followed, which was across the football field behind the community centre, then cutting through his gran and grandad's garden to access the steps through the park at the end of his street. Once home, he ran straight upstairs and threw his bag in the corner of his room. His mum was likely sitting downstairs ready to go so he knew time was of the essence.

Sam quickly used the facilities and gave his face and hands a good wash. Also fixing his hair with his wet hands. He was satisfied with his appearance. Sam trotted downstairs to see where his mum was, and, as predicted, she was sitting on the couch with her jacket on, her handbag on her lap and a container of soup beside her on the side table.

As Sam walked in, his mum stood up, clearly ready to leave, which was fine by him. She handed him the container of soup, and they headed for the door. As they walked out of the house and towards the swing park, Sam was conscious he wasn't really listening to his mum, he was on high alert watching out for his foes. He did seem to be getting away with mmm hmms and occasionally nodding in agreement though.

The pair had made it without incident to the lockups behind the swing park, now was the crucial period as

Sam would be able to see if the white van was parked outside Slater's or not.

As they turned left to walk down to the cut through, there was no sign of Slater or his van. This was a huge relief to Sam. He scanned all around the swing park, including up to the top entrance but nothing. He felt better. The Hamills navigated the cut through and the short hop up from the road to the front of Mrs Young's house without incident and circled around to the back door in order to enter. Sam figured Slater was at work so the earlier they got in and out the better it would be.

Mrs Hamill knocked lightly as they walked in, Sam placing the soup on the kitchen counter. They wandered through to the sitting room, Mrs Young sitting in her big armchair, which had been moved directly in front of her fire. She sat looking at the television with a tartan rug covering her legs. Mrs Young looked much better than the last time Sam had seen her, but she was still looking pale and fragile. Her face lit up when she saw them walking in and she beckoned them over. "Come on in. What can I get you two?" she asked.

Mrs Hamill stepped in before Mrs Young could stand up. asking her to stay where she was. "We're here to give you a hand, not the other way around. We brought you soup, and Sam is happy to get you anything you need from the shops." Mrs Young thought better of trying to move and let her guests do what they had come to do.

Sam's mum went through to the kitchen to boil the kettle, leaving her boy and Mrs Young in the living room. "How are you feeling?" Sam inquired.

"Much better now, son. Although I probably wouldn't be here if it wasn't for you. Thanks for helping me out, I still don't know what happened." Mrs Young responded.

Sam followed up "Do you think you just fell?

"Yes, I think so. I had been pottering around outside and the last thing I remember was going upstairs to the bathroom." she answered.

"So, nobody else was in the house?" asked Sam.

"No, son? Who else would be here? It's always just me. The doctor thinks I fainted."

"Sorry to hear that, Mrs Young. What does the doctor think caused you to do that?" Sam asked.

"They don't know. Could be my blood sugar."

Just then, Mrs Hamill came through with some tea and biscuits on a tray for everyone.

"I'm probably getting low on supplies, hen? Do you think I need anything?" Mrs Young asked Mrs Hamill.

"You could do with a few things." Sam's mum replied. "Maybe you could do a list for us, and Sam could run up to the shop while we're here?"

Mrs Young liked this idea and asked Sam to retrieve her notepad and pen from the kitchen drawer. They sat sipping their tea while Mrs Young laboured to jot down a list of her usual must have items from the Co-op. After a few minutes, the tea was finished, and the list was done. Mrs Hamill gently took the notepad from Mrs Young and tore the page out with the list on it. She took a quick scan, nodding as she went. "Sam will be fine to get this while I help pick up around here."

Mrs Hamill passed the note to Sam and asked him to run up the road to the shops. Mrs Young asked Mrs Hamill to take a twenty-pound note from her bag to cover the costs. "You might want to take my roller bag, son?" Mrs Young suggested.

Sam gave a swift "I'll be fine, Mrs Young." in reply. There was no way he'd be seen around the village with a tartan shopping bag on wheels. Sam headed for the door, list and money in hand, and started jogging as soon as his trainers hit the pavement. Still no sign of Slater or Bairn, long may it stay that way, he thought.

It was only as he entered the Co-op that Sam looked at the list. It was mostly basic items on there… bread, cheese, butter, jam, milk, tea bags, rich tea biscuits, more soup for her pantry and dog food. The last item was ever so slightly surprising to Sam, seeing as Mrs Young didn't own a dog, and there was already some in her pantry just last week. He wasn't there to ask questions, so he just bought everything on the list and headed back down the road. Sam was now feeling some regret for not taking the wheeled shopping cart, as it was a fair old load he was carrying, and the dog food was awkward and heavy. He wedged the cardboard box of tinned pedigree chum under his arm, which made carrying the bags of everyday items a bit easier and wandered back down to Mrs Young's with her purchases.

When Sam arrived at Mrs Young's back door, having been relieved once again at the lack of a white Ford Transit outside Slater's house, he discovered a note on the kitchen counter that his mum had gone on to his gran and grandad's and he was to meet her there. Mrs Young was still in her armchair when he walked through, having temporarily put her shopping down beside his mum's note on the kitchen counter.

"That's everything on your list, Mrs Young. I'm going to put it all away before I go."

"Thanks, son. You and your mum have been a godsend. She washed the dirty cups in the sink and put them away before she left. Thanks for my shopping, I really appreciate it."

"No problem, I'll leave the change in the bowl on the hallway table." suggested Sam, having seen keys and change in the bowl before. "I got everything on the list, but do you mind me asking, what's the dog food for?

"I get it for my grandson. He picks it up from here as it saves him going to the shop himself."

This seemed a bit odd, but Sam nodded in acknowledgement and asked if he could put anything away for Mrs Young.

"Everything can go in the pantry except the dairy foods, son." She explained.

Sam put the milk, butter and cheese in the fridge and then placed the pantry items on the shelves closest to the pantry door. The only item he placed elsewhere was the case of dog food, which he left on the floor, where the now absent cases of Whiskas and Pedigree had been.

"That's me, Mrs Young. Anything else you need from me before I go?" Sam asked. "Are you able to get up and down the stairs ok?"

"I'm fine, son. I just lost a wee bit of confidence with the fall and need my strength back. I'll get up to my bedroom fine though." she replied.

"If you're sure?" Sam said, double checking.

"You're fine to head off, son, can't thank you enough. Get away to your gran's now." Mrs Young assured Sam.

Sam bid Mrs Young farewell and, as he left the back door, decided to pop his head around the corner of Mr Slater's house to see if the van, and therefore the auld git himself, had returned. It wasn't there, so Sam decided to take a quick look at the freshly seeded area at the bottom of Mrs Young's garden to see if there had been any germination, although he realised it had only been a few days. There hadn't been much change, but it did look like a few minuscule blades had started to poke through the soil. Sam thought about watering but decided against as there had been plenty of rain over the last few days.

As he walked back up towards the back of the house, Sam thought to himself that he'd aim to return to check on the grass in a few more days. After everything that had happened to Mrs Young in recent days, he really wanted to get her grass back to full health for her. It was a very minor thing, but it made him feel good, and he even managed a little smile as he thought about it.

Sam had allowed himself, for one brief moment, to not focus on Slater or Bairn being after him. His guard was down for the first time in a few days and then he saw someone out of the corner of his eye. It was Slater standing on his back step smoking a cigarette, his face once again slightly obscured by a cloud of exhaled smoke, which was preferable. Sam thought about turning around and climbing over the fence at the bottom of Mrs Young's garden, but he felt it was too late and would make him look like he was running away, which he absolutely would be doing. He had no option but to walk past him.

"Visiting your wee pal again? How nice." Slater sneered, creating another cloud of smoke in front of his face as he spoke.

"Yeah, I was checking on her to see if anyone had done any harm to her." Sam sneered back, finding some courage in front of his nemesis somehow. As the elevated discussion continued to unfold, Sam had continued walking and had managed to manoeuvre himself to the other side of Slater and he was now on the side nearer to the path and his exit.

"If that's meant to be some sort of loose reference to me, both you and her are off your heads. The auld bag has been knitting with one needle for years, but you should know better. I was told she fell. If you think someone broke in and hurt her, it certainly wasn't me. If you're looking for suspects, you'd be better looking closer to home." Slater retorted.

Sam was taken aback by the "closer to home" comment and couldn't think of anything to say. Did he mean his mum? Ridiculous, he thought. Unable to think of a sharp response or a witty retort, Sam just said "ok, bye." and walked quickly along the side path.

As Sam walked the short distance to his grandparents' house, he pondered both what Slater had said, and also that he had been on his own and Slater hadn't done anything more than sneer at him, which is what he had always done, so Sam was taking this as a positive development.

After a few minutes, Sam was walking into his grandparents' kitchen where he could hear his family's voices coming through the wall from the sitting room. He wandered through and sat with them and put his thoughts of Slater, as well as Bairn, to the back of his mind for a while at least.

Chapter Fourteen
Planted Seeds

Thursday was turning into a busy day. Now that school
was over, Sam had his usual Thursday night Co-op shift
in an hour or so and had decided to shoehorn in a visit to
see Redpath before it, which would have a dual purpose.
Firstly, he wanted to know if any headway had been
made about the cat mutilator, as it's been well over a
week since Sam showed Redpath the clearing in
Pitgarvie Woods. Even though he suspected Slater, there
could possibly be some background detail that would
help his case. Secondly, and definitely the more pressing
of the two issues right now, Sam needed to know why
Bairn was in the police station the other night. Was there
more evidence recovered? Had Bairn's alibi collapsed?
Hopefully Redpath would set him straight.

Sam decided to just head straight into the police station
as soon as the bus dropped him off. It was a bit of a risk,
as Redpath might not be there, but he knew he could
always do the same thing tomorrow, before his Friday
fruit machine gig, if he wasn't.

Sam stood outside trying to see what activity was going
on through the window, but he couldn't really tell so he
just walked in, with a growing feeling of trepidation. He
contemplated that the passage of time was starting to
play its part in his comfort with making himself at home
at the police station. It had been a second home to Sam

while his dad was running things, but he felt increasingly awkward now.

There was nobody at the front desk, but Redpath spied him from the other side of the room and motioned with his hand for Sam to head over where he was.

"Good to see you, Sam. What brings you in today?" inquired Redpath.

"Just thought it would be good to catch up, but I do have a couple of things I wanted to ask about," Sam said, champing at the bit to ask about Bairn.

"No problem at all, Sam, what can I do for you, then?"

"The other day I was passing, and I saw Bairn being led inside the station. Was that in connection with Lauren's disappearance?" asked Sam.

Redpath took a little mini look around the room before answering, speaking in a softer voice at this point. "You know I can't really divulge anything relating to live cases… but, between you and I, it wasn't, we have other inquiries he's helping us with."

"You look worried." Redpath said, obviously noticing Sam's demeanour. "Why would Bairn being interviewed make you concerned?"

Sam explained "Bairn grabbed me outside The Railway Tavern, blaming my dad for him getting lifted before and threatened to batter me if he got lifted again."

"What? I can have him brought in and charged for that."
A clearly disgusted Redpath promised.

Sam put his hand up "No, please don't. I'd rather just
leave it."

"I get that, but we can't have thugs like him throwing his
weight around." Redpath explained. "Anyway, given the
circumstances, I will tell you that we brought Bairn in
for a general interview about Westwood's operations. I
can't really say much more than that."

Sam breathed out, clearly relieved. "Thanks."

"What was the other thing? asked Redpath.

"Oh, I just wondered if you'd found out anything more
about the cat disappearances… timeline, number of calls,
as well as anything more on the site in Pitgarvie
Woods?" Sam explained.

"I made a start on it, but I am getting pulled in every
direction, so I still need to follow up on some things.
Can you give me a couple more days, and I will update
you?" Redpath promised.

"Anyway, let's lighten things up a bit. How are you
handling Dunfermline's push for promotion?" laughed
Redpath.

Sam laughed too. "I am feeling the pressure. I think
everyone is. I am going to East End on Saturday."

"Oh yeah, who are they playing?"

"Stranraer. A bunch of us from school are meeting at Dunfermline fire station and going to the game together. Pray for us." Sam said, laughing again.

Redpath smiled and then turned serious again "Watch yourself. Lots of young lads are looking for bother at the games these days."

Sam nodded. "I know, we're not planning on getting into any trouble. Hopefully another win to celebrate, that's all we're interested in."

Redpath nodded in agreement as Sam stood up, shook his hand, and headed for the door. "I'll be in touch and I'll either find you or leave a message with your mum." Redpath called out, as Sam was departing. Sam acknowledging with a wave.

Sam had allowed plenty of time for his chat with Redpath before work and now he was debating whether or not to run home or to just go to work early. Maybe Mr Kelly would let him start and finish early? It was worth a try.

Sam walked across to the Co-op and headed straight for the storeroom at the back, where Mr Kelly was likely to be. And he was. "Hi Mr Kelly, any chance I can start early tonight?"

"I don't see why not. As long as you get everything done, it doesn't bother me." Mr Kelly replied. "I was meaning to ask you, I saw you having a conversation with Mr Slater the other night. What was that about?"

"Oh, nothing much" said Sam, lying through his teeth. "He was asking how Mrs Young was getting on."

"Just checking. It seemed a bit odd, but I missed you at the end of your shift, so I thought I'd ask. He's an odd bugger, Slater, but he can also be quite funny. You never know what you're going to get from him." continued Mr Kelly.

'Funny?' Sam thought. 'Yeah, funny looking'. He wanted so badly to query the statement from his boss, but he thought better of it. It seemed Mr Kelly did not adhere to the universally held view in the village that Slater was a prick. In Kelly's defence, he lived in Rosyth, so would only see Slater when he was in the store.

His shift went slowly but he was home 45 minutes earlier than usual, which was a nice bonus. Sam wondered if he should ask if he can permanently move his shift, as getting in earlier would be great.

Sam sat with his mum, who was settled down to watch Eastenders. "How was your day? She asked. "Are you not a bit early tonight?"

"Pretty good, mum." Sam replied. "Yes, I was ready to start early so they let me finish early too."

"That's good. Do you need anything to eat?" she asked.

"I'm fine, I ate earlier in the break room." explained Sam. A perk of the job is that the later day staff can help themselves to any leftover pies and pastries from the hot food counter, as they get discarded at the end of each day in any case.

"If you have time, do you want to pop in with me to see Mrs Young again tomorrow after school. I know you are working but she really appreciated our help last time – especially yours with getting her messages – and I wanted to make sure she had everything she needs before the weekend." Mrs Hamill suggested.

"That's fine with me, mum". Sam replied, just as the EastEnders music was starting, which was his cue to head upstairs. Sam took his schoolbag up and rummaged through it, checking his schedule to make sure he had no unwelcome surprises tomorrow. His life had been exceptionally busy for the last month and, with the Easter break on the horizon, Sam was looking forward to a bit of a rest.

With nothing seemingly needing to be done for school, Sam had a think ahead about his weekend plans. After school tomorrow, he had his visit to Mrs Young's house, and, in all likelihood, a quick trip to the shops for her, then his driving gig with Derek. Saturday, he would be catching the bus into Dunfermline with Gub and Shug to meet up with the rest of the high school crew for the trip to East End Park. And Sunday he had another work shift. Action packed indeed, he thought to himself, and that didn't even include any evening extra activities with the boys.

With Sam getting in earlier than usual, it almost seemed like he had a night off. Sam certainly had more time than usual before bed, so he decided to sort through his cassettes. It was a growing collection, and it felt good to go through what he had. Sometimes something from the bottom of the pile would end up at the top of his playlist, so it was always a worthwhile exercise. Quartet by Ultravox was a good example. Neglected of late, but the cassette was now being placed into the tape player as Sam continued to curate his collection. The tape was at the beginning of Side B, which was good news for Sam as his favourite track from this album, Visions in Blue, was first on that side.

As he sorted through his tapes, Sam thought back to what Redpath had told him about Bairn and Clint Westwood, and he wondered what had been going on. Westwood was revered like some sort of celebrity around the Dunfermline area but there was always something off about him. Sam's dad never had a good word to say about Clint and that was good enough for him.

Westwood was always in the paper for charity work or some event or other going on at one of his bars but there were always rumours swirling around about drugs and other nefarious activities going on. Plus, if Bairn was one of your employees, that doesn't say a lot about your judgement.

Of course, the positive side of all of this was that Bairn had no reason to bother him, so that just left Slater and, based on their argument last night, it didn't seem like he was going to do anything more than snipe from the sidelines anyway. Sam undoubtedly felt better about his safety when travelling around the village in any case, and that was all that mattered.

Sam went to bed not long after and much less weighing on his mind since his meeting with Redpath and his interaction with Slater the night before. He had brushed his teeth, washed his face and went to bed thinking about his forthcoming football day on Saturday. It was just over 24 hours away and the excitement was building. Sam had been to plenty of games before with his grandad but never as a co-ordinated event with so many pals from school. He couldn't wait.

The football match was still fresh in his mind and was the first thing to enter his head as Sam woke up from his slumber. This time tomorrow he would be getting ready to catch the bus into town. He just had to get one more day of school and some work out of the way first.

Sam's good mood had been enhanced by the fact it was a beautiful sunny morning. Birds were chirping outside, and chinks of sunlight were getting through the gaps where his bedroom curtains weren't overlapping. Today was going to be a good day, he thought to himself.

Sam jumped out of bed and ventured to the bathroom, turning on the taps over the bath so that the hot water heater would kick in while he brushed his teeth. Seeing the steam now rising from the bathwater he flicked the switch so that the water was now diverted through the shower attachment which was fixed onto the wall. Sam climbed over the tub side to enter, immediately realising he had forgotten to put his music on in his room so he would be showering in silence. No matter, his mood would not be ruined by this oversight.

Probably due to the lack of accompanying soundtrack, Sam's shower was shorter than was typical. He dried himself with his towel and headed back through to his room to get dressed. Once he was suitably attired, Sam opened his curtains only to find that the sun had disappeared, and it was starting to spit with rain. It now looked like one of those typically Scottish spring days where the next hour could bring anything; sunshine, hail, rain, maybe even some snow blowing in the wind.

As he arrived at the foot of the stairs, Sam's mum asked him if he wanted toast, to which the answer was 'yes please'. As he seated himself at the table for his quick breakfast, Mrs Hamill reminded him about them paying Mrs Young a visit after he finished school.

"I remember, mum. Will I see you here before or just meet you there?"

Mrs Hamill thought for a second before replying and suggested they meet at Mrs Young's.

School had turned out to be fun and the day went fast. At lunch, the gang of four sat with Walshy and some of the other lads who were heading to the big game tomorrow. Excitement was high and there was a real buzz around for the day out, and hopefully a crucial victory as Dunfermline marched towards promotion. Even Tommo was getting carried away with things and had now agreed to go to the game too, which was a real novelty for him. Sam just had to get through his busy night, and he'd be able to enjoy things the next day.

As agreed earlier that morning, Sam went straight to Mrs Young's from the bus stop. Not having to adopt his covert tactics certainly made things easier. Sam knew what to expect at Mrs Young's this time, it would be more or less a repeat of the other night. Quick bit of chit chat and then a swift visit to get some messages in for her for the weekend.

Sure enough, his mum was already there making a cup of tea for them both. "Would you like a cuppa too?" she asked Sam as he walked in. "No thanks, mum." Sam responded, knowing time was of the essence and he needed to get his shopping trip over and done with before heading home to be picked up by Derek.

"My list, as well as the money, is on the kitchen counter, son." Mrs Young advised. "Thanks, Mrs Young." Sam said, grabbing the small pile of cash and paper and heading expeditiously out the door. He was worried about his time, so he jogged up to Station Road and flew into the Co-op like a bat out of hell. Mr Kelly was standing talking to one of the women at the checkout and gave Sam a quick, half-hearted wave as he entered the store.

Sam unfolded the note so he could see what he needed to get and, knowing the store layout like the back of his hand, what order to get the items in. As soon as he could see the list of things Mrs Young wanted, one item jumped out at him... dog food. This was strange enough the other day, but again? Sam recalled that it was quite a large pack and how could she need the same again already? He had no option but to buy it, along with the other items; pan drops, marmalade, and digestive biscuits so not as much as last time, which was much easier to manage.

The checkout woman, who Sam didn't know at all despite working there two evenings a week, placed everything else into a plastic bag, which allowed him to sling the box of dog food cans under his arm again. As Sam headed back down the road, he pondered if this grandson of Mrs Young's was running a kennel.

Unlike last time, Sam's mum was still at Mrs Young's. He hadn't been very long, and she was in the kitchen tidying up their teacups when he returned. Sam put the plastic bag on the counter and then did the same with the dog food.

"Got everything on the list, mum. Will I just put it in the pantry like last time?" asked Sam.

"Yes, I think so." She replied. Sam proceeded to put everything where he thought it should go. Again, leaning the carton of dog food on its end on the floor against the pantry wall, in the space vacated by the carton Sam had placed there only two days ago. Sam estimated that Mrs Young was at least in her early seventies and wondered why her grandson was making her get something so heavy, especially when he imagined he could easily get it himself.

Sam had his next appointment, doing the money collections with Derek, to look forward to, so he grabbed his school bag, which he'd left by the back door.

"Are you coming, mum? I need to get home before my shift."

"Yes, let me just check on Mrs Young and say cheerio."

As his mum ran through to Mrs Young's sitting room, Sam was left to his own devices in the kitchen. He was staring at Mrs Young's Janus stove which had two faces looking away from each other as its logo. He was familiar with this image as it's the same on the fireplace on the other side, through the kitchen wall. Sam knew who Janus was and liked the fact the two-sided appliance had a two-faced logo. It was a nice touch, he felt.

His mum had said her goodbyes, so they were ready to leave, Sam shouting cheerio to Mrs Young from the kitchen as they exited through the back door. They pulled the back door closed as they left and turned the corner to walk alongside Mr Slater's side wall towards the cul-de-sac. No van again, so Slater was still at work or elsewhere.

As they cut through the path towards the swing park, they hadn't really said anything until Sam broke the silence.

"Not that I mind, as she's a nice lady, but why aren't Mrs Young's family doing anything to help?"

"I think they are, a little bit anyway, but Mrs Young's daughter has personal issues, and I don't think it's easy for her. Her husband is away a lot." Mrs Hamill replied.

"What about the rest of them? She mentioned a grandson."

"Well, you will understand this, he's busy with his job all the time." she answered.

"I'll understand? What do you mean?"

"Derek. Derek is her grandson and he's always working, isn't he? I thought he was full time for the vending company, as well as the nights he does with you?"

"Derek?" said Sam, in astonishment. "How did I not know that Derek was her grandson?"

"I thought you *did* know." Mrs Hamill responded.

"Nobody has mentioned this to me. Not him, not you, not Mrs Young, not even Mr Slater."

"Slater? What's he got to do with it?"

Sam ignored this question. "Is Derek her only grandson?"

"Pretty sure. Arlene, Derek's mum, is her only child."

As the discussion continued, rain had started teeming down from the skies. Luckily, they were only yards from home. In order to avoid an instant soaking, they both ran the last few dozen steps.

As they burst in their front door. Sam said. "I really can't believe it."

"Why don't you ask him about it when you're with him tonight?" Sam was still shellshocked but nodded, conveying that he would ask.

Sam bolted upstairs to get ready. He didn't have long before Derek would be at the door. He dumped his bag against the wall of his bedroom and turned his stereo on. he had too much on his mind, and was short on time, so he didn't bother raking for anything handpicked to play. Instead, he ran the gauntlet of turning his stereo to the radio setting and hoping for something good.

If he didn't already know, Sam was reminded of the correct time, with Newsbeat ending and Bruno Brookes coming on air with his teatime show. It was 5.45 pm, which meant he had 15 minutes to get ready before Derek arrived.

A quick wash of his face, a fast brush of his teeth and his hair, and then through to change clothes from his school garb into a clean t-shirt and fresh jeans, topped off with a new Benetton jersey he'd bought recently with the money he got from Mrs Young. The heavy rain could be heard drumming on the roof above his head, making Sam think twice about putting on his precious Adidas ZX 450s but, after weighing up the fact he'd be mostly in the now clean van, he put them on anyway.

Just as he finished putting his trainers on, he could hear Derek honking the horn from the van outside. Sam ran down the stairs at high speed, missing out a number of steps on the way, such was his rush. Sam shouted bye to his mum as he was departing, keeping up his pace by running in the rain out the front gate to the idling brown van.

It felt like a long time since he'd seen Derek, a lot had happened since they last met, even though that was only three days ago.

"Alright, cock?" announced Derek, while laughing.

Sam laughed in response saying "Yes, thanks."

And they drove off. It was a truly grim weather outlook, and the rain was lashing down. It was only 6pm but it was dark and gloomy, almost as if it was nighttime already.

"I was at your gran's right before you picked me up?"

"My gran's?" Answered Derek appearing slightly perturbed by the statement. "How do you know my gran?"

"Me and my mum have been helping her with things since her fall." Sam responded.

"Oh, thanks. That's nice of you both. I don't get to see her as often as I'd like." replied Derek, slightly defensively.

Derek changed the subject "How's your Slater investigation going?"

"He got annoyed with me the other day but everything's fine now." said Sam. "He's not a fan of yours?"

"Oh, really? He's a nosey old prick and I've never hidden my dislike for him."

"Is that why your gran doesn't like him?" asked Sam.

"Probably. She hasn't said anything much to me about him." said Derek turning the volume up on the car stereo, clearly more interested in his music than idle chit chat. "Got any plans for the Easter holidays? We might have extra work if you're interested."

"I have nothing planned, so just let me know" replied Sam.

"Good, good." said Derek. "You must be doing ok money wise now?

Sam nodded. "Yep, much better. Even treated myself to some new clobber." He said as he pointed at the Benetton logo on the jersey he was wearing."

Derek gave Sam a look, clearly unimpressed with the purchase. "Whatever floats your boat." he said with a wry smile.

This little interchange had helped pass the time nicely and they were now at The Wander Inn, their regular first stop. The cash collection team were old hands at this now and immediately sprang into action, Derek with the machine keys and Sam ready with the cash bag. In and out in no time.

They were making excellent time and had only a couple of the Dunfermline locations to go before they would head back to Oakley via Crossford and Cairneyhill.

The penultimate stop was The Langham, which may evoke thoughts of a classy establishment with oak panelled walls and high-end cocktails, but, in reality, it was an old man's pub with veneered tables and fluorescent lights.

They never really had any interaction with anyone in any of the pubs on their route. Occasionally, a patron might be playing the fruit machine and etiquette is to let them play their next go and then ask them to briefly step aside while the machine is emptied. Other than a brief pause, the gaming experience is unaffected.

As they entered The Langham, their solitary fruit machine was being played by an old, bearded man who had dragged his bar stool over and had made himself quite comfortable for his game playing experience. His pint was resting on top of the machine, which is frowned upon at DLB, and his dog, which was a Black Lab, was sitting patiently by his side as he played. That was until the boys walked in.

The dog, which was not wearing any sort of leash or harness, immediately bounded over to the two of them as they walked towards the machine. What was noteworthy is that the dog entirely ignored Sam but was all over Derek, jumping up on him, sniffing his Doc Martins and his black jeans profusely.

Derek being a big kid was unphased and was tumbling around on the floor with the dog while Sam stood to the side, waiting patiently while swinging the empty white cash bag in his hand.

Eventually, the dog lost interest and Derek stood up brushing himself off. The old man had stopped playing the machine to watch the chaos between Derek and his dog unfold. "Well, she likes you, son. She usually doesn't bother anyone. You must have a good scent or maybe you forgot to empty that bacon out of your pocket" he said. Both boys laughed and got on with the task in hand and speedily getting back to the van.

They started to drive the short distance to the final Dunfermline pub, The Park Gates. "I told you dogs love

me" announced Derek. Sam certainly couldn't deny it based on that interaction. That comment shook loose something in his brain. He'd forgotten about the dog food. "Talking of dogs, how come your gran buys you dog food?"
Derek looked at him as they turned left out of Bridge Street and onto Pittencrieff Street.
"I'm not following." A confused Derek responded.
"I've been getting your gran's shopping, and she's asked me to get a multipack of Pedigree Chum twice in three days "for her grandson". Isn't that you?!
"I think she might be losing her marbles. I don't know anything about that." Derek replied, quite brusquely.

Sam was troubled by the dog food conversation. Derek didn't seem like he was being honest with him and some of the details just didn't add up. He was Mrs Young's only grandson so either she *was* losing her faculties, or he was lying. And her losing her mind wouldn't explain where the previously purchased dog food went.

There wasn't much further to go until their next pick-up location. Nobody was talking now, and Sam sat looking at the rain running down the front window as they drove to the next pub, which was the final one before heading out of town. The raindrops were making little lines on the glass, their shadows casting identical lines on the dashboard when they drove under streetlights.
They were now at the pub, so Derek pulled abruptly onto the pavement outside of the Park Gates Inn.

As they exited the van, Sam suddenly had a thought. 'Assuming Derek *was* lying, what was the dog food for? Mrs Young didn't have a dog, and he wasn't allowed a dog at his house. Was he feeding someone else's dog? And then it struck him. Millie. Derek had often asked about her and has repeatedly mentioned wanting a dog. It would explain Millie disappearing without a trace.

Once again, they opened the machine, filling the cash bag in no time, locked it up again and headed back out into the rain. As Sam threw the bag of shrapnel in the back of the van, he couldn't hold it in any longer, he had to ask the question. He didn't know how to phrase it, so he just blurted it out. "I know you have her, where is she? What have you done with her?"

Derek's eyes widened and his face turned ashen-white, the rain making loud tapping sounds as it bounced of his black leather jacket. He suddenly gave Sam a hard shove to the chest, making him fall back onto the ground, Derek then slamming both rear doors of the van shut.

Sam didn't have time to react. The van was screeching off down the road before he knew what was happening. He stood up, immediately feeling a massive wet patch on the back of his jeans from sitting momentarily on the ground. Sam pushed his soaking wet hair back off his forehead with his fingers and wiped water from his eyes. As he looked along Pittencrieff Street, the two rear lights of the van faded into the distance and out of sight.

Chapter Fifteen
Keep Your Enemies Close

Once Sam had given his predicament a modicum of thought, he came to the unavoidable conclusion he would have to walk. He was already soaked through and the road outside of The Park Gates was quiet, so he felt that walking back into town to the bus station was probably his best bet.

As Sam trudged towards the town centre trying to catch a lift, his mind flitted around between shock at Derek's reaction to the Millie accusation, misery at the pouring rain he was walking in. He also allowed himself a brief distraction to a man his grandad used to talk about who lost all the fingers on his right hand, except his thumb, after catching his hand in a shaft door at the pit. His nickname was The Hitcher and Sam reckoned he would have been a worthwhile walking companion at this juncture.

Sam had no money on him but was thinking he could maybe sweet talk the bus driver into letting him on for free. There was also the option of getting a taxi and having his mum pay once he got home, although this would be expensive. Given the current high winds and incessant rain, it seemed like it would be money well spent.

It really was a thoroughly grim evening. Sam trudged towards the brighter lights of the town centre for about five minutes when he reached the intersection where

Pittencrieff Street met Chalmers and Bridge Streets. Out of the corner of his eye he saw that someone in a vehicle was flashing its headlights in his direction, but Sam ignored since he assumed it wouldn't likely be directed at him. As he started to cross the road, the flashing stopped, and a few loud toots of the horn could be heard instead. Sam looked in the direction where the sound was coming from, but he couldn't see anything, not helped by the darkness, or the raindrops that were running into his eyes. As he reached the other side a white van pulled up alongside him and as the window was rolled down it revealed Slater's wrinkled face smiling at him.

"Have you been swimming? Slater said with his trademark fake laugh. "C'mon, jump in and get out of the rain."

Sam thought twice, or maybe even three times, about it, given his recent run ins with, and suspicions about, Slater. Even though Sam seemed to be adding to his list of enemies recently, he was not about to turn down the chance of a lift in a dry, warm vehicle, whoever was driving it.

"Why on earth are you out walking in this weather? You're soaking." added Slater.

"I was abandoned outside the Park Gates by Derek." Sam sniffed a little pathetically.

"Well, I can't wait to be saying 'I told you so' very soon. Let's go and get something to eat and you can tell me all about it."

The drive was all of three minutes to Mancini's on Chalmer's Street. They parked across the road and ran over to get out of the rain, not that Sam could really get any wetter.

"Two please" Slater said, motioning to the girl behind the counter with two fingers, Richard Nixon style in case of any misunderstanding about the number requested.

"We're sitting in?' Sam asked, clearly surprised they weren't heading back home with their food.

"Oh yes, this is my Friday night treat. Proper chips in a posh chippy. I do it every week."

The waitress then led them into the back room and sat them down at a small table with an off-white veneered top.

"Fish and chips ok?" Slater asked Sam.

"That would be great" Sam answered enthusiastically. He was starving and could murder a good fish supper. Slater indicated that's what they wanted, along with two cups of tea, to the waitress and they were all set.

"So, what happened with the black clad beanpole?" Slater inquired the second the waitress left to put in their order.

Sam still had good reason to be suspicious about Slater, he had followed him, as much as was possible, for the last week or so and had seen little to shift his view about Slater being front and centre of the cat murders. However, it wasn't lost on him that Slater had made a nice gesture tonight and, in the absence of any actual evidence against him, he was happy to cautiously go along with this, whatever it was, for now, and perhaps revisit when he wasn't in such dire need of assistance.

"I've been getting Mrs Young's shopping since her fall, you see, and it struck me as odd she was getting dog food in. you know, given she doesn't own a dog."

"Yes, that is certainly odd, she's never owned a dog since I've lived next door, and that's been over ten years." added Slater.

Sam nodded. "So, I asked her who it was for, and she said her grandson. I thought fair enough, but then when I had to get more only a few days later, I asked my mum who her grandson was, and she said Derek. I had no idea."

"That's how I know him. He used to visit next door with his mum when he was younger, then he was staying with her a while back." offered Slater. "He hasn't been staying there for a long time though, at least six months, I think."

"So, the dogfood was obviously weird on its own, but when we were collecting the fruit machine cash earlier today this dog went nuts for him. I mean crazy. The dog completely ignored me and was bouncing all over him, so I figured it was either the scent of another dog or the smell of the dog food itself. Either way it just made me think. And the more I thought about it the more annoyed

I got, so I just asked him outright if he had Millie. That's when he shoved me over and drove away. It was just a hunch before, but I'm certain he has her now."

"What makes you think it's Millie and not just some other dog?"

Sam outlined his thinking just as the chips and tea arrived. "I suppose it could be any dog, but why push me over if it isn't Millie? Also, he asked about her a lot, more than normal I'd say. It just dawned on me that something about the whole thing was off. Why get your gran to buy the dog food in the first place, unless you were trying to keep it secret?"

They started tucking in immediately, both were obviously starving. Much as Sam was grateful to Slater for the lift and the food, he had developed a real dislike for Slater over the last few weeks, and he had to hide his true feelings for the time being. Even with this temporary cease fire, it was hard not to allow those feelings of disdain to return, especially when watching Slater eat. He tended to thrust the chips into his mouth without opening it particularly far. Pushing his food through a soft wall of rubbery lips, like a sphincter in reverse. Sam decided to concentrate on his own food.

"So, what do you propose to do about it?" Slater asked.

Sam was slightly taken aback, as they had eaten in silence for the last five or so minutes. "About what?"

"Derek Paton and your dog."

"I am going to go to his mum's to confront him."

"When are you going to do that?

"Tonight is my plan. I can't stand the thought of Millie being there a day longer."

"I'll give you a lift, how about that?"

They finished up their food and teas, Mr Slater paid for the meal.

"Thanks very much, Mr Slater."

"No problem, lad. I can wait on you for a bit then I've got to take the dogs out.

Sam was highly suspicious of Slater, particularly as he was acting out of character by being so nice tonight. They left the chip shop and ran across to the van. It was still belting down.

As soon as they set off on their journey back to Oakley Slater seemed to revert back to his usual persona.

"So, why were you and your wee band of bum chums following me around, then?"

Sam was somewhat taken aback by this and could only muster a defensive response. "What do you mean?"

"Don't act all coy with me, sonny Jim. You were all standing staring at my house, and I saw you following me a couple of other times. C'mon, spill the beans."

"We, weren't following you, just keeping our eyes open with everything going on in the village." Sam explained, somewhat unconvincingly.

"So, Mrs Gowans was making it up when she said you were raking in my coal bunker?" Slater inquired.

Sam was stunned by this as he'd forgotten he was caught red-handed standing over the bunker, but felt he had to tell the truth to some extent. "I can explain that" he said, trying to think of something to say. "I saw you with a bag going in and out of the woods and I had to know what it was."

"What did you think it was? Asked Slater

"I had no idea" said Sam, lying but hopefully not too obviously.

"Coal."

"Sorry?" replied Sam.

"The bag was full of coal." Slater explained. "When I'm walking the dogs, I see the guys who work on the coal trains chucking huge lumps off into the woods to collect at a later time, and I just go and collect it myself, before they get the chance."

"Oh" said Sam, realising that this blew a hole in his whole cat murderer theory, although this only explains the mystery of the bag and not the various other elements Slater was connected to.

Sam was keen to move away from the current line of questioning. "During the miners' strike, what made you decide to break the picket line?"

Slater turned toward Sam, giving him a puzzled look. "Who was talking about that?" he inquired.

"Oh, nobody specific. I just knew you had done that."

"Well, it was a chance to make some extra money, nothing more. Well, I knew it would annoy exactly the right people, so a little bit of it was that as well."

"Who were you trying to annoy?" queried Sam.

"There were a lot of people around the village who were very vocal about the strike and the reasons for it. A lot of it was propaganda and I wanted to do something to get under their skin. Becoming a scab was the best way to do that. A year ago, they'd shout insults right to my face, now they just whisper behind my back."

It was still pouring with rain and there seemed to be no let-up in it. It seemed much later than it actually was, because of the dark clouds hanging in the air. It had been an interesting drive, and the discussion had taken their minds off of the dreadful conditions.

The inclement weather had brought with it cold temperatures and. as they approached the outskirts of the village, they could see numerous chimney stacks coughing out their grey smoke. When they pulled up outside Derek's house, it didn't look like anyone was home. There was no brown van, and no lights were on inside. Sam decided to check anyway.

There was no real game plan here other than confronting Derek about Millie and, ideally, forcing him to hand her over. Sam wondered if there was a kennel out the back. Considering the Patons didn't approve of Derek having a dog, maybe he pushed his luck and kept Millie outside? Sam hadn't looked out the back when he was there a few weeks ago, mainly because there was so much to see inside.

Slater waited in the van while Sam walked up the three concrete front steps and gave his trademark knock on the door, which was a hard tap, two light taps and one final hard tap. He then retreated back down one step to wait to see if there was a response, the rain still tap dripping on Sam's face. There was no answer, so he repeated exactly what he'd just done one more time. This time the hall light switched on and he could see a dark shape walking closer to the door through a frosted side window.

The door opened slowly, and the ghostly white face of Mrs Paton could now be seen through a small gap between the door and the door frame.

"Hello. What do you want?" she said.

"Hi Mrs Paton, sorry to bother you. It's me, Sam Hamill. I'm looking for Derek."

"Derek? Sorry son, but he's been staying at his gran's for a long time now, probably a year or so." Sam knew that this wasn't true, but Mrs Paton seemed sincere. Maybe this was news to her? "I saw him earlier today, he usually visits me a few days a week, but he went to work, and I probably won't see him again until Sunday now."

Sam didn't really know how to respond to this. Derek definitely had *not* been staying at his gran's, and for over six months, according to Slater. "Do you know if he has a dog?" was the best Sam could come up with.

"A dog? No, I'm allergic so he couldn't have one here, and I know his gran wouldn't let him have one, she's always had cats. Why do you ask, did you see him with a dog?" Mrs Paton replied.

"No, I think it's just a misunderstanding, Mrs Paton. I'll leave you in peace now." Sam blurted out quickly, retreating from the doorstep with a wave. As he walked down the front path, he glanced back to see her watching him from her front window.

As Sam jumped back into the dry and warm white van, he explained his findings. "She says he hasn't been staying there for quite a while, and he's never had a dog there, or anywhere else to the best of her knowledge. She seemed genuine."

"What now then? Slater posed.

"If you don't mind, can you drop me off at my house? I need to get out of these wet clothes anyway.

"Do you still think he has your dog?" Slater asked as they rolled down the hill away from the Paton residence.

"If he doesn't, why the dog food, why shove me and drive off? He's been picking up the food from his gran's regularly. The key questions are, where does he have her and where is he staying?"

"Does he have access to anywhere through your work?" Slater inquired.

Sam hadn't thought of this. "Yes, actually, he does. Although the lock up in Oakley is really small and I don't see how he could keep a dog there without anyone knowing. The other place is in Dunfermline, and is much bigger, but I don't think he's the only one who uses it. Plus, he'd have to go back and forth all the time."

"Is it possible there's another property you don't know about around here. Or through the pubs you visit, would anyone give him access to their storerooms or outbuildings?" Slater asked, continuing his run of good questions.

Sam tapped his chin, in deep thought. "Not that I know of, on both counts. He hasn't shown me any other lock ups, and he hasn't ever engaged with any staff when we've been in the pubs we visit. Oh, except Bairn at The Railway Tavern a couple of weeks ago, but that was brief and didn't seem very friendly."

"Bairn? Don't get me started on that big clown. Doing the bidding of Clint Westwood will catch up with him at

272

some point. The stories I could tell. I'll spare you the details and tell you when you're 18." Slater said, laughing at his own statement, seemingly finding it funnier than he ought to.

As the van pulled up outside Sam's house, Slater leaned in. "I really hope he doesn't have your dog, but I do hope you get her back. Dogs are the best of us, and I'd do anything for mine, so I know how you feel. I'll keep wracking my brain about where Derek, and possibly your dog, might be. If I think of anything useful, I'll let you know."

"Thanks for the lift and the chips, Mr Slater" Sam announced as he leapt back out into the wet evening before running up his front path. His mum was nowhere to be seen when Sam walked in, Sam looking back out to the street as the white van's rear lights disappeared into the distance. Slater had surprised Sam tonight, although he didn't have time to think about it too much as he had Millie on his mind. As he started to get out of his wet clothes, Sam did wonder if he'd been well wide of the mark with his Slater theory. While he could undoubtedly behave strangely, and was certainly annoying, the more Sam found out about Slater, the less likely it was that he was capable of anything like the cat killings.

Sam had been scared to look at his precious trainers as he knew they would be in a sorry state, and they were. Completely soaked through and with little streaks of dark dirt across the toe area, so he decided to use his old football boot technique and crumple some newspaper into balls and stuff them inside each shoe, depositing the wet footwear in the airing cupboard. He also wet a cloth and wiped all around the uppers of his shoes to clean off the dirt. Next for Sam was to put all his wet clothes into the washing machine. Normally, he wouldn't run the machine with such a small load but because his entire outfit was soaked through. The sheer weight of his drenched jumper, jeans, t-shirt and socks was probably about the same a full load so he threw it all in with some Daz and clicked the machine on, running upstairs in his underwear – they would have to wait until the next load.

Next up, was a hot bath so he started filling it with some Matey bubble bath, which his mum had been buying him since he was little and, as long as none of his friends found out, he would happily continue to use. Sam's music of choice for this evening was a home-made compilation of New Order tracks, starting with Everything's Gone Green.

Sam was too anxious to stay in the bath too long so rather than top it up with hot water, as he usually did, he just climbed out when the water started to get cold. He'd only been in there about ten minutes, but that was enough. He was warm now and threw on an old Adidas Ivan Lendl t-shirt and some comfy tracksuit bottoms for chilling in front of the tv. Without any idea of where to look for Derek, Sam was in for the night now.

Despite Sam's fish and chip feast not so long ago, he had grabbed a couple of chocolate digestive biscuits and poured himself a glass of Ribena. No sooner than he had settled down to watch tv with his snack, there was a light knock on the door.

Sam thought it might have been his mum, who'd possibly left without her keys, but, when he opened the door, he was surprised to see Slater there, soaked to the skin with his two dogs. Sam didn't really want to invite him in, but he felt guilty.

"Do you want to come inside, Mr Slater?"

"No, son. Were all thoroughly soaked anyway, and we'll just bring all the water inside with us. I was thinking some more about places I might have seen Derek around the village, while we were walking, and there is a place that came to mind. Across from the main entrance to Pitgarvie, there's the entrance to the chapel…"

Sam nodded.

"Well, right next to that there's a wee dirt road that goes quite far back behind the chapel and at the end of that road is an old cottage. I used to walk that way years ago, but the fields are all overgrown now and full of ticks."

Sam's ears pricked up at the mention of ticks and, of course, the cottage. He knew exactly where this place was, albeit from the back end via the woods.

"It wasn't until I really thought about it, but I reckon I've seen Derek at least half a dozen times, driving out of that dirt road. Now what would he be doing back there, I wonder? It used to be the farmhouse for about two or three potato fields back there, but it hasn't been occupied in a very long time."

Sam remembered the cottage; he had almost walked over there on 'tick day'. It was completely decrepit and surrounded by old appliances and other rubbish. Not a very nice place to live but the ideal place to hide a dog, he thought.

"If you want to go and check it out, I'll take you down there tomorrow morning? Added Slater.

"Thanks. That would be great, Mr Slater."

"Give me your phone number, son, and I'll call you in the morning to arrange." suggested Slater.

Sam grabbed the pen and notepad from the phone table and proceeded to write down the digits of the Hamill home phone for Slater, who put the piece of paper in his inside pocket before heading off with a 'cheerio'.

Sam went back to watching TV for a moment before letting what Slater had just told him sink in. Sam was in no doubt that this is where Derek had been staying. It was local but also remote, meaning nobody would just wander by. It just seemed right. Sam thought for a minute before deciding that he couldn't wait until tomorrow morning. If this is where Millie was, he couldn't wait a second longer. He had to go right now to find her.

Sam knew going out in the pouring rain meant he was going to get soaked again, but he didn't care. He had no option but to wear his old trainers, seeing as his good ones were drying out in the airing cupboard, and the clothes he was wearing this time couldn't really be ruined by getting wet. He grabbed an old school rugby top, his cagoule and his dad's torch again, for providing protection as well as light. From what he'd learned about Derek these past few weeks, he didn't see him as much of a fighter, but if he did want any trouble then the heavyweight torch would come in handy.

Sam pulled the door shut and walked out into the darkness, leaving a few lights on for his mum to return home to. He assumed she was at his grandparents' house, as she hadn't said where she was going, and probably would have if it was somewhere else. As Sam stepped through the front gate, he thought briefly about walking towards the cottage via the railway line, but the weather put him off. The street would at least be lit, while trudging along the tracks would be pretty miserable in this weather.

Sam strolled at a brisk pace out of Hill View and up towards Station Road, turning right to head directly downhill towards the chapel, and the dirt road adjacent to it. It was only as he got closer his mood changed from determination to nervousness, as he started to think about the moment when he would catch Derek red-handed. It hadn't escaped Sam that it had taken a strange sequence of events to lead him to this point. For Sam to find out about Derek being Mrs Young's grandson, the dog food, and not living at either address he was meant to be at. Bizarre indeed, but he was glad it had all happened as otherwise he wouldn't be on his way to get Millie back. And, despite all the butterflies that were fluttering around in his stomach, he was very grateful for that.

Sam was getting close. Despite the lack of good lighting and the still pouring rain, he could see the outline of the railway bridge over Station Road coming into focus. Once he walked past that, he would be at the beginning of the dirt road. He had plenty to mull over and, as he did, so the penny dropped about why Derek's room, when he had visited before, was immaculately clean and tidy, while the van and the local lock up were absolutely filthy. It was because he didn't live there and hadn't done so for some time.

Sam also thought about the abandoned, or maybe not abandoned, cottage. It probably didn't have working utilities so what did he do for electricity and water? He knew from Mrs Young and Mrs Paton that they saw him regularly, even though he didn't live at their houses. This would be where he showered and got his clothes cleaned, as well as picking up supplies, such as Pedigree Chum.

It seemed like a lot of trouble to go to though. It also explained his visits to newly constructed houses, although that backfired when he realised they weren't all plumbed in.

Sam walked under the railway bridge and as he walked up the slight incline towards the chapel, he could see the twin roads ahead of him. As he reached the entrance to the dirt road, Sam stopped for a second to gather himself and take a deep breath. The road looked fairly long, and he couldn't see the end of it or the cottage it led to. Nevertheless, he started his trek along it.

The dirt had turned to a mixture of mud and standing water and, beyond a few scattered areas of medium sized stones and grey driveway chips he could momentarily stand on, Sam was doing his best to avoid the deeper puddles. As he moved further away from the main road, the light from the streetlights was now fading. It wasn't completely dark, but it was close. Sam didn't want to alert Derek to his presence, so he did his best to navigate along the path as best he could without using his torch.

Sam could now see the cottage in the distance. Even in the dingy evening light, he could see that it likely used to be white but was now an off grey colour with a number of darker stains which ran down the walls from the roof. He had seen the back of the house before, which was littered with discarded materials. Now that he was getting close, Sam could see the front was no tidier. One thing that was conspicuous by its absence was Derek's van. Sam had imagined Derek's van parked here during his entire journey to the property. There was no way that, if it *was* here, it could be anywhere else than right in front, as the road stopped at the front of the cottage and there was no apparent way around for something the size of a vehicle.

Had Slater been mistaken? Had Sam's belief that this was where Derek was keeping Millie been misguided? It was the only place that had been mentioned as a possible location, and Sam was here now so he thought he might as well check it out in any case.

With no sign of Derek, or his van, Sam felt he could utilise his torch now. He aimed the bright light onto the side of the cottage, illuminating the faded blue door as well as a broken window adjacent to it. It looked in even worse condition than he had expected. Sam wondered about how many wild creatures had found their way in through broken windows or elsewhere in the dilapidated property, which gave him a mini dose of the creeps.

Sam walked up to the door and tried the handle. Locked, or at least stuck. He flashed his torch inside via the broken window to show what at one time was a kitchen. There were black bin bags everywhere. On the floor and on what he assumed used to be countertops.

Sam jumped down from the step and looked to his left. There was no way through, as there was a large clump of overgrown bushes encroaching on this side of the cottage. Even if he was able to hack his way through that, there was a rusting fridge on top of a large pile of loose bricks immediately in front. Sam decided to move along to his right to see what was around the other side of the building, dodging old metal drums which were covered in a thick layer of flaky rust. Sam stopped for a brief moment to shine the torch up onto a large window, also broken, that may have provided light to the sitting room. He couldn't really see in as, without a step ladder, or something else to climb on, he was too low to see anything other than the room's ceiling.

Sam continued on, now turning the corner around the side of the cottage. There was nothing much to see on this side, and Sam was losing heart that this was where Derek was hiding out. Having observed two windows on the front, albeit broken, there were no windows on this side, and, beyond mounds of rubbish, which had clearly been there for some time as some had grass and weeds growing on them, there was little else of note.

Having already seen the rear of the property a few weeks ago, admittedly from a distance, Sam knew there was more old machinery and other random waste on this side. As he turned the corner and aimed his torch over the junk strewn around in the long grass, he didn't see anything that made him think any differently than before. There was no real sign of life here.

There was another large window on the back of the building, so he stood on top of what looked like an old freezer to get a better look. This window was, unsurprisingly, broken, like all the others he'd seen so far, but with a much smaller hole, about the size of one of the stones he'd walked on during his journey down the dirt road.

Sam aimed his torch into the room, flashing a bright beam through dirty glass and airborne dust inside. He could see what looked like the side of large wardrobe and there was a pair of old curtains either side of the window frame, so he assumed this had been a bedroom. He was running out of places to check now, knowing he had only the final side of the building to look at.

Sam jumped off the old appliance onto the wet grass, stepping back from the wall of the cottage and retreating back so he could shine his light and get a better look at the entire building. He could see the roof was partially caved in on this side, and there was a dead tree branch protruding from the hole. As the rain continued to slap down onto Sam's face, it was a sobering reminder that nobody would be able to live in there. There was no shelter from the elements at all.

Somewhat disheartened, Sam headed for the corner of the cottage. As he turned, something moved in the dark, which caught his eye. He aimed the light right at it and a large rat was looking back at him. Sam's heart skipped a beat. What he saw next made it skip another. The rat appeared to be eating the remnants left over from a can of Pedigree Chum which was laying on the ground.

Sam edged towards the can, the rat launching itself into a pile of wood nearby. As Sam shone the torch down onto the grass near where the rat had been, the ground was littered with more dog food cans. As he aimed the torch back towards the house, he spotted a black metal railing about three feet away from the outer wall. As he walked closer to the cottage, he could see a set of steps leading down underneath the crumbling structure.

Clearly someone had been here recently, and the dog food convinced Sam that the theory about Derek keeping Millie here was bang on the money. If it wasn't for his dog potentially being inside, there was otherwise no way Sam would even consider entering the basement of the cottage. But he was here, and the steps led down to a weather-beaten black door which Millie could very well be right behind.

Sam hesitated, holding the metal railing with his left hand, for a brief moment. Having taken a short breather to regain his composure, he was now walking down the concrete steps to the basement door. He tried the handle, it was locked. However, the door moved in the frame just enough to suggest the lock could give quite easily with a good shove. Sam had seen his dad do this to their hut on occasion, which needed a bit of assistance at times. Copying his dad's technique, Sam put his full weight into the door with a strong shoulder barge. The door flew open and slammed against the wall behind it.

As soon as the door was open, Sam could hear a tapping or scraping sound, almost like metal on metal, from further back inside. He wasn't exactly sure what he was hearing but it was not a million miles away from the sound Millie's leash made when she dragged it around as she walked. Sam called out. "Millie! Millie, I'm coming!" he stepped into the pitch-black angling his torch once again to try and get a feel for the layout and hopefully lay eyes on his beloved pet.

Even with the light from the torch, it was difficult to navigate around the basement. There seemed to be a number of ways he could go with multiple internal doors to open. The first door was just a cupboard and had some cleaning products and an old broom inside. The next door was a tiny bathroom with little more than a skinny chest of drawers in it. Aside from a toilet itself, the only other items of note were yet more black rubbish bags strewn around. The third and final door had to be the one. Sam opened the door and was immediately hit with a rank smell, which had been sealed inside that room. If Millie had been mistreated, there would be hell to pay. Covering his nose with his arm, Sam pushed the door further open. Immediately on shining his torch inside, he could see the outline of a metal dog crate inside. This made sense as the noise sounded like the metal on the end of leash on metal.

Sam directed his torch towards the cage, fully expecting to see an excited Millie looking back at him. Instead, he could not have witnessed a more shocking sight. Inside the dog crate was a naked young woman, kneeling on all fours on a filthy mattress. Her emaciated body covered in welts; her skin caked in dirt. She was either shaking or shivering, or perhaps both. Sam uttering a whispered exclamation to himself on seeing her "Oh, for fuck's sake."

Mrs Hamill arrived back at her front door and could hear the phone ringing inside. She fumbled for her keys, trying to rush inside. No sooner than she had opened the door, and lurched forward to answer the phone, it stopped ringing. She took her jacket off, hanging it in the airing cupboard, as the phone started ringing again.

"Hello?"

"Hi Janet, it's Constable Redpath here. I was looking for Sam."

"Let me see if he's here." She replied, shouting upstairs to see if Sam was there. "He doesn't seem to be in… can I leave a message?"

"He's been onto me for a week or so about the cat disappearances, which we haven't really been focusing on, due to the ongoing investigations into Lauren Smith's and Michelle Polson's cases. Well, because of his persistence, I've been looking into it today, and I found something very interesting. Coincidence possibly, but I can say unequivocally that the cat disappearances stopped the same week as Lauren Smith was abducted.

We were getting two or three calls a week, and we haven't had one since late October."

"Really?" Mrs Hamill said, sounding a little shocked. "What do you think that means?"

"We haven't come to a fixed position on that yet, but my personal view is I think it means whoever was stealing the cats is the same person who abducted Lauren and Michelle. It's a classic escalation."

"Oh god, that's truly awful" said Mrs Hamill "Does that help you with any suspects?"

"We're not there yet, but it's certainly useful information." Redpath advised.

"Well, thanks for calling, I'll let Sam know." As soon as she hung up the phone, she heard a knock at the door.

"Hi, Janet." said Tom Slater. "Is Sam in? I tried phoning a few minutes ago, but it was just ringing out."

"He's popular tonight." She explained. "He's out though, I'm afraid, Tom."

"Out? Do you know where he is? I got the impression he was staying in. I picked him up soaked through in the town earlier and we came to the conclusion that Derek Paton had Millie."

"Derek? We were just talking about him earlier as we've been helping his grandmother."

"I know. Derek's been letting on to his mum that he was staying at his gran's and vice versa to his gran. We discovered he's staying at neither of their houses." explained Slater.

"How does this mean that he has Millie?"

Perhaps not Millie, but a dog. Sam is convinced it's Millie though. Derek's been collecting dog food regularly from his gran's. and, when Sam asked him about it, Derek kicked him out the van and left him in Dunfermline. That's where I found him."

"What? Is Sam ok?" Mrs Hamill asked, clearly concerned.

"Yes, he was drenched, but otherwise fine. I bought him some chips while we tried to solve the dogfood mystery. After that we drove back here and visited Mrs Paton's house, and she confirmed Derek hadn't been staying there for some time. She thought he was at Mrs Young's. We knew straight away he wasn't there. Last time I saw him hanging around over there, I caught him kicking her cat off the back step. I told her but she didn't want to believe it and has hardly spoken to me since."

Janet Hamill put her hand over her mouth and her eyes widened. "Did you know that Sam found the remains of that cat in Mrs Young's garden?"

"No, I did *not* know that" replied Slater, mouth agape. "That maybe explains a few things though."

288

Mrs Hamill looked at the phone table to her right and then back to Slater. "Constable Redpath had just called for Sam saying that the cat abductions stopped when Lauren disappeared."

A sudden realisation fell over Mrs Hamill's face. "Where did you say Derek was staying?"

"I don't know for sure, but I thought he might have been hiding out in the old farm cottage behind the chapel, because I've seen him leaving there quite a few times. I said I would take Sam to check it out tomorrow morning. I was worried he would be too impatient to wait until tomorrow. You don't think he will have gone there tonight?"

Janet Hamill thought for a brief moment "I know my son. If he thought Millie was there, he will have convinced himself it couldn't wait until tomorrow."

"Ok, jump in the van." said Slater "Let's go and get him."

"It's ok, I'll get you out." Sam announced loudly as he moved quickly toward the cage. There was no response. The girl was clearly conscious, as she was moving, but as he shone his torch on the upper part of her body, he could see her head was covered by a black cloth bag. He could also now see the metal scraping noise was the sound of handcuffs on her ankles and wrists which were attached to the bars on the sides of the crate.

Sam tried to reach inside the cage to remove the bag from her head, but there was a piece of rope tied around her neck, keeping the bag in place. He needed both hands to untie it. He placed his torch down on the floor so he could still see. The beam of the torch highlighting various things on the floor of the crate, such as blood, clumps of hair and what looked like faeces.

Sam reached inside the crate with both hands and was able to undo the rope and pull the cloth bag off of the girl's head. Sam could now see that she had duct tape wrapped around her ears, eyes and mouth which was stuck fast to her matted hair. He didn't recognise the girl, but it definitely wasn't Lauren, as this girl's hair was brown rather than blonde. He had to assume it was Michelle Polson. Whoever she was, she had clearly been through a horrendous ordeal and, unless he could get her out, it was going to continue. Sam tried to undo the tape, but it was hard to see without holding the torch and when he did, he only had one hand free which made the task impossible.

Sam thought it would be much easier if he could free her from the cage first, but he needed tools that weren't immediately available. He shone the torch onto the cage door and could see there was a large padlock keeping it locked. He aimed the torch around the room, desperately looking for keys to the padlock and the handcuffs, even tools so he could break them off. Unfortunately, while the room was full of junk, there was nothing useful that he could see. Another mattress, which he assumed was where Derek slept, a disgusting bowl which was caked with dried dog food, empty plastic jugs and other food waste, and yet more black plastic bags. Sam figured Derek kept the keys with him.

Starting to panic at his inability to free the girl, Sam grabbed his torch and ran back outside the door to the hallway to see if the keys were possibly hanging on a hook in one of the other rooms or in the hallway itself. He remembered there was a chest of drawers inside the bathroom, but the drawers were just full of useless junk.

Sam walked all the way back to the entrance door and hadn't spotted any keys, but he did see something which made all the air leave his lungs. While he was standing next to the open basement door, he could see two beams of light shining across the garden of the property and then shut off. He then heard the loud thud of a vehicle door closing. It had to be Derek.

It would be fair to say that Sam's view of Derek Paton had completely changed tonight. Derek had gone from being a close friend, albeit with some major quirks, to something quite far removed from that. And, in the last few minutes, he had gone from being a misguided fool, who had potentially kept Sam's dog from him to a sadistic kidnapper and probable killer.

Cornered in the basement was the last place Sam wanted to be, so he quietly pulled the outer door shut behind him and ran up the steps looking for somewhere to hide outside. He put his torch on and shone it away from the steps to see if there was a good hiding place. He was desperate, and so ran to the same large pile of wood the rat escaped to. It was large enough to hide behind for a short time, as long as Derek didn't suspect Sam's presence at the cottage. He also hoped that the rat was long gone.

Sam knelt down behind the wood pile, while still trying to keep an eye out. He couldn't see Derek yet, but he knew he was coming as the light from *his* torch jumped around on the surrounding bushes as he approached. Sam ducked down as the light got brighter, praying that Derek wouldn't know he was here and enter the cottage as normal.

Sam held his breath, trying to be as quiet as he possibly could, while, at the same time, listening out for Derek to open the basement door. There wasn't much in the way of footsteps to listen out for, with the rain softening the ground and creating a naturally cushioned floor under foot. Sam listened intently, trying to ignore the sound of his racing heartbeat in his ears, Derek now appeared to be walking down the concrete steps.

Sam gambled on a quick glance over the top of the wood pile and could see a definite glow from the foot of the steps and could now hear the jingle of keys being tried in the door. He assumed this would be Derek opening the lock and wondered if the padlock and handcuff keys would be on the same key ring as the door keys.

Sam suddenly had a horrible thought. In his rush to get out, he didn't have a chance to check if he'd broken the lock altogether or, in an ideal world, if the lock clicked shut when he pulled the door behind him. Even the better of these two scenarios would only buy Sam maybe two more minutes, as Derek would undoubtedly see the bag had been taken off the girl's head and know that someone had broken into the cottage.

Sam pondered whether he should be making a run for it now or waiting until Derek went inside. He needed as much time as he could get, so he decided to wait in the hope that Derek went inside. It sounded as if the door opened and closed again which, with Derek inside, would buy him precious extra time to get away.

Sam flicked his torch back on and ran as fast as he could from the woodpile to the corner of the house, aiming his light ahead of him as he went – the still falling rain lighting up in a plethora of thin streaks ahead of him.

As Sam turned the corner to run along the back of the house, he could hear, almost instantly, what could only be described as a loud roar from inside the house. The ear-splitting cry was more like something a large animal would emit, rather than the sound of a human. Sam assumed Derek had discovered that someone had been into the cottage.

As Sam sprinted along the back of the house, he heard the door to the basement slam loudly, startling him. His momentary lapse in concentration causing him to slip on the wet grass. He slid forwards, trying to balance, but instead landed on his backside, letting his now soaking wet torch slip from his grip as he put his hands down to support himself.

Sam scrambled to get back on his feet and imagined Derek closing in on him even though he had a little bit of a head start, although not as much as he'd hoped. In his panicked state, he launched himself forward again grabbing the torch as he went, which was still turned on and had been shining a low beam through the grass behind him. At least this made it easier to spot.

"Sam!!! I can see your torchlight." He could hear Derek scream loudly into the night air behind him. "I know it *has* to be you!" Sam glanced back and couldn't see anything. He just kept running as fast as he could.

As he reached the end of the building, Sam made a snap decision to head along the treeline to the field behind the cottage rather than go towards the main road, where he could be easily caught. Derek had his van and could catch him up in no time, if he went that way, so Sam considered his best chance of escape was to disappear into the darkness of the woods and then run to get help in the village.

"Saaa-aaam!" Derek shouted again, this time in a sinister sing-songy way. Sam kept going, doing his best to keep his footing on the wet ground, all the while wrestling to keep hold of the heavy wet torch as he went.

"I can see you, you wee prick." Roared Derek once more. Sam had the horrible realisation that he was probably telling the truth this time as his torch was beaming forth along the edge of the field. He had no choice as it was the only way he could see where he was going. Then, a loud bang echoed around the night sky, causing a shocked Sam to fall again this time his torch flying out of his hand ahead of where he was.

'Jesus Christ! He has a fucking gun?' Sam thought to himself, his already racing heart speeding up markedly. His breathing quickening further. He needed to get out of here.

"Did I hit you?" Derek shouted menacingly. He also sounded closer than before, and Sam needed no invitation to duck into the woods. He hid immediately behind the first few trees and peeked out to see where his torch was, but it was nowhere to be seen, and he didn't dare leave his hiding place to go and look for it. Derek's torch was easy enough to see, however, as a shaky light could be seen moving towards the woods from across the field.

If the farmer's field was dark then the woods were pitch black, but Sam knew the terrain, and would manage the steep slope down towards the railway track as best he could in the dark.

Sam's eyes had adjusted just enough that he could see the outline of the trees and he was doing his best to slalom through them as quickly as he could. Sam had a continual feeling that Derek was closing on him and that every second counted. He just needed to put some distance between himself and Derek so he could contact the police.

Another roar went out behind him. "SAMMMM!!!" Derek sounded deranged, which, given the scene inside the cottage, he obviously was. The slope was very steep so Sam worked his way down diagonally to limit the incline as best he could. Another gunshot rang out. It was loud and sounded much closer than before. Sam assumed Derek was firing the gun into the air as there's surely no way he could see him now.

Sam was becoming seriously concerned as, with the advantage of having a torch to light his way, Derek would undoubtedly be gaining on him. The shouting and the gunfire sounded worryingly close. Not having his torch with him was a big disadvantage for Sam.

Sam took a quick glance behind him, horrifyingly he could see the beam from Derek's torch not far behind. Derek definitely *was* closing in on him, Sam's heart sank. He made a determined effort to pick up his speed and to try and navigate the slope in a more direct fashion. However, there was risk involved as he was mostly operating in near total darkness.

His increased pace seemed to be working, Sam couldn't afford to take a look to see where Derek was, in case he fell, but he felt like he had opened up a gap between the two of them. The only noise Sam could hear, in between Derek screaming and firing his gun, were his own footsteps on the leaves and twigs beneath his feet and his elevated breathing.

Suddenly, Sam stumbled over what felt like a tree root and fell forward. Unfortunately, being on such a steep slope, this propelled him forward and he started to roll out of control downhill at what seemed like great speed. He tumbled head over heels for what seemed like a few full rolls until his momentum was stopped. Not by a tree stump or flatter ground, but by a splash landing into water. He knew immediately on impact that he was in the black hole.

Having convinced themselves that Sam had put himself
in harm's way by attempting to rescue Millie at the
cottage, Slater, accompanied by Janet Hamill, was now
driving his white van at high speed down Station Road
towards the chapel. They both sat in silence looking at
the amber streetlights reflecting onto the wet road,
hoping that Sam was safe and sound, also hoping that
they were very wrong about Derek.

It was a dreadful night, with rain was still falling heavily
from the overcast sky, as Slater turned onto the dirt road
that led to the cottage. It only took them a matter of
moments to realise that this was very likely the place
where Derek was hanging out as they saw the tell-tale
brown van parked outside.

Fuelled by guilt about having told Sam about the cottage,
Slater was driving the van much too fast for the road
conditions and had to slam on the brakes to prevent
hitting Derek's van ahead of him, the van skidding
slightly before coming to a halt. They both jumped out,
firstly, running to the front door and trying the handle. It
was locked, so Mrs Hamill banged on the door while
Slater looked for access around the left side of the
cottage, but it was blocked by debris and brush.

Having raised no response at the front door, and with no
way around the left side of the building, they headed the
other way towards the rear of the property in the hope of

finding some other way inside. They were moving fast and arrived at the basement steps in no time. Again, they tried the door, which was locked, but there were multiple muddy footprints on the steps which told them they weren't the only ones who had climbed the steps tonight.

Slater kicked the door where the lock met the frame with his steel-toed boot, and it swung open quite easily. Using his torch, Slater led the way as the two of them opened and then closed the couple of doors immediately inside before reaching the third and final door at the end of the short hallway. This door was partially open and as soon as Slater shone the light inside, they could see straight away what they were dealing with. Janet Hamill conveyed her horror at the sight of the imprisoned girl with an audible shriek.

They both scrambled to the cage to help but were met with resistance in the form of a large padlock. Slater shining his torch around the room, looking for keys, just like Sam before him, but there was nothing except filth.

The captive girl, whose head was still wrapped in duct tape, could obviously hear the pair beside her and was becoming more agitated in her bonds, scraping and rattling the cuffs against the steel bars of the cage. Frustratingly, there was little Mrs Hamill or Mr Slater could do to free her without keys or bolt cutters but at least Janet was able to pull some of the duct tape from her head while Slater provided light for her to see what she was doing.

Janet painstakingly pulled the duct tape off one piece at a time. it had been wrapped around the girl's head what seemed like dozens of times, forming a thick layer about a quarter of an inch thick. The outer layers could be removed fairly easily as the tape was effectively wrapped around the head on top of previously applied pieces of tape. Once these outer pieces were removed, Janet had much more difficulty with the older pieces, the entirety of which was stuck fast to hair and skin. As Mrs Hamill pulled at the tape, she could see the adhesive pulling the girl's skin away from her face, so she had to be much more careful and deliberate at this point.

As the tape was gradually removed from the girl's face, there were visible cuts and bruises, dark circles under her eyes, as well as black sticky lines where previously used pieces of tape had obviously been applied. With her mouth now more or less free of tape, the girl was noticeably grimacing as the last remnants of sticky tape were removed from her face. "Please... please help me get out of here" the girl sobbed.
"We're trying to get you out, hen. We're here to help you." Mrs Hamill said trying to comfort the captive girl.
"What's your name, honey?" Slater asked softly.
The girl was noticeably shaking "Michelle. My name's Michelle."
"We're trying to get you out of here Michelle, but we don't have the keys. Do you know where they are? The girl shook her head, her eyes red and streaming with tears."
Slater and Janet looked at each other, realising that the only way to rescue the girl was to go and fetch help.

"We also need to find Sam." Janet suggested firmly to Slater. Who nodded.

"Was someone here just before us? Janet asked the girl.

"I... I think so, I couldn't see but I could hear someone different, before that evil bastard arrived. It wasn't all that long ago." Michelle offered.

"Sam." Slater said, confirming what Janet was already thinking.

"I think we need to find him quickly and get help to come here." she replied.

Michelle, realising that this meant they were going to have to leave her here, started to get agitated again. "No, you can't leave me. Please don't leave. Please!"

"It breaks my heart to leave you, but I promise it won't be for long. We're going to get help for you." Janet said, clasping the girl's shackled hand briefly.

The girl seemed to understand but was sobbing heavily as they left the room.

As they left via the back steps, Slater noticed a few discarded cans on the grass. "This is how Sam caught him out. Derek, I mean. The dog food Sam was buying for Mrs Young was really for him."

Janet shook her head in disgust, realising that this meant the dog food had been fed to Michelle, as they walked quickly back towards the van.

Slater then noticed something else. As he shone his torch to light the way, he could see the footprints, made in flattened down wet grass, heading away from the rear of the cottage.

301

"I think Sam went this way" said Slater pointing at the newly discovered tracks.

"Why would he go towards the woods?" Asked Janet

"He was trying to confuse Derek, maybe. No other reason to go that way."

Janet Hamill looked at Slater. He said "I'm going to follow the tracks. Here, take my keys and get the van up to the police station.

"I can't drive though. I never learned." She replied.

"Ok, come with me" Slater said as he grabbed Janet by the jacket sleeve and ran with her in tandem with the torch, in his other hand, providing the necessary light to get back around to where the van was parked.

Slater put his torch away, then fished his keys out of his jacket pocket and jumped in the driver's seat, putting the key in the ignition. The open door activating the overhead cabin light so they could easily see what they were doing. The van roared into life, and the characteristic rattle of the diesel engine was keeping them company now.

Slater manoeuvred the van around, so it was facing back towards the main road and invited Janet to swap places with him. "Jump in", he suggested.

As Janet Hamill sat in the seat Slater reached in and grabbed the bar under the front seat and pulled it forward a touch, to make reaching the pedals easier for her. He leaned forward again, depressing the clutch with his left hand and using his right hand to press down on the brake. Slater then asked Janet to move the gear stick into first gear, which she did quite straightforwardly. Slater, then asked her to put her foot on the accelerator and gently push down, as he lifted his hands off the pedals. Ducking back out of the van, Slater then advised Janet to release the handbrake.

"Nice and slow now. Once it's down, the van will start rolling forward. Don't bother trying to change gear, just keep it in first and go nice and slow, but fast enough so you don't stall. It'll be enough to get you up the hill to the cop shop. If in doubt, press the accelerator down further. You know where the brake is, if needed. I'm going to head along the field behind here to find Sam."

"Thank you," said a nervous Janet.

"You'll be fine. Slow and steady wins the race."

"Please bring my Sammy home."

Slater nodded and shut the door as she slowly spluttered off. He watched her for a few minutes to make sure she had the hang of it, she was staying in the middle of the dirt road and appeared to be getting up to what looked like a spicy five mph.

Janet appeared to be doing enough to stop it stalling, which would be quite hard to do in any case, and that was all she needed. Station Road would be deserted and, as long as she could manoeuvre up the hill to the police station, she was home free.

Slater turned back towards the rear of the building and flicked his torch back on so he could follow the tracks as best he could.

Sam gathered himself but found it hard to fathom how he ended up back in the freezing cold water of the black hole again. He was treading water in what he felt was the middle of the pond, having got his bearings back ever so slightly. Sam cast his eyes around the dark surroundings to see what he could make out, with a view to finding the area missing the barbed wire, where he undoubtedly fell in, so he could climb back out. Obviously, there were plenty of trees and bushes which appeared to him in various shades of black, charcoal and grey. He could just about make out the barbed wire, as well as the gap, when he spotted a dark shape that made his heart sink. A figure appeared to be standing a few feet from him on the side of the pond. It could only be Derek, and Sam realised he was now in a very vulnerable position.

Derek clicked on his torch and held it under his chin, using the upward facing beam to create a sinister looking face. "Here's Johnny" he said, while laughing maniacally. He appeared to step closer to the edge of the pond. "I've been keeping this a secret for months, but you just had to stick your neb in, didn't you?"
"I thought you had Millie." a disconsolate Sam replied from the middle of the black hole, through chattering teeth.
Derek sighed loudly "How many times have I told you, I wouldn't have done that! Even though I would love a dog, I wouldn't have deprived you of yours."
"I know that now." replied Sam, despondently "Can you please help me out of here, it's freezing."
"Oh Sam, Sam, Sam. Out? Who said you were getting out?" Derek said, shining his torch onto his other hand to highlight the pistol he was carrying.

Sam's heart sank. He gulped and subconsciously moved himself further away from Derek, towards the back of the pond. "You know I won't say anything." said Sam, his nerves and the extreme cold causing him to chatter incessantly.

"Oh, is that right? I'm not sure I can take that chance, pal. That troublesome little honest streak of yours means you would definitely blab." Derek scoffed. "I can't decide whether to shoot you now or wait until you get either too tired to tread water any longer or hypothermia sets in. It must be freezing in there. Your body won't handle that temperature for long."

Sam, realising that his only chance was to get out quickly, made a lunge for the side of the pond.
Derek put this attempt in check by firing another ear-splitting shot towards Sam, the bullet momentarily whizzing close to Sam before making contact with the water.

"I have plenty of bullets, so don't be trying that again. I'd rather have you die in an unfortunate drowning incident, it's much tidier whenever your body eventually turns up, but, if you keep that up, shooting you it will have to be." Derek advised firmly.

Sam felt utterly dejected and helpless. He started to sob as he backtracked further towards the rear of the pond.
"Don't worry, I'll keep you occupied while you slowly expire. I can bore you with some details about all the things I've done, the mistakes that I've made, while you continue to tread water. I'll keep talking until you can't swim any more, and, if you try to get out..." Derek

highlighting his pistol again, tapping it with his torch. That would save me from making another mistake. I've made many in the last few months." Derek said with an audible sigh.

Sam was in an extremely precarious position, so he figured that trying to engage with Derek was his only chance of survival. "Mistakes? What mistakes have you made?" he asked.

"Well, the dog food was what brought you here, so that was a definite oversight. I should have just bought it myself in Dunfermline, where nobody would know me, instead of getting my gran to get it for me. In fairness, I didn't anticipate you'd be buying my gran's shopping for her. Oh well. Then there's your dad."
Sam forgot about the cold and the treading water related fatigue for a minute. "My dad?"
"Oh, yeah. I feel really bad about this, but I gave someone an idea as to how they could get your dad out of the picture because he was investigating them. I knew your dad's routine, so I helped set a trap for him, mainly because I thought he was starting to get suspicious about me too. Turned out he had no clue, but he had been in to see Slater and my gran, and I thought he'd made a connection to me, so I explained how to lure Millie with some dog food, when they were on their evening walk, and if they waited long enough on top of a coal wagon, your dog and your dad would be standing below the metal door. I thought it was a good plan in theory, but I didn't dream it would be the perfect crime. Sorry, pal. That's probably tough to hear, but I thought you should

know. For what it's worth, I wish I hadn't gotten involved in that."

Sam was devastated. Derek had helped someone kill his dad and gotten away with it. If he was standing beside him, he would have attempted to avenge his dad right there and then, but he could do nothing while stuck in the water.

Sam, fighting back tears, pleaded "Who was it that wanted my dad dead?"
"You won't be around to do anything about it, so what does it matter?" Derek scoffed.
"It matters to me." Sam spluttered from the freezing pond. "Were you there? Did you help them do it?"
"You're making me feel responsible. I was there to show them where to put the dog food for Millie, that was it. I didn't do anything else." Derek replied, becoming more defensive,
So, you never saw my dad or Millie?" Sam probed.
"No, I honestly didn't see them!" Said Derek, sounding more than a little exasperated.

Sam, sensing that he had gone as far as he could with the subject, decided to move on "What about the cats? Why did you start killing them?"
"Nothing specific. I've just always really hated cats. You never know what they're thinking, they hiss at you, they arch their backs, and they don't like me. Nasty little fuckers. Hurting them brought me joy."
"How many have you killed?"

Derek pondered this question for a moment, appearing to tap his head with the barrel of his gun, then said "I honestly don't know. A lot. I felt bad about Ginger Rogers, but only because I knew my gran loved that cat and would be upset. I have zero regrets about any of the others. I have made a bunch of mistakes, but I don't regret my cat killing spree whatsoever."

Sam's strategy of keeping Derek talking seemed to be working. He wasn't so threatening now. Maybe if he could last a while longer Derek would let him out? He really didn't have much else in the way of options so treading water and talking was all he could do.

Derek continued on, saving Sam the trouble of asking another question "That brings me to my biggest mistake of all… Lauren."
"You killed her?" asked Sam, hoping for a negative response.
"Yep, afraid so."
"Why would you do that?" Sam asked, letting his emotions get the better of him again.
Derek's voice sounded sincere "I didn't mean to. She lived right across the road from me since we were wee. I always liked her, we were in the same year at school, we hung out together when we were younger, but she changed in high school. I probably did too, to be fair. I had always fancied her, so when I got the van, I asked her out and she laughed in my face in front of her friends. I thought I could have taken her into the town, gone to a nice place to eat, but no. She decided to embarrass me instead. It stuck with me for a long time,

so when I was emptying the machine in The Railway Tavern, early on the night of their Halloween Party, I saw her drinking and decided to wait for her outside. I don't know why I did it. I was getting bored of the cats, I suppose, and also wanted to teach her a lesson. So, I took her. She was drunk and accepted my offer of a lift home. I just didn't go home. She passed out in the passenger seat, so I tied her up in the cottage and decided to keep her."

"But didn't the police search around the cottage?" queried Sam.

"They did, but during the days when they were around the chapel, the cottage and the field behind, I just drugged her, put her in the van, and drove around until they were done. I also had access to the lock up so I could stay out of sight with her. Once they stopped coming around, I felt I could invest in some more serious hardware and restraints, and she was permanently mine. It was all going well until she died."

"How did she die?" asked Sam, not really wishing to find out.

"My guess is that being chained up and isolated was too much for her, and she had a heart attack, or maybe a seizure. Anyway, she croaked. But I knew this was what I wanted to do, so I had to get a new one."

The matter-of-fact way that Derek dealt with Lauren's passing was chilling. "A new one? The girl in the cage now, or have there been others?" Sam asked, his teeth beginning to chatter again.

She's number two. She was walking right along the road in front of the Abbeyview lock up and I picked her up when I was leaving. The dirty wee hoor thought I was taking her out for the night. I am getting a bit bored of her now, so I'm thinking maybe Margaret should be next. She'd make a great pet, don't you agree?"

Sam knew Derek was trying to wind him up, so he didn't say what he wanted to say and stayed quiet instead. Another reason to make sure he got out of this mess.

"Aww, is that striking a wee raw nerve?" Derek said mockingly.

Sam wanted to move the conversation on. "So, it was you who tidied up the cat murder scene?" He was getting more and more breathless now and knew he couldn't last too much longer treading water.

"Certainly was. I saw you pass my house, and I knew exactly where you were going. I followed you and Tommo in and watched you from a distance. As soon as you were gone, I cleared everything away as I knew you'd go running straight to the cops. That was actually a smart move by me, but I panicked, and I didn't want the police extending their search down this way, so I sneaked some of her belongings into the office above The Railway Tavern to try and frame one of the staff there. The police obviously didn't buy it. It was a stupid thing to do as, in hindsight. I never considered that it would make it obvious that someone from the village was responsible for her disappearance. Not that those clueless clowns have any idea, mind."

Sam was fading fast. He felt seriously fatigued and knew he was going to really struggle to keep going for much longer. "Please! Derek, I can feel the grass starting to brush against my feet. This also happened the last time and I don't want to get tangled and drown." Sam called out in desperation.

"The last time? You mean you've been in there before? Ha, ha. Well, that's very unfortunate. You getting tangled and drowning would be fine by me, but there's no grass or any other vegetation in there. I know, I've looked. There's no sunlight for plants to grow, the water *is* probably full of bacteria though. It is good to hear one of the old stories about kids drowning in there again, though. You know all the parents just made that up to stop us playing here."

"Wait. Does the material wrapping around your feet feel like strands of hair, by any chance?" asked Derek, after a moment of silence.
"I suppose so." said Sam, confused and shivering.
"It's the only thing I can think of that could explain what you're saying because, other than you, the only thing in there is what's left of Lauren Smith. Nobody ever comes here, or so I thought, so I tied an old iron headboard to her feet, and she sank like a stone. Unfortunately, she doesn't seem to have gone all the way down."

Sam suddenly felt sick and wanted to launch himself out of the pool right there and then. He swam towards Derek, who burst out laughing. "Two's a crowd, eh? I'm afraid you still aren't getting out though and he pointed his pistol at Sam. But Sam kept paddling forward, hoping the darkness would make Derek miss if he did shoot. "One more stroke and I'm pulling the trigger." Undeterred, Sam pushed forward, and a loud bang rang out, stopping Sam instantly.

"That was your final warning shot, the next one is going to be a direct hit." Sam stayed where he was, much closer to the edge now but still in the chilly water.

"You know what's pretty exciting?" Derek suggested to Sam. "If I kill you and then Michelle, I'll officially be a serial killer as that will be three murders. Although, if you drown, nobody will know I helped you on your way, so maybe not officially, but I'll know. Maybe I should just shoot you after all?" Derek, who seemed to be having a debate with himself, had lowered the gun temporarily but was now pointing it at Sam again. Sam didn't know what to do or say. He didn't want to inflame the situation so just stayed quiet, hoping for Derek to have a change of heart.

"It's actually sad you will never feel the rush of knowing you could take someone's life at any moment. I am enjoying all this newfound power and pointing a gun at you is quite the thrill." Derek opined while continuing to aim his pistol at Sam. "OK, I am getting bored waiting, you've lasted much longer than I would have thought. I think I'm just going to have to end it now, old chap."

Sam held his breath. This seemed genuine and Derek is clearly capable, given all that he's said in the last ten minutes. Derek raised the gun slightly and Sam closed his eyes, waiting for the gun to fire. "Wait a second, I did promise to tell you who killed your dad, didn't I?"

Thud! Not a gunshot but a very strange sound. Almost as if a sledgehammer had been used on a piece of concrete. Followed quickly by a loud splash. Sam's eyes had been closed but he could now see someone was floating in the water beside him and another figure was standing on the edge of the pond. As his eyes adjusted again, he could just about make the figure out, it was Slater.

"Come on, son. Get yourself right to the edge and I'll get you out." Sam swam the last few feet to the edge of the brick circle and reached out, Slater grabbing his arm with both hands and pulling him up onto dry land.

"I've never been so happy to see anyone in my entire life!" Sam gushed through chattering teeth. "How did you find me? "
"There were trodden down tracks in the grass all the way from behind the cottage to about three quarters of the length of the field by the treeline. "I followed them until they stopped and then I heard a gunshot from inside the woods, and I knew that's where you were. It was easy."
"How did you knock Derek into the water?" asked a breathless and shivering Sam.
"At the same point where the footprints stopped, I found this shining in the grass." Slater lifted Sam's dad's torch

in the air. It weighs about five times what mine does and Derek felt the full weight of it on the back of his head."

"Do you think he's dead?" asked Sam, turning to look back at the body floating in the water.

"I think probably yes." Slater said." C'mon, let's get you out of here. The police are coming, and they will fish him out. Your mum and I followed you down here and just missed you. We saw the girl in the cottage, and your mum is away to get help while I came to find you. Let's get back to the cottage and see if they're there." Slater put his NCB jacket around Sam and ushered him up the slope towards the farmer's field. Slater using the large torch again, this time only for lighting the way.

"He told me my dad was murdered."

"Your dad? How do you know?" a shocked Slater inquired.

He was telling me all sorts of stuff when I was stuck in the water. He obviously didn't think I'd live to tell the tale."

"Did he say what happened?"

Sam spent the next five or so minutes retelling Derek's confessions to Slater as they hurried back to the cottage - it helped to keep Sam's mind off the fact that he was soaking wet and frozen.

As the pair got within touching distance, they began to see the blue lights starting to flash on and off from the other side of the cottage. Slater and Sam arrived back at the rear of the property as a number of police officers ran across the back garden to presumably head inside and rescue Michelle Polson.

Slater led Sam straight to a waiting ambulance at the front of the property, idling beside Derek's van with the back doors open in anticipation. A paramedic immediately rushed over, recognising Sam as someone who needed assistance, and draping him in a metallic looking blanket and sitting him down in between the open doors at the back of the vehicle.

No sooner than Sam had parked his behind, Redpath walked over. "Well, someone's had an eventful night. What were you thinking tackling him on your own?" An emotional and exhausted Sam blurted out "I really thought he was hiding Millie down here, that was it. I never in my wildest dreams would have imagined any of this.".

"Fair point. Nobody did." Redpath replied.

"Derek also confessed to Sam that Bill was murdered.". Slater offered.

"What?" A stunned Redpath exclaimed. "My god. I didn't ever consider that your dad was a part in all this." Sam nodded solemnly. "Derek said he helped whoever did it. He also admitted killing Lauren Smith, her body is in the pond, as is Derek's thanks to Mr Slater."

Redpath nodded and immediately spoke into his radio, conveying the message through to the wider investigative team. "I'm hearing two bodies could potentially be in the pond, over." The radio crackled with someone saying something inaudible back to him.

"A couple of officers were already on their way down to the pond via the railway line. They'll set up a cordon and recover the bodies and preserve the scene. I'm sorry, Sam, that's awful about your dad. We'll get to the bottom of it. Is there any way you think he was making it up?"

315

Sam said, "It's possible but given all the other things he *did* do, then probably not."

Redpath nodded "I take it he didn't actually say who it was who killed your dad?"

Sam shook his head. "He said he was going to but the next thing he was floating in the water."

"Once things have calmed down, I'd like to get a statement from you. Your information will be vitally important to make sure we get justice for your dad and the other victims. And it doesn't sound like we're going to be able to ask Derek to corroborate anything." Redpath advised.

"I doubt it. He was about to shoot Sam, so I gave him a real crack on the back of the head, and he fell like a tree into the pond. He was floating face down on top when we left." Slater said, acting out how he hit Derek with the torch for effect, as he spoke.

"He had a gun?" queried Redpath "I hadn't heard that piece of information."

"Yep, no idea where he would have got that from." said Sam wearily.

"If you hang around with Clint Westwood then things like guns become easy to get." offered Slater.

Sam turned to look at Slater. "Westwood? Are you sure? I thought Derek couldn't stand that lot?"

Redpath just shrugged his shoulders before leaving to join up with the other police officers for a while.

Sam received further treatment from the paramedic. He had his temperature taken, was given a flask of tea and generally fussed over. After a few minutes, another vehicle arrived on the scene, it was Janet Hamill in

Slater's van, although it was being driven by a police officer. They both jumped out and she ran to Sam, giving him a fierce hug.

"Oh my god, Sammy! Are you ok? What happened?"

"I will tell you everything, mum, I'm just too tired right now." an exhausted Sam answered.

"Ok, that's fine. I'm just glad you're ok. If something had happened to you, I don't know what I would do." Sam's mum said, hugging him again.

The paramedic came back and advised a still shivering Sam to get out of his wet clothes as soon as he was home, continue to drink hot drinks and take a warm shower. The advice was clearly aimed at Mrs Hamill who nodded back at the paramedic throughout. Slater offered to give them both a lift up the road and Redpath nodded his approval, so they all left.

As they climbed in the van, they could see the emergency service personnel helping Michelle Polson to the ambulance. She was wrapped in a blanket and looked extremely thin but was walking, albeit with some assistance. The team led Michelle into the ambulance where they started to check her vital signs. Given they didn't immediately leave, the assumption was that her general health was better than expected.

"That poor girl. I hope she is going to be ok" Janet Hamill said, her voice conveying her emotions.

"You helped save her, Sam. You gave us a fright by going tonight instead of tomorrow as planned, but who

knows what would have happened if you hadn't gone."
Slater chimed in.

As they were just about to leave, Redpath jogged back
up to the van, Slater rolling down the window of the van
to see what he wanted, as Sam and his mum looked on
from inside. "Tom, you're sure Derek went into the
water?"
"He's not there?" Queried a shocked Slater. "He was
definitely floating on top of the water after I knocked
him out."
"I swam past his body to get to the edge of the pond so
Mr Slater could grab me." Sam added, underscoring
Slater's remarks.
"Well, there's no sign of him now. he must have been
unconscious and came to." Redpath proposed. "I doubt
he'll get far. Wherever he's gone, we'll find him."
"I sincerely hope so." Janet Hamill observed. "He needs
locking up. Do you think he'll come after Sam?"
"I doubt he'll be seen anywhere near the village again
after this, so I wouldn't worry." added Redpath tapping
the door of the van. "Sam, I'll be seeing you soon. Get
yourself some rest tonight and I'll be in touch."
Slater gave a brief wave as he slowly peeled out of the
parking area at the front of the cottage. Driving out of
the property towards Station Road, Slater allowed
himself one final glance in the rear-view mirror,
breathing a deep sigh of relief as he left the emergency
vehicles behind him.

Chapter Eighteen
Aftermath

Sam looked up at his bedroom ceiling. It was bright in his room, the sunlight was creeping in around the edges of his window, and he had to squint for a bit until his eyes could open all the way. Glancing across at his alarm clock, he saw he had slept until noon, which was the latest he'd slept in a very long time. It was entirely understandable, however, after his antics the night before.

He had followed the instructions the paramedic had given to the letter. A late-night bath and three cups of tea meant he felt significantly better by bedtime, although he virtually passed out from exhaustion as soon as his head hit the pillow.

He hadn't let last night's events keep him from sleeping but, now that he was awake, Derek and his dark deeds were doing their best to infiltrate Sam's brain. He couldn't get the image of the cottage basement out of his head and a wave of anxiety crept over him as he thought about Derek's attempts to do him in at the pond.

Sam swung his legs out of bed and walked over to his window, opening his curtains, where he squinted once again as the sunlight hit his face. After the rain event of the day before, it was a pleasant surprise to look out at a sunny day. He could see from the items hanging on the washing line, that his mum had already washed and hung all of his wet clothes. No long lie for her.

Sam wandered downstairs. He was starving. Mrs Hamill heard him coming down the creaky stairs and popped out of the sitting room to meet him on the bottom step, giving him another big hug. "I'm so glad you're ok, son. I would be lost if something happened to you."

"Mum, I need to tell you something."
"Ok, but there's no rush, son. You can tell me whenever you feel up to it. Do you want something to eat first? Constable Redpath has been on the phone and wants me to call him as soon as you're up. He says he'll bring you anything you want to eat."
"Is he going to ask me about what I know about Derek?"
"I would think so. I think he has to write his report as quickly as possible."
"Ok, can I have two bacon rolls, then, please?"
"I'll call him, and I'll put the kettle on."
Mrs Hamill fired up the ring on the stove to boil the kettle, before they both walked through to the sitting room while they waited on Redpath.

Sam was sitting uncomfortably perched on the end of his dad's armchair. "Mum, I didn't want you hearing this from Redpath, so I'd rather tell you now. Derek told me last night that dad was murdered. I should have told you last night, but I was spent, and I didn't want to burden you with that after everything else that happened."
Mrs Hamill breathed in sharply, and audibly, and covered her mouth with her hand. "What? Murdered? Do you think he was telling the truth? Who would want to murder your dad, and how would Derek know?"

Sam sat upright as he detailed the unfortunate details "I don't know if it's true or not, and he could have just been trying to torment me, but he seemed to know a lot about it. He said Millie was lured to the coal wagon with dog food so that dad would be under the metal door. Who knows? He's a sicko, so he could be making it up, I just have a feeling he wasn't."

"I just don't know what to think. Why kill your dad?" asked Mrs Hamill.

"He didn't say but he mentioned dad sticking his nose into something."

"I've known Derek since he was wee. I've known his mum since school. He used to be such a nice boy. How did he turn into a monster?"

"I don't know, mum. Some folk just turn out rotten." Sam offered, with a tone of disgust.

They sat in silence for around a minute, when the whistle of the boiling kettle interrupted their discomfort.

As Mrs Hamill ran back through to the kitchen to take the kettle off the red-hot hob, there was a knock at the door. It was Redpath, and in record time.

"Food delivery!" Redpath announced from outside.

Mrs Hamill welcomed him inside and they walked through to the kitchen to get plates and organise the tea.

"How's he doing?" inquired Redpath in a hushed voice, as he nodded towards the sitting room.

"Oh, ok, I think. He's been through an awful lot." Janet replied, appearing understandably rattled. "I badly need this tea after what he's just told me."

Redpath nodded, knowing that she was referring to her husband's murder.

"Plus, I didn't sleep a wink thinking about all that happened last night, as well as the idea of Derek coming after us with his gun."

"I know it's easy for me to say, but I don't think he'd take the risk of coming back here. If he does manage to avoid capture, he'll be putting Oakley in his rear-view mirror." replied Redpath.

They convened in the Hamill's sitting room to consume their food and drink.

"Still no sign of Derek then?" asked Sam, working under the assumption that they would have heard if he'd been caught.

"Nothing yet" replied Redpath "and we still have divers trying to retrieve his gun from the pond."

"Could that mean he took it with him?" a concerned Mrs Hamill asked.

"Possible, but unlikely he held onto the gun if he was knocked out. Whatever that vent shaft or draining channels is, it goes pretty deep and is pitch black so finding anything in there isn't easy."

"How come Lauren didn't sink all the way to the bottom, in that case?" asked Sam.

I'm told that it's angled at points, which would explain it." Redpath responded.

The questions subsided after that as they all tucked into their breakfast rolls and tea.

"Sam, I took some calls for you this morning... Tom Slater checked in on you, he's going to swing by at some point to see you, Steve Wilkins wanted to know if you were still ok to do your shift tomorrow evening, both sets of grandparents and your Uncle Tam have been on to see how you're doing, and Shug called about the football but understood when I explained you couldn't go."

"Was he still going?" Sam inquired.

"It sounded like it. He said they were getting ready to get the bus into town, so I assumed so."

"How come you said I couldn't make it?" asked Sam.

"I didn't think it was a very good idea, given the ordeal you had last night." His mum promptly responded.

Sam reluctantly nodded in agreement.

"I didn't really have to explain either, he had already heard about everything." Mrs Hamill explained. Derek's exploits have already made the news."

"That quick?" a surprised Sam asked.

"Yes, the operation to rescue Michelle last night attracted a lot of attention in the village and snowballed from there. By this morning, we were getting dozens of calls from the media. There's a press conference at the station this afternoon." Redpath advised.

"They're not going to be interested in me, are they?" Sam asked with a growing note of panic in his voice.

Redpath was quick to calm Sam's nerves "Don't worry, we're not releasing anything indicating your, your mum's, or Mr Slater's, involvement at this time. You can breathe easy. Talking of the press briefing, I need to get your statement recorded. Can we sit through in the kitchen and get your story down?"

"Sure thing" said Sam, keen to get it over with.

"Oh, before I go through, what did you say to Mr Wilkins?" Sam asked his mum.

"I said I'd ask you. I can call him back once you've decided." she replied.

"I think that'll be fine, no point in missing out on getting paid. Who did he say would be picking me up?" Sam wondered.

"He said it would either be him or another vending employee. They'll get you here."

Sam gave his mum a little smile and a nod and walked through to the kitchen.

As the two sat down at the kitchen table, Redpath got his notebook out. He broached the elephant in the room first by asking "Is your mum doing ok, you know, with the news about your dad?"

"I think she's in shock, to be honest. It just brings all of those memories back, and to know that it was deliberate will be difficult to take." replied Sam.

"I get that. You can't fathom what disturbed individuals like Derek will do. He isn't wired like the rest of us. There is something very wrong with him and nobody noticed until you stumbled into his sick world. If he's telling the truth about your dad, we will get it all out of him when he's in custody." Redpath stated.

Over the next half an hour, Sam outlined how he had come to have suspicions about Derek in the first place, why he thought Derek had stolen Millie, why he went down to the cottage and how he ended up in the black hole with Derek on the verge of killing him.

"He admitted to the cat killings as well?" asked Redpath.
"Yep. Almost sounded pleased with himself." replied Sam.
Redpath shook his head. "What have you got on for the rest of the day?"
"As you probably heard, I was supposed to be going to the football, but I'll listen to the radio instead." Sam replied, sounding a little disappointed.
"I think it's good you're getting some rest after yesterday's events. Maybe your mum will get you something good for your tea?"
"I'm asking for chips again." Sam said with a smile.

Redpath's radio suddenly squawked into life. "Redpath receiving. Mmm hmm. Yes. Understood. Over."
Again, Sam could hear someone on the other end but couldn't make out anything they were saying.
"No sign of Derek or his gun yet. We'll keep on it. Tell your mum not to worry. He'll be trying to run away from here, not coming back."
"Will do." Sam said.
"Well, I better get your statement up to the station so we can get our ducks in a row before the press conference. Thanks for giving up your time, I know you're probably knackered."
"No problem, and thanks for the rolls." said Sam as he showed Redpath out.
"I'll maybe try and check back with you later." Redpath shouted as he exited the front garden and climbed into the squad car.

Sam had a couple of hours before the football broadcast, so he decided to get some clothes on and go for some fresh air. The sun was still out so a wander around the village seemed to be a good idea. He didn't take long to get dressed and, given it was sunny and fairly hot, decided to opt for just a polo instead of his usual hoodie or tracksuit top. Another recent purchase, an Adidas Lendl special edition, along with his good jeans. The height of fashion, he thought. If his trainers were dry from last evening, then he thought he would look about as cool as anyone could. He went to check on them.

Incredibly, the airing cupboard/newspaper technique had worked already. They were completely dry. He threw the balls of newspaper in the rubbish bin and slid his stocking feet into the trainers. They felt, possibly, a little tighter than normal – he assumed because of the quick dry in the airing cupboard – but he reckoned they would stretch back out after a wear or two.

Now that he was ready, Sam stuck his head around the sitting room door to alert his mum to his plans and headed up towards the centre of the village. He wasn't hungry so there was no need to visit any shops, and he knew his pals were all on their way into Dunfermline, so he walked along Wardlaw Way with a different destination in mind.

He had never knocked on this door before but was compelled to do so now. He knocked, awaiting a response. A woman who looked as if she was in her late thirties answered the door.

"Hello, is Margaret in?"

"It's Sam, isn't it?" said Margaret's mum.

Sam nodded. "Yes, I am a friend of Margaret's from school. I wondered if she was interested in going for a walk?"

"I'll check for you, son. I'm surprised you're out and about after your exploits last night."

"You heard about that?" Sam asked, a bit taken aback.

"Oh yes, my friend phoned me late last night and another couple of friends called about it this morning. That must have been terrifying. Everyone's glad you're ok." explained Mrs Stafford.

"Thanks. I'm fine, honestly." said Sam, who couldn't think of anything else to say.

Mrs Stafford went inside and, a few moments later, Margaret came to the door. She looked pretty, even though she was just wearing old jeans and a worn-out t-shirt, her long brown hair up in a ponytail. It felt like a long time since Sam had seen her. She glanced back inside her hallway before stepping onto her front step and giving Sam a big hug.

"Are you alright?" My mum told me Derek is the one behind everything that's been going on, including Lauren's disappearance. I can't believe it."

"Yeah, it all happened so fast. I was helping his gran, although I didn't know she was his gran at the time, and all these things kept happening which convinced me he had my dog and, when I challenged him about it, he went daft. I still didn't know what was really going on until I found where he was hiding out. It was shocking.

327

It was like a bizarre story you hear about on TV, but I was thrown into the middle of it."

"My mum said he had a gun." a shocked Margaret queried.

"He did, and he was going to use it on me until Mr Slater stepped in."

Margaret adding "I'm so glad he didn't. Where is he now?"

"Despite Slater knocking him out, he somehow got away, but the police are after him and believe they'll catch him soon." Sam explained.

Margaret was clearly shocked by what she was hearing. "I'd love to come out just now, and hear more about last night, but my mum is making my lunch. Maybe we can go out another time though? The Easter holidays are next week so maybe we could do something then?"

Sam was a little embarrassed Margaret wasn't able to head out but did his best not to show it. "That sounds good. I'll definitely see you around during the holidays. I missed you at school last week."

"I was off a couple of days. After all the shocking news about Lauren's clothes being found etc, I just wasn't feeling up to it."

"Glad you're better now." Sam said, waving goodbye as Margaret headed inside to get her lunch.

The next stage of Sam's walk took him down the lane past Tommo's and on toward The Black Dog. As he walked alongside the pub, he made the snap decision to go into the newsagent for a can of juice. The little row of shops which housed the newsagent also included the salon where Lauren used to work. As he walked towards the glass door of the newspaper shop, his eyes were drawn to a cluster of deflated yellow balloons hanging around the corner of the hair salon's large front window. The balloons were likely hung there around the time of Lauren's disappearance to show support for the efforts to find her. It didn't escape him that the balloons, which were once shiny and vibrant, were a sad metaphor for Lauren's, now confirmed, demise. He hadn't noticed them until now, and he wished he hadn't.

With his cold can of Coke now in hand, Sam considered walking up towards Derek's house, but he thought better of it. He didn't want any part in whatever was going on up there. Goodness knows what all of this was doing to his mum. She was already wafer thin and pretty much translucent, likely attributed to the stress of her life. He wondered if she was previously aware of Derek's behaviour before everyone else, or was her health and mental state due to Derek's dad's transgressions?

Having decided to avoid 'the flat roofs', Sam's only options were to go back up towards Station Road or cut through towards the railway line. He decided that it was better to stay on the beaten track rather than off it, so he walked back towards the shops, this time going along Sir George Bruce Road so as not to repeat his outward journey completely.

As Sam reached Station Road he couldn't see over the brow of the hill, but he could hear some noise in the distance. As he walked closer, he could hear it was a crowd of some sort and as he reached the top of the road, he could see what it was. The press conference was taking place at the front of the police station, and it was big. There was a large crowd of reporters and photographers, supported by various press vehicles which were parked on both sides of the street.

Again, Sam didn't want involved in whatever was going on and was terrified someone would spill the details of what really happened, so he cut down Hill View towards the swing park and thought he would go and see if Slater was at home. He was slightly nervous in case he bumped into Mrs Young, but he was also aware she hadn't done anything wrong, and, more importantly, neither had he.

Slater's van was there so, unless he was out walking his dogs, he was likely there too. A different feeling than the last time Sam had been hanging around at the back of Slater's house, given he wasn't spying on him any longer.

Sam knocked sharply on the back door but there was no response. He wondered if he was walking the dogs as there was no sound at all from inside.
"Oh hello, son." said a soft voice from nearby.
Sam looked over at Mrs Young's back step and she was peering around her door frame at him.

Sam didn't know what to say to her about the whole Derek fiasco. He wandered over tentatively to see how Mrs Young was. "How are you doing, son? I've appreciated you doing all my shopping for me lately. Do you think you could go again soon?" she asked.

Either she was in denial about Derek, or she didn't know yet. Sam's money was on the latter option, and he certainly wasn't going to be the one to tell her. He also wanted to get back to listen to the football, so right now would hopefully work for her.

"No problem, Mrs Young. I'll be happy to go for you. "With the Sunday shop closures, I can either nip up for you now, unless you want to wait until I'm on the way back from school on Monday?"

"Now would be great, son. Here's my shopping list. I already wrote it out." Mrs Young said, having, somewhat presumptuously, prepared it before asking him.

"That's great. I'll run up now and get it out the way." Sam promised, not trying to sound rude but he had other plans for this afternoon.

"That's wonderful, son. See you in a wee bit."

Sam could have done without this, but he was feeling guilty for some reason, probably because he knew she would be sad when she heard the news about Derek. The one benefit in doing it now is that he was already halfway there, and it would only take a matter of minutes to get to the Co-op from her house.

Sam headed out onto the Blairwood Terrace and continued past the miners' welfare to the co-op. As he nipped across Station Road, he unfurled her list for the first time and his theory was proved correct as soon as he read it. One of the main items on there was Pedigree Chum. Mrs Young didn't know. He also wondered how

Derek had explained to his gran that he needed so much dog food; it was a multipack every couple of days it seemed.

It took no time to grab all the items and head to the checkout. To say he was familiar with the shop was an understatement, as he had probably filled the shelves with the very things he was now removing.

Sam was back on Mrs Young's steps in ten minutes, tops. He didn't want to be rude, but he didn't feel comfortable hanging around there. He knocked, announced his return, and went inside. Sam was relieved to hear Mrs Young answer from through in her front room. He put the dog food in her pantry, in the full knowledge that this time it wasn't going to be collected. He further mused about the fact that Derek must have been there to pick up yesterday's pack before going to the cottage last night. Sam left the rest of the items on the counter along with her change, shouting cheerio only a few moments after he'd shouted hello.

Now that he'd said his goodbyes, Sam headed back home through the swing park. It wasn't long until the radio broadcast would be on. He was looking forward to hearing how the Pars would do as they continued their push for promotion. He could also do with a rest as he felt like he'd been walking for a long time.

Sam's mum was through in the kitchen as he walked in the front door. "Oh, hi Sammy. Cup of tea and a biscuit?"

"That sounds perfect, mum." said Sam as he walked through to take a seat in the sitting room. As soon as he sat down, there was a light tapping on the front window. A quick glance towards where the sound was emanating from told him that it was Slater, who then pointed towards the front door. Sam was keen to find out why this unorthodox method of communication was being utilised, so he went to the door as instructed, to see what Slater wanted.

"Sorry, I saw you walking in the front door right ahead of me, and I didn't want to bother your mum. She's seen enough of me the last 24 hours, plus I've got the mutts with me." Slater advised, while standing on the front path. "How are you doing today?"
"Fine, thanks. I slept late so feeling better. Thanks for all your help, again. I might not be here without it." Sam said, keeping his emotions in check.
"You're welcome, lad. I'm glad it all worked out for the best. Any news about the lanky psycho?" Slater pondered.
"Nothing since last night. I saw Redpath earlier and he doesn't think he'll come back to the village."
"I agree, although I doubt for the same reasons Redpath is giving. As I said to you before, Derek was a little too close to Clint Westwood and his cronies, and my guess would be he'd reach out to them for help. They would make certain Derek would never be seen again, rather than allow any connection between him and their seedy operation to become known."
"Do you mean they'd help him escape or kill him?" asked Sam, a little troubled by Slater's synopsis.

"Oh, the latter." Slater said, quite definitively.

"What do you mean by seedy operation, I thought they ran pubs?" Sam asked.

Slater was firing on all cylinders now, and not a good word to say about Clint Westwood. "That's what everyone thinks, but Clint has layer upon layer of businesses that are all hidden in an endless loop of phantom companies or shell corporations. He can't afford any of that to become public knowledge. His business empire has tendrils into pretty much anything you can think of in West Fife, he has the police in his back pocket as well." Slater suddenly realised he had veered onto personal territory and didn't want Sam to think he could have been referring to his dad. "I am certain Westwood wouldn't have any of our village police on his payroll, but he definitely has some in the town. My advice would be to steer clear of him and his ugly empire."

"I will." Sam confirmed authoritatively. "How do you know all of this?"

"I have my eyes open, son. There could be an eclipse, or some other major celestial event that Patrick Moore would be harping on about, but I wouldn't notice it. There's always far too much going on down at ground level around here."

"Right. The dogs are getting restless; I better keep them moving. Good to see you're in fine fettle. Will catch you later." Slater remarked as he headed off down the road.

Sam went back inside, and his tea was sitting on the coffee table. A thin wisp of steam climbing above the cup before disappearing into the air. A couple of chocolate digestives were sitting on a small plate beside it. Bliss. This will set him up nicely for his football listening afternoon, he thought.

Mrs Hamill was busy pottering around in the kitchen so, instead of a little chat, Sam made do with whatever was on tv while he drank his tea. There was nothing on, however, so he drank up, ate his biscuits, and retired upstairs to find Radio Scotland on his stereo. Once the channel was located, Sam lay back on his bed to listen in.

Given Dunfermline were in the third tier of Scottish football, that game wasn't featured. It was the Rangers game instead, but the commentary team would go 'around the grounds' at various intervals for updates, and that would have to do.

Sam woke up with a start and didn't know where he was. The radio was on, and the scores were being read out, presumably at the end of the news bulletin since the clock was saying 5.33pm. He had missed the whole game. He listened intently for the result. 'Here we go', he thought to himself as the score was announced "Dunfermline Athletic 4, Stranraer 1". 'A convincing win, that's just what the doctor ordered'. He imagined the boys on the bus, bouncing along somewhere on their journey home. Sam assumed that the result would have made it a great day out, and he was sorry to have missed it.

Sam turned off his radio and wandered downstairs, still feeling a bit groggy from his unplanned nap.

"How did they get on?" asked his mum.

Sam didn't want to admit to having slept through the match so simply said "4 – 1." adding a thumb's up for good effect.

"Is that good, then?" she added.

"Yes, great result. Keeps us on track for promotion. Not all that many games to go now and if we win a few more we're in the First Division."

"Good. Do you want to celebrate with something good for tea?" Mrs Hamill proposed, realising the question was almost rhetorical given she already knew his answer.

"Can we have chips?" Sam posed.

"Yes! I knew you'd say that, but only if you go and pick them up." she replied.

"Deal!" replied Sam as he was already heading towards the door.

"Hold on, let me give you some money. I'll have a white pudding supper, please, with everything on it." Mrs Hamill handing Sam a £10 note as she detailed her order.

It had been a long time since Sam had eaten his breakfast rolls and, as a result, he was now starving. He was out the door and on his way to Vincenzo's at high speed. He hadn't decided what supper to get for himself yet and was planning to see what looked good inside the display case when he was ordering.

After the very sunny and pleasant day he had enjoyed earlier, the weather had now turned wet and Sam's face was being subjected to a light drizzle. Undeterred by the conditions, he was driven on by his desire for hot, greasy food.

Sam walked straight to the counter and ordered his mum's white pudding supper, as well as a fish supper for himself. It wasn't too busy for a Saturday night, which was good news, especially as it was just Vince on his own. He wondered where Mrs Torretti or the wondrous Angela were, as there was usually at least two of the family working on busier nights. It was almost always Mr Torretti and one of the girls, but not tonight.

Once Sam had ordered, he stood to the rear of the shop so as not to appear to any other patrons that he was still deciding. As soon as he found his spot, there was a loud thump on the window directly behind him, startling everyone in the shop, including Vince. Even though the window was coated with condensation, Sam could tell immediately, thanks in no small part to the two mops of unkempt red hair on Tommo and Shug, that it was the boys getting back from the football. Sam went outside to get the scoop.

On arriving outside the shop, the three pals erupted in cheering and clapping, jumping on Sam as if he'd scored the winning goal in today's match. "Here he is, the local hero." Shug shouted.
Sam went red and tried to brush it off as quickly as possible, but they were having none of it.

"C'mon, tell us what happened." Tommo implored.

"We've all heard bits and bobs around the village but let's hear it from the horse's mouth." pleaded Gub.

Sam explained "You've probably heard it all already, but it would appear that Derek is an evil bastard. I brought him into the group as well, I feel really bad about that."

"Oh, rubbish. You didn't know. None of us had a clue, and that includes the police." said Tommo "Is it true he pulled a gun on you?"

"Yeah, I wouldn't have challenged him at all if I knew he had a gun. No idea where he would have got hold of one of those."

"From Clint or one of his crew." offered Shug.

"How come everyone seems to know about his connection to Clint Westwood's gang except me?" asked Sam.

"I don't think it's well known, he does seem very chummy with Bairn, and I've seen him talking to Clint himself a few times." Shug added.

"Anyway, I'm glad I found where he was hiding Michelle. Although I feel awful about Lauren." said Sam.

They all nodded in agreement.

"Anyway, enough sad stuff, how was the footy? I see you decided to go, Tommo."

"Yeah, snap decision. Glad I went, it was really good." replied Tommo.

"It was a great game, but the best part was the atmosphere. Lots of singing. Everyone was really up for it." Gub explained.

"Walshy was asking for you." added Tommo "He'd heard all about your brush with death as well."

"Fuck's sake!" exclaimed Sam. "I can't believe everyone has heard about it."

"It's all good. People are bumming you up." Gub offered.

Behind them, Vince appeared from the chip shop doorway with a large, neatly wrapped package. The steam emitting from the top giving away what was inside.

"No charge, Sam. A treat from my family for what you did last night." Mr Torretti advised while showcasing a beaming smile. Both the free food and smile were unprecedented. The gang looked on in awe.

"Thank you so much Mr Torretti, that's so kind of you." Sam said as Vince nodded and went back inside.

"Are you doing anything tonight?" asked Tommo.

"I think I'm just going to sit in with my mum. She's been through the wringer as well." Sam explained. I might swing by tomorrow and see what's happening, although I'm working at night."

"Who'll be driving you now?" inquired Shug.

"That spivvy guy that runs the vending company, I think." Sam advised. "I better head off, the steam from these chips is scalding my hands." He added while laughing.

The guys all patted him on the back as they bid him farewell, and Sam headed off back down the road for a much more tranquil night than the previous one.

Chapter Nineteen
Old Scores

Sam was up bright and early compared to yesterday, which wasn't a significant achievement given how much he had slept the day before, mainly as he had plenty to do today. He had already eaten breakfast, had a bath, got dressed and was currently taking advantage of the fine weather for a long walk. He had stopped telling himself that this was another chance to search for Millie, he knew there was no chance of finding her now.

Having convinced himself that Derek was hiding her at the cottage, his hopes, as recently as two days ago, were sky high that he'd get Millie back. Then for him to find out that he couldn't be more wrong about what Derek was hiding there, his hopes of finding her were finally dashed.

If nothing else, it was an excuse to go a bit further afield than his usual strolls, deciding firstly to walk along to the cottage to see how it was looking after the drama of Friday night. Sam would plan his next destination once he had been able to check out the village's very own crime scene.

Sundays were typically very quiet in Oakley but, as it was Easter Sunday, it was completely dead. Most shops were shut and the only people about seemed to be older folk in their best duds heading to church. Many of them doing that very thing across the road from him right now. Sam continued on down the hill towards the railway bridge not really knowing if the cottage would still be alive with police or if it would be left as though nothing had ever happened there.

When he arrived at the dirt road, there was nothing stopping him from walking down there, so he did. As he turned the corner and the greyish white walls of the cottage came into view, he could see there was a fair amount of blue and white police tape strung up around the front door, and also between the end of the house and the more or less blocked direct route to the basement steps.

As before, Sam had to walk around the entire perimeter of the cottage in order to get to the basement steps. As he turned the final corner, Sam looked at the woodpile and his heart pounding escape from Derek came rushing back to him. He could see without heading down the steps that there was police tape across the basement door too, so that was far as he decided to go.

Having revisited the first crime scene, Sam's nose was now bothering him, so he re-traced his steps back around the rear of the cottage and headed west along the treeline to see if he could see where he had been chased by the armed maniac on Friday night. It had been raining on and off overnight, so whatever tracks that may have been are now gone, but he did have a rough idea of the area where he fell and dropped the torch, and also where he had entered the forest.

The birds were chirping, the sun was out, and the circumstances could not be any more different than they were two days ago. As Sam continued to walk along the field, he stopped at a little gap in the trees to his right. This seemed like it was familiar to him. Could it be where he had cut down through the woods? It was so much easier to navigate, as there was enough light getting through that he could see the initial slope going downhill.

No tumbling down the slope this time. He was being careful where he stepped, actually being able to see the terrain made all the difference. As Sam was attempting to locate the black hole, Friday's events suddenly took over his thoughts. This was the area Derek was last seen at, so Sam suddenly became concerned that he may have hidden from the police and was potentially still here. Sam convinced himself that this would be the last place Derek would be, so he continued on.

And there it was. The black hole, where he almost met an untimely end, was directly ahead of him. Easily identifiable now, with a plethora of blue and white police tape looped around the barbed wire fence at various different heights. It gave Sam an uneasy feeling thinking about what unfolded there on Friday night. Another shiver went down Sam's spine when he thought about Lauren's body having been in there on both occasions he had gone in the water.

Sam walked up to the top end of the pond where the fence was broken and eased through a gap between two lines of tape. It felt a tad chilling standing by the edge of the pond where he nearly met his maker. He leaned forward, peering into the water to see if he could see anything at all in the murky water. As he craned his neck forward, he nearly fell in again when he saw a grey face looking back at him. Sam quickly realised that it was his reflection in the poor-quality light. It was enough to make him reconsider his little sojourn to the pond.

Sam decided to head back via the railway line, which meant heading further downhill until he met the tracks. His little interaction with his own reflection had given Sam an elevated heartrate again, but it wasn't beating as fast as on Friday. The wind had started to blow through the trees and the sky had become overcast, making the woods suddenly seem even eerier than they already did.

Sam was somewhat relieved when he reached the bottom of the hill where the trees ended, and the railway tracks shot off in two directions. He had spooked himself more than anything, but the trauma of Friday evening was obviously still with him.

For a split-second Sam thought about turning left towards the Dean Viaduct and Blairhall, but he decided against it as it would add about an hour onto his already long walk by the time he circled back via the main road. Sam headed back directly towards the village instead.

Sam didn't know why he went this way as, once again, he'd be walking past the siding where his dad died. It was always a challenge before when he thought his dad had died in an accident there, but, now that he knew it was murder, it was even more difficult. Sam hoped to never see Derek again but one reason for seeing him would he once last chance to talk to him to find out who had murdered his dad, and for what reason. Sam certainly wasn't going to rest until he found that out.

Sam walked fairly briskly past the rail siding and put the thoughts about his dad and those who sought to do him harm out of his mind as best he could. He was now heading along towards the signal box. He glanced down to his left, into the trees, half imagining Slater down there picking up the large, discarded pieces of coal.

It didn't take him long to get to the main road. Easing out of the railway property through the little gap between the signal box and the metal gates for the level crossing. With all his walking, Sam had worked up a thirst, so he made a beeline for Mr Baresi's shop.

Of course, it didn't escape Sam that this was the very spot where Bairn had lifted him off the ground with one arm only a week ago. Naturally, he took a quick scan across to The Railway Tavern and the surrounding area, before he entered the shop. The coast was clear.

As Sam opened the shop door, Mr Baresi appeared from behind the plastic strip curtains, which separated his front of shop from his back room, as if by magic. The two of them went through the usual pleasantries as Sam purchased a can of Red Kola and a handful of

McCowan's penny chews, which he grabbed from the box beside the till.

Once back outside, Sam made the decision to pop in on his gran and grandad, slurping on his can of juice as he wandered up the road to their house.

Sam took his final sip of juice as he walked in the back door. "It's just me." he shouted as he entered the kitchen, dropping his can off in the rubbish bin under the sink on his way past. Sam entered his gran and grandad's sitting room, and they were both on their feet waiting for him. His gran embracing him as soon as he walked in the door and his grandad extending his hand for a handshake immediately thereafter.

"You had us worried, son." His grandad said with a trembling voice. His gran lifting a handkerchief to her eye to wipe away a tear. "Let's have a seat." She proposed, as they all sat down.
"So, this Derek was some sort of nutcase?" Sam's grandad inquired.
"That's about the size of it, grandad."
"Those poor girls, and all those cats. Awful." added his gran.
"And he's on the run?" his grandad asked.
"Yep, but Constable Redpath says they'll get him."
"I hope so." Sam's gran stated. "Let's get a cup of tea in you." Rising from her chair and departing for the kitchen.

"Your mum was saying you had a wee swim in that flooded air shaft again?" His grandad said, with a wry smile on his face.

"I don't think anyone would call it swimming, grandad." Sam replied, laughing as he said it.

"Hopefully with that clown out of the way, the village can go back to normal."

"Hope so. Either the police will get him or, according to Mr Slater, Clint Westwood's thugs will." Sam advised.

"The wee fat guy that runs the pub? He's some sort of gangster?" Sam's grandad inquired, looking puzzled.

"Apparently so." said Sam, as his gran came through with the teas. "He has quite the empire, I've been told."

"Was that not a bit dippit to confront that idiot Derek on your own, if he's involved in all of this stuff with these crooks?" His grandad asked, sternly.

"I didn't know any of that then." Sam said, shrugging his shoulders.

Sam's gran doled out the teas as they sat quietly for a minute.

"What's on for the rest of the day, son?" She asked.

"I'm working tonight?" Sam replied.

"Still liking it then?" asked his grandad.

"Yes, it's good money and there's not much to it. The only bad thing is it eats into my weekend a fair bit." explained Sam.

"Wasn't it Derek Paton you were doing that with?" asked his gran.

"Yep, it'll be someone else tonight, obviously. As long as they're alright, I'm not bothered." Sam responded.

346

"Well, they can't be any worse than him." His grandad scoffed.

"Talking of work, I better get up the road and start to get organised." Sam said, as he stood before taking the teacups through to the kitchen with him. His grandad shouted cheerio, and his gran followed him through.

"Look after yourself, especially when you're out tonight. We worry about you, son." Sam's gran said, followed with another tight hug.

"Thanks gran. I will." Sam said as he gave his gran one last squeeze and headed out the door.

Sam walked down through the back garden, his mind full of jumbled thoughts about Derek, the cottage, and his shift tonight. So much so, he forgot to hold his breath as he walked past the manure barrel. He was looking forward to getting paid more than anything else, and he assumed that he would be owed Friday's pay packet as well, despite not finishing the shift. Although that was hardly his fault.

Sam had a few hours until his shift and he was looking forward to relaxing for a bit beforehand. He was now walking towards his house, and as he walked in the front gate his hopes were immediately dashed. Sam thought he could hear voices from inside and, as he glanced in the front window on his way up the front path, he could see they had visitors, although couldn't tell who.

On entering the house, Sam was summoned into the sitting room by his mum. It was Lauren's parents who had paid them a visit.

"Mr and Mrs Smith have come to see you." Mrs Hamill said.

The Smiths stood up and walked over to Sam, who was still standing by the doorway. We wanted to say thank you for giving us some peace regarding Lauren. If it wasn't for you, we might have never known what happened to her." Mr Smith said, choking back his emotions. We got you a card and have put a wee something in to for you." he continued, giving Sam a light blue envelope.

"Thank you, you didn't have to." Sam replied, a bit embarrassed.

"We know, but we wanted to." Mrs Smith said giving Sam a hug.

The Smiths sat back down so Sam felt he'd better sit down too, sitting in his dad's chair next to the TV.

"We're glad we caught you. we've been busy talking with the police and we're also getting ready to move next week." explained Mr Smith.

"You're moving?" inquired Sam's mum, clearly a little surprised at the news. "Where are you moving to?"

"We're moving into the town. Too many bad memories here and we want a fresh start. Dunfermline is where we both work, and we just needed to get away from here. Our house looks directly at the Patons', we just have to escape the daily reminders of what Derek did to our daughter." Mr Smith continued.

"We will never forget but we need a clean slate." Mrs Smith added, tears beginning to roll down her cheeks. Sam's mum moved over to the couch and gave Mrs Smith a hug. "Well, you'll be sorely missed around here, but that is totally understandable." Mrs Hamill opined.

The Smiths rose from the couch and said their goodbyes as they headed towards the door. "Please keep in touch" Mrs Hamill said.

"We definitely will." Mr Smith replied as they were walking out.

Sam and his mum stood and watched them walk up the road from their doorway.

"That was so nice they came to see you, Sam." Mrs Hamill while waving to the Smiths one last time.

"It was. They really didn't need to do that." Sam said in response.

"I know." replied his mum. "But I think it helped them too, if you know what I mean."

Sam nodded. Just as they were about to go inside, they could see a police car slowing down to a stop at their front gate. It was Inspector Paterson and Constable Redpath.

"What now?" Sam wondered out loud.

The Hamills welcomed the two officers inside and they all ventured through to the front room and sat down.

"Can I get everyone tea?" Sam's mum asked.

No thanks, Mrs Hamill, we can't stay." answered Inspector Paterson. "We just wanted to tell you that Derek's body has been found."

"His body? So, he's dead?" asked Sam.

Mrs Hamill. gasping at the news. "Oh my god. Really? Where was he found?"

"Yes, he's dead. He was discovered in the burn underneath Dean Viaduct near Blairhall." The inspector explained.

Mrs Hamill "How terrible. I feel so bad for his mum."
"Yes, another awful event in this sorry affair, I'm afraid." added the Inspector.
"Do you think he managed to drag himself along there after being in the pond and then passed away?" Sam pondered.
"That would have been my first guess too, but he had injuries consistent with falling onto the rocks below from the railway line on top of the viaduct." The Inspector continued.
"Fell? That must be 40 feet high!" exclaimed Sam.
"60 feet, if you ask me." Redpath interjected.
"Do you think he jumped, then?" Sam asked.
"Yes, we are working on the assumption that he took his own life." The Inspector said, now back on his feet. "We wanted to tell you personally as you were involved in the events on Friday night, and I know there was concern that Derek was still at large. That matter is now closed."
Sam nodded. "Still seems a little bit strange he would kill himself."
"Why do you say that?" Constable Redpath asked.
Sam explained "When he had me trapped in the pond, he seemed proud of what he'd done. Moreso with the cats, but he didn't show me anything that made me think he was sorry for any his actions."
"We can't know what was going on in his mind. Maybe he was worried the net was closing in on him and knew he'd be going to prison for a long time? We can't speculate, we can only go on what we see." Inspector Paterson explained.
"Thanks for letting us know." Mrs Hamill said, with Sam nodding in agreement.

"We're off to tell Mr Slater now, among others." added Redpath, as they made their way back out of the house.

"Can you believe it, Sammy?" A shocked Mrs Hamill said.
"What a crazy weekend this has been, mum." he replied.
"At least we're not going to be worrying about him coming back now." Mrs Hamill added.
"True. This whole thing doesn't seem real." said Sam, shaking his head as he spoke.
"I feel like I need a cup of tea. Do you want one, too?" his mum inquired of Sam.
"Yes, I could really do with one." Sam replied.

His mum went through to the kitchen to make tea, while Sam sat staring at the empty fireplace for a few minutes. He was trying to comprehend everything that had happened over the last 48 hours but was having a very hard time making sense of any of it.

Sam just wanted things to go back to normal in the village, as much as they ever could. For the last six months everything has been turned upside down. While the events of this weekend have been difficult, he was coming around to the conclusion that at least, hopefully, a line would be drawn now, and everyone could just move on.

Mrs Hamill came back in with the tea as well as a cheese and ham sandwich and a biscuit for each of them. "This should tide you over until after your shift" she said.

Sam was hungry and already had a mouthful of sandwich so just gave a thumbs up.

Just as they were finishing up their meal, the phone rang. Sam's mum answered the call and, after a few minutes of chatting, shouted to Sam that it was Mr Slater checking in. Sam took one last gulp of his tea, which was tepid now anyway, and walked out to the hallway where Sam's mum passed him the receiver.

"Hello."

"Hi, son. So, you had the police over today, to tell you the big news?"

"Yep, they said they were going to your house after us." Sam replied.

"As soon as they said he'd committed suicide I thought, 'aye, sure he has'."

"You think someone made it look like suicide? Sam responded.

"Seems a little too convenient, if you ask me. He now can't answer any questions or give any evidence against Clint now." Slater seethed down the phone line. "I'm telling you, they did him in."

"That's true. What I said, but was shut down, was that he really didn't seem to have any regret for what he'd done. Was happy with himself. Seems a bit of a leap to suicide, no pun intended." Sam replied, having a quick look over his shoulder to see where his mum was.

"That's true as well. I also think that's such an odd place to pick. I wouldn't have picked there, it's quite an effort to get to. I occasionally go past there with the dogs, but I tend not to look over the sides of the viaduct. And, if he

352

didn't want found, he could have gone off the Forth Bridge. I don't know why I'm explaining all of this as I don't think it was suicide at all. More like a quiet place, off the beaten track, for someone to murder him." Slater said, getting louder in Sam's ear.

Sam nodded despite Slater not being able to see him.

"Still think it was someone in Westwood's crew?" Sam inquired.

"Yes, I do. That's how these people operate." Slater said definitively. "Anyway, I had better stop ranting over the phone at you. Let me know if you hear anything else."

Sam agreed and placed the receiver back on top of the handset.

Sam's mum was through in the sitting room.

"That seemed like an animated call?" she said sardonically.

"He doesn't seem convinced that it was suicide."

"What does he think happened then?" asked Sam's mum.

Sam didn't want to get too deep into this with his mum, so he just said, "He was just speculating, mum."

"Ok, fair enough." was all Mrs Hamill said in response.

Rather than get involved in any further chat about Derek's death, Sam made his excuses and went upstairs to play some music. It had been quite a busy day and listening to some good tapes would help him relax before his shift.

Sam had about ten minutes before he was getting picked up. He'd taken the wrapper off of a brand-new TDK D90 cassette for the purposes of recording the Top 40 on Radio 1. Of course, he wouldn't get more than 45 minutes of it as he wouldn't be in to turn the tape over. He might grab a few good new songs though, so it was still worth it.

Just as he was about to put the tape in the cassette deck on his stacking stereo, he could hear a knock at the door downstairs. 'Not another bloody visitor' he thought. As he was running downstairs he wondered if it was his lift for the vending gig, perhaps a bit early. It wasn't, it was Redpath.

Before Sam could even contemplate the fact that it was very odd that he was back again, having only been by earlier this afternoon, Redpath said "We need to talk." Judging by Redpath's demeanour, it didn't seem like a conversation to be had in public, and it was pouring with rain, so Sam ushered him into the close which ran between his house and the house next door.

"I don't know what's going on, but something is very wrong." said Redpath.
"What do you mean?"
"I mean the story I've been going around telling everyone this afternoon is a load of rubbish."
Sam's eyes widened. "You mean about Derek's suicide?"
"Yes, I don't think that's what happened at all." The constable said, looking anguished.
"Well, you're not the only one who thinks that." Sam stated.

"I know you were saying earlier that he didn't seem like he would do that." Redpath said.

"I don't mean me. Slater has a theory about it all which could be closer to the truth."

Redpath queried. "What theory?"

Sam continued "He thinks that Derek will have reached out to his pals in Westwood's gang, thinking they'd help him escape, but they will have killed him to stop him telling anyone about the catalogue of illegal activities they do."

Redpath leaned closer, almost whispering. "You can't tell anyone about this, not even your mum, but I saw his body at the bottom of Dean Viaduct. Derek was laying on his back on the rocks, but his face was all battered and beaten. Two black eyes, a bloody nose, and what looked to me like a broken jaw. I was the last of four police officers to arrive and, by the time I got there, they'd already concluded suicide. It was too fast, and I genuinely don't think they can really think that. I'm playing along for now, but we're taught to question everything we see, and nobody seems to be questioning this, not publicly anyway. How would his face be all beaten up if he landed on his back? Also, how could he even land on his back, facing away from the viaduct, if he jumped forwards. I obviously haven't tried it myself, but I wouldn't have thought jumping off tall structures backwards was common. He was also a decent distance away from the viaduct, almost like he was picked up and thrown off."

"Who do you think could have done that?" asked Sam, also leaning in and talking softly.

"I honestly don't know. Do you have any theories? That would take some amount of strength."

Sam simply said one word… "Bairn."

"You think?" said Redpath.

"I know Derek was over six foot tall, but so is Bairn who is also ridiculously strong. He lifted me off the ground with one arm last week."

"Lifted you with one arm?" Redpath exclaimed.

"Anyway, you could be onto something, but I can't trust anyone. I don't know if Paterson is just passing on what he's been told or is in on it. or maybe even orchestrating it."

"What's your plan, then?" Sam asked softly.

"I'm going to sit back and bide my time for now. I don't know who to trust, so I'll just keep doing my job until I feel like I can say something." replied Redpath. I can't arrest anyone without evidence, and I need to see how far this thing goes. Anyway, I better get going. I need to get home as I've been working non-stop since Friday night."

"I need to get my skates on too, I'm working tonight and getting picked up at any moment." added Sam, as Redpath nodded and headed back out the close into the rain and towards his car.

As Redpath drove off in his squad car, Sam noticed a light blue Ford Escort van sitting slightly further back up the road, just behind his dad's car. This will be his lift for money collecting, and, sure enough, the car manoeuvred around his dad's car and stopped outside the Hamills' front gate. Sam aimed a single finger towards the steamed-up driver's side window to convey he would just need a minute. He ran back inside his house, momentarily, to shout goodbye to his mum and to get a waterproof jacket. He raced back outside to the van, jumping in the passenger seat without looking.

"What did *he* want?" said a voice from the driver's seat. Sam was frozen with shock as he saw a shaven headed, white t-shirt wearing giant sitting next to him. It was Bairn.

Sam immediately fumbled for the door handle to his left and started opening the door.

"You've got nothing to worry about." Bairn scoffed, grabbing on to Sam's right arm. "Didn't anyone tell you I'd be getting you for the vending machine job?"

A confused Sam said, "I don't understand, *you* work for the vending company?"

"Mr Westwood's my boss and, seeing as he owns the company, he requested that I should fill in. I've done it before."

"Westwood owns the company?" said Sam thinking out loud, suddenly realising that Slater's point about Westwood having many fingers in many pies was true. Also realising any attempts to heed Slater's advice would be difficult since he was already working for one of Westwood's network of businesses.

Bairn nodded towards the ajar car door, saying "Shut that and let's get a move on."

Sam felt like he had no option but to oblige.

"Oh, right. Here you go." Bairn said, appearing to remember something, as he fumbled in the small storage area under the radio, passing Sam a manila envelope "Mr

Westwood apologises for you getting left behind on Friday night. That's Friday and tonight's pay in there, plus a wee bit extra for the hassle you had. We should have a new permanent driver by the end of the week." Sam took the envelope and folded in half, stuffing it into his jacket pocket without checking it.

"So, what was PC Plod wanting?" Bairn asked again.
"He was just coming by to tell me they about Derek Paton."
"Ah well. Good riddance. He won't be missed."
Sam sat for a second, taking in that comment. No 'what about him?' Or what happened?' there was only one conclusion to draw from this. He already knew.

"So, you've done the cash pickups quite a few times?" Bairn inquired, jolting Sam from his deep thought.
"Yeah, probably half a dozen at least. Derek would empty and I'd put the full bags in the van."
"Well, a wee change tonight then. I'll keep watch, you do the money. The bags are in the back, although they're just plain ones, the cops have the bags we usually use. Luckily, we have spare keys. Here you go." As Bairn handed Sam a large keyring with a multitude of keys on it, initials engraved into each key. 'WI' for the Wander Inn, SPH for Shooters Pool Hall, and so on.

As soon as they set off, what little conversation there was entirely ceased. A regular feature of Derek's driving duties was the musical accompaniment, but Bairn chose to have the radio turned off. On prior money collecting nights there would be various interludes with idle chit

358

chat, but there was none of that tonight. Bairn sat stony-faced staring ahead, his tattooed forearms sticking straight out ahead of him and his giant mitts at ten and two o'clock on the steering wheel.

Sam didn't really need to chat or to be told what to do anyway. He had done this many times, he knew where the machines were and the handy key/pub initials combo on the keyring meant that he already had the correct key in hand before arriving in front of the machine to unlock the cash compartment. Despite Bairn's lack of assistance, Sam was able to open, empty, close and depart with money bag in super quick time. As soon as Sam threw the full bag in the back of the van and sat in the front passenger seat, Bairn was already rolling to the next location.

As there was no hanging around or hijinks at any of the stops, they were setting a really quick time. Sam was on autopilot, in any case. Throughout the entirety of tonight's cash-collecting gig, his mind wasn't really focused on doing his job, money or vending machines, he was thinking about Derek's last moments and how he met his end. From what Redpath had told him, he had formed a pretty clear picture in his head of what went down.

Derek would have made it to a telephone box to make arrangements to meet. No doubt thinking that reaching out to Westwood would result in him being spirited away to some safe haven but, instead, Bairn meting out a violent and bloody beating before throwing him from the top of the viaduct to his death. If Slater was right about Clint having members of the police on his payroll, Westwood's crew didn't even have to try to make it look like Derek took his own life. As long as it looked even remotely believable, then that was enough.

It suddenly dawned on Sam that, in all likelihood, this would have been more or less the same story with his dad's death. The only enemies his dad would have made would be Clint and his crew, and, if Bairn was the enforcer, then was it hard to imagine anyone else that could have dropped the door down on his dad. Sam turned to look at Bairn, who was still staring straight ahead, the unbridled anger began rising in him. His breathing quickened, his face started to redden, and his hands formed fists as he looked at the man that, in all probability, took his dad away from him. Just as quickly as the hate had consumed him, a cold dose of reality washed over Sam. In truth, what could he do about it? Bairn was twice his size and, if Sam challenged him, he'd probably end up the same way as Derek did.

Sam wasn't going to forget, however. He would just have to sit on his feelings for a while. Sam would bide his time and make sure that Bairn got what was coming to him, at some point.

Sam continued his cash collecting while Bairn drove from pub to pub. Sam didn't feel threatened tonight somehow. Bairn, nor anyone else involved in Westwood's operations, wouldn't likely see him as any type of threat, which suited Sam for now. He just wanted to get this shift over with and get back home.

The thoughts running through Sam's head had taken his mind off of the job and, before he knew it, he was being dropped off at his front gate. "Someone will call you through the week about Friday." said an emotionless Bairn, through the open driver's window, before he tore off down the street. Sam just nodded and walked inside.

His anger at the events of the last few months had focused his mind. Sam had admired his dad and everything he did as a police officer, but he had never considered following him into the police service. For the first time, he was more than open to it.

Sam had been hoping that the village could have drawn a line in the sand after everything that had happened, but, having sat next to his dad's probable killer tonight, he felt burdened by the realisation that this wasn't going to be the case. Clint Westwood's network of criminality wasn't going anywhere, and it would take a real, concerted effort to do anything about it. He knew what his future held for the first time, and he was pleased about that. He would go and see Redpath this week and find out how to go about applying for Fife Police.

Sam sat at the kitchen table leafling through his dad's old notebooks and contemplating the huge change that was about to impact his future. He was lost in his thoughts as he imagined a day when Clint and his cronies didn't run West Fife. If the police were as corrupt as Slater and Redpath had said, then he'd have his work cut out for him, but events had lit a fire inside of Sam and he now felt that had to see it through.

As Sam sat in a silent kitchen, pondering the life changes that were about to come, a Border Collie with no collar and no leash made her way in the fading light of the day towards the village.

THE END

ABOUT THE AUTHOR

John Crawford is a crime fiction writer, originally from Fife, Scotland, now residing in Maryland, USA.

His first book, Risingson, which is set in the small village of Oakley in West Fife, is the first in a series of novels featuring Sam Hamill.

John's other career is as a public relations consultant representing clients in the UK and the United States.

Born in Dunfermline, John started life in the small mining village of Oakley, before moving into the city of Dunfermline at a young age. John's career path has meandered through the UK civil service, followed by advertising and politics, before he started his own public relations consultancy, and has taken him to Edinburgh, London and the Washington, D.C. metropolitan area. John and his family reside in Severna Park, Maryland.

Printed in Dunstable, United Kingdom